C000102904

Available by Beyond Death Publishing Ltd

Unredacted Cthulhu Almanac Vol I -

1816: The Year Without Summer

Coming Soon

Unspeakable Doodles & Drabbles –

100 Lovecraftian Reimaginings

Love Beyond Death

Future Expected Titles

Unredacted Cthulhu Almanac Vol II

Doodles & Drabbles – 100 Forbidden Mythos Delights

1816: THE YEAR WITHOUT SUMMER

Edited by Dickon Springate

Beyond Death Publishing Ltd

Copyright © 2019 by Beyond Death Publishing Ltd and

Dickon Springate, Brett J. Talley, Chuck Miller, Jonathan Oliver

Michael J. Sellars, K.T. Katzmann, Rob Poyton, K.C. Danniel, Geoff Groff

Charles P. Dunphey, Stacy Dooks, C.K. Meeder, G.K. Lomax

Russell Smeaton, Mihail Bila, Sian Brighal, Steve Lillie, Shayna Diamond

and Sardonicus

All Rights Reserved

Beyond Death Publishing Ltd

Email: BeyondDeathPublishing@gmail.com

https://twitter.com/ThatCthulhuGuy

https://www.facebook.com/IndiePublishingHse/

First Published: April 2019

ISBN: 978-164570787-5

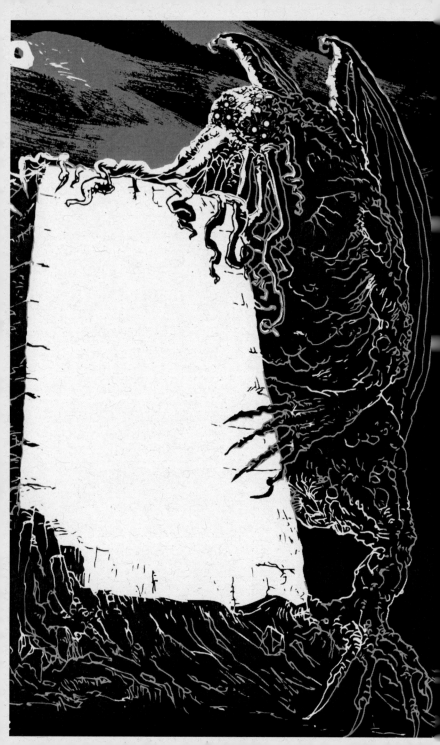

1816: The Year Without Summer

Contents

Foreword

by David Southwell

This book started on my sofa. Its editor and publisher is an old friend. Not just the sort of old friend you agree to write forewords for, but the sort you bury bodies with. The type of friend you would call on if you had got yourself involved in some eldritch malarkey and needed back-up.

I tell you all this not only for transparency, so that my bias toward Dickon is exposed and available for you to autopsy, but because I am ridiculously proud that 1816: The Year without Summer started on my sofa. There were no portents, no odd auguries, just good company and conversation.

One of the powerful beauties of the Cthulhu Mythos is that stories about it can happen anywhere in time and space and also way beyond those two fixed points of human perspective. It has endured beyond Lovecraft, Clark Ashton Smith, Robert Bloch, endured beyond August Derleth, because it offers others everything to explore. Yet often much of the strength of a good mythos story comes from the specifics of where in infinity, when in time. The Lovecraftian stories that tend to snare our imagination, snag our memory, are not only ripe with sense of place and period, but because there is something at stake. It may be the sanity of one man or woman, it may be the fate of an embattled expedition or whole culture, maybe even a whole planet, but there is always something to be lost.

1816: The Year Without Summer

What is at risk, in the stories collected in this anthology, is the shape of history itself. Some say history is delicate, easily bullied into telling whatever story the powerful and victorious want. Some regard history as a skin of lies pulled uncomfortably taut over available facts to make propaganda drum. Yet most of us tend to agree on the established, if somewhat vague, form of past itself. We all know that, not only didn't the world end on the 18th July 1816 as predicted in the Bologna prophecy, or even yesterday, but we can also agree and trace the trajectories from then which structure the now. As 1816: The Year without Summer shows, history as we think we know it is a sham, the whole outline of the old is at constant risk from the occulted force of the Cthulhu Mythos.

Remove a scientist or artist too early in the game and the whole shape of a society can be subtly shifted. Topple a queen, alter the course of a cardinal or break the mind of a key general and nations may fall. In these collected tales, we can see how it is not only the obvious battles of blood, fire and suffering echo across time, but the veiled engagement against forces far more ancient than man. Forces with their own much longer history have threatened our very existence, threatened to bend and end our own story as species.

Delve into any year in human history and it always becomes about an archaeology of stories. We are built on layers of memory, layers of narrative. As the included authors ably demonstrate, 1816 is a rich bed for any story excavator. The modern world is built on its inventions – whether Davy's Lamp, Stirling's Engine or Mary Shelley's Frankenstein. It is also built, as you are about to find out, upon the bones of the strangest of creatures, the trace evidence of the violent wreckage of cosmic forces deeply buried in our collective chronicling.

As a writer myself, I have an added reason for welcoming this collection beyond the pride that it started on my sofa, beyond the pleasure of reading a bloody good Lovecraftian story. It is the first book from Beyond Death Publishing, a company who from page one has consulted with authors, artists and audience on fundamental matter of fairness. By buying this book, you are helping to support the sort of publisher we writers need. Not just independent, not just creative, but committed to manifesting stories in an ethical fashion.

Now, stop reading words by someone you have never heard of, and start digging through the unredacted history of 1816.

Prologue

In April 1815, the centuries dormant volcano of Mount Tambora on the Indonesian island of Sumbawa suddenly and inexplicably erupted.

Official records state that around 71,000 souls were lost in the immediate aftermath of the eruption, but this huge and tragic number is itself dwarfed by the final toll of more than a million lives that are estimated to have perished globally, due to the climate change that impacted and enveloped both hemispheres for the next three to five years at the very least.

Though only known to a handful, the real cause for this calamitous event began 1,000 years ago on the eastern tip of the Avalon Peninsula on the large Canadian island of Newfoundland.

The Sepulchred Conflagration

By G. Groff

Apaata stood patiently on the banks of lake Quidi Vidi, overlooking the seal breathing hole. In his mitted hands he gripped his long harpoon tightly as he waited for a seal to emerge from the icy depths below and come up for air. His vigil had already been over an hour long and to ensure his reflexes were sharp, he continued to make a series of tiny muscular trembles, just enough to warm them through without exerting them or disturbing his perch by the water's edge and thereby alerting the seals.

Out of the distant mist that exists at the verge of the horizon, where blinding ice snow meet pale, puffy clouds, came a low rumbling. Apaata could not make out what was causing the noise, but whatever its origin, he could tell that it was edging ever closer. His seal hunting training, the calming watchfulness that had served him well for decades, ensured that he did not run, hide or indeed make any movement at all that would give away his position; he just continued with his internal flexes and waited nervously.

As the thunderous cacophony approached, it got louder, and although he could not hear any clear voices, Apaata felt sure that underlying the maelstrom was the repetitive sound of barely shod feet stampeding across the ground towards him. This explanation would have made sense, except that he knew heading eastward from the lake was nothing but craggy rocks and the never-ending watery expanse beyond.

Prologue ~ The Sepulchred Conflagration

Confusion and doubt wrestled in Apaata's mind, until suddenly a giant dragon's head emerged through the dense mist, complete with large, sharp teeth and flaming, midnight black eyes that also somehow appeared to glow with fury. Despite all his training, nothing had ever prepared him to face such an almighty foe, and even as the internal debate continued as to whether or not to stand ready and await this incredible fiend, he caught sight of a headlong rush of dozens of humongous, strangely garbed warriors, with round, wooden shields and long, blond hair trussed up and tightly plaited.

Quickly gaining ground across the fresh snow towards him, the intruders carried a huge wooden craft, the likes of which Apaata had never seen, though he guessed it must be a massive canoe like vessel, as it had sections for paddles along both sides, and its prominent figurehead was what he had earlier mistaken for a dragon. Judging by their clothes and outward appearance, these men were clearly foreigners from a distant land, as not only were they two heads taller than himself, but also, instead of wearing pelts made of caribou and polar bear skin, their garb matched their demeanour–dark, yet vividly colourful–not at all suitable for the biting, wintery blizzards.

Tensing in still readiness to fend off the first of the advancing invaders, Apaata suddenly felt a sharp stabbing pain as a wicked barb tipped arrow pierced the thick polar bear skin that he was wrapped in and embedded itself in his chest. Blinding pain coursed across his torso, followed by a second arrow strike, landing a little less than a handspan away from the first; this one plunging deeper as it punctured a lung. These new and unexpected sensations were all too much for Apaata, who had never so much as needed to raise a fist in anger before, and as his irrelevant harpoon fell from his limp hands and clattered noisily onto the ice, he tilted his head sideways to get a better look at what had struck him. This curiosity lasted only a second or two, as, moments later, his lifeless body flopped onto the discarded harpoon; felled by a single, cruel blow from a war axe wielded by a powerful, tattooed arm.

As his blood flowed out and instantly began to congeal and solidify on the freezing ice, Apaata was unaware that his death was only the first among many, as the berserking hordes encroached from the coast and mercilessly hacked their way through anyone that stood in their way in search of treasure, whether they resisted or not.

When these strangers at last chanced upon the Esquimaux settlement, they could not believe that so many people would live together with barely a rudimentary wooden fence encircling the encampment, presumably more to keep the cattle in than any invaders out. The dwellings were arranged in a vast, broken circle, perfectly and symmetrically aligned around a large central ice sculpture that seemed to be of a deformed whale with a long spear protruding from its snout; their god Katkannaalu, the staunch oceanic protector of their primary god, Sedna.

The invaders knew not the ways of the tribal elders, nor cared about the weak or feeble gods they worshipped, for these blond giants came from a harsh land where life was fierce and barbaric and their gods equally so.

With detached authority, they swooped down upon the community and overran the bewildered villagers, smashing and defiling the statue with their hammers and axes, until Katkannaalu's former likeness was little more than a melting collection of slush and broken shards of ice.

Taking what little valuables and dried food there was, the strangers took turns in savagely violating some of the tribe's diminutive young girls, before mocking the former deities one last time as they magnanimously strolled out of the village and retreated towards the coast from whence they came.

Prologue ~ The Sepulchred Conflagration

The villagers who remained alive after the rampaging horde had left looked on in dejected misery at their fallen idol. As they began to console one, all thoughts and voices began questioning how Katkannaalu had failed to protect them, or, more worryingly, wondering if he had deliberately chosen not to.

As his waking eyes flew open, the elder village shaman, Kumaglak, came out of his trance and feared the worst. It had been the same frighteningly confusing dream vision that he had been plagued with for weeks, and though he still did not believe in any blond giants approaching from the frozen wastelands of the east, the repetition and violent nature of the dream troubled him deeply.

Trying to gain some context, Kumaglak rose and shuffled to the entrance of his hut where, having pulled aside the thick hide curtain, he could see, low on the horizon, the now familiar vividly colourful sunrise.

Kumaglak had still been young when the tribe had settled along the coast a handful of years ago, before the changes in the skies began. At first, the rose hues were so brilliant that the entire tribe gathered to watch the sun slowly sink below the horizon, however after months of similar dusks its beautiful novelty waned and nobody except Kumaglak observed it gradually receding back to normality.

It was a few weeks afterwards that the autumn feast was held and with it, the annual ceremony. Those in the tribe who wished to participate split into two teams; The Ptarmigans and The Ducks. A mark was drawn across the ground and a sealskin rope laid across it. The teams then gathered on opposite sides and took hold of the rope. Kumaglak stood next to the mark, raised his hand and looked to each team.

Upon Kumaglak dropping his hand, both teams began pulling on the rope in an attempt to drag the opposing side across the mark. Both struggled towards their goal for several moments, with neither seemingly gaining any footing, and as seconds extended into minutes Kumaglak watched on with a furrowed brow.

Finally, The Ptarmigans gained a small footing as The Ducks attempted to hold their position. What felt like hours, was only moments, as The Ptarmigans gained more footing, edging The Ducks closer to the mark. Then there was a snap as the rope broke and The Ducks collapsed backwards into one another. The Ptarmigans yelled at their victory as The Ducks rose to the feet to yell along with them.

Once the celebration had ceased, Kumaglak made his customary proclamation that the winning team would be a mark of the weather to come, and with The Ptarmigans as the winners, this indicated that a harsh winter was approaching. Only a few took notice of his expression as he finished and departed from the remainder of the ceremony.

Several days afterwards, Kumaglak, still wracked with troubled dreams, called those at the village to a tribal gathering. With the sunset behind him, he related the visions he had seen, doubt thick in his voice, but determined not to miss out even the slightest detail, less he omit some vital clue that the chief and his head advisors could make best use of. The chief and his council exchanged many subtle nods as Kumaglak relayed his visions, and even before he had left their presence, the pair were deep in hushed conversation.

As nightfall descended on the encampment, Kumaglak drank a sleeping draught of nettles and wild roots, desperate to prevent another night of interrupted slumber. His concoction worked and though he would forever regret this tiny act, Kumaglak fell into a deep, untroubled sleep.

It was not the everyday sounds of the community rising that woke him the next morning, rather the sound of heavy rock slamming and crushing a smaller boulder, occasionally skipping as a poorly aimed strike connected badly. Though unusual, due to his extended sleep, Kumaglak took longer to come fully to his senses. When he finally did so, it was with a possessed urgency that he hastily threw across his shoulders a thick fur-skin and dashed out into the freezing winds outside.

The vision that met his eyes was confusing at first, but as he scanned the horizon, he realised with horror and dread what had happened. What he saw first was the body of the fisherman Apaata, lying dead on a lattice stack of wooden logs, two arrow shafts visible in his torso. Beyond that he saw, standing by the pyre, the chief and his advisor, both holding a flaming torch in their hands and frantically urging all the remaining men, women and children of the tribe to destroy their talismanic ice sculpture as if their very lives depended upon it. Everything was exactly as he had seen in his dreams, with the calamitous exception that the culprits defiling their protector god Katkannaalu was not a group of strange, blond giants, but faithful tribesmen whom he had once called friends.

Trembling with frustration, Kumaglak threw himself at the enraged mob, intent on preventing further insult and humiliation to the likeness of their gods, however an accidental backwards blow sent the shaman tumbling to the ground, where he lay stunned and mumbling incoherently. The strike had clouded his mind and disorganised his thoughts, so he could not be sure if what he saw next was a genuine premonition, or just the effects of concussion, but in his mind's eye, he saw a dancing fireball descend upon the settlement, leaving nothing but a crater of ash.

Bitter tears leaked from Kumaglak's eyes as the full realisation struck home that not only had his chief completely misinterpreted his prophetic warnings, but the whole community had now blasphemously destroyed their god's image in his name. What soul-rending retribution this might have he could not begin to image, but, like all tribesmen, he was familiar with his divine lore and knew well that neither Sedna not Katkannaalu were worshipped for their abundance of forgiveness and leniency.

* * *

Though he could not possibly have known it, at that exact moment, at the furthest edge of the solar system, two floating asteroids collided. The larger of the two barely had its orbital trajectory perceptively altered, while the dwarf asteroid fragmented into a number of spinning shards; two of which seemed to speed up as they shot out across the void and headed unerringly towards planet earth.

For almost a thousand years, the two earthbound shards flew ever closer, defying the shifting gravity wells of celestial bodies as they came; their cores slowly heating up, despite their surroundings, almost as if they were no longer simple far-flung impact debris but eldritch messengers traversing the cosmos with a singular mind and hellish purpose.

It was not until mid-1815 when the leading shard entered the earth's atmosphere a few months ahead of its smaller twin companion; somehow navigating a direct route that sent it tumbling out of the sky without a single telescope observing its fall. With its abnormally fiery core burning fiercely, it plunged into Mount Tambora, Indonesia, reigniting its century-dormant heart and causing one of the largest and most destructive eruptions in the history of man; sending up noxious gases that blackened the sun and, ultimately, led to countless deaths for years to come.

A few months later, as the climatic changes were still being felt all around the world, the smaller twin entered the earth's atmosphere, though none below could see it. Its intent was not to cause mass carnage and fear, but the more focused goal of complete and total obliteration of an Esquimaux settlement, long since abandoned by its original occupants and now settled and built upon by westerners boasting European descent.

Prologue ~ The Sepulchred Conflagration

*   *   *

August 19, 1914

Gaubert N. Beaumonts

Chas. E. Goad Company

Montreal, Quebec

Mr. Beaumont,

Enclosed, please find several sheets of notes comprising what appears to be a short journal that was discovered during our insurance survey of St. John's, Newfoundland. As the condition of the writing is poor, likely due to the age of a century, I have taken the task of typing them in completeness to the best of my ability. There are a few sections where the ink is incredibly faded and thus illegible to my eyes. While there is no assigned date, the contents suggest a date shortly after the fire of early 1816.

Among the notes was a German newspaper published in December 1816, which contained an article mentioning the discovery of a new comet by astronomer Jean-Louis Pons, during late January of that year. Although some research has determined that this comet would have been too faint to be visible to the unaided eye, the date would corroborate with the story.

Additionally, the library has archived newspapers, including some dating back to the early 1800s. Of interest is the first publication after the fire, in which, among the dead, is an Elias Abner, aged 54.

The nature of the contents seems fantastical even to myself, yet oddly enough, there are a few corroborated details. Amazingly, if demonstrated beyond reasonable doubt, this would provide an explanation for the unusual number of fires that have plagued the city over the last 100 years.

1816: The Year Without Summer

Sincerely,

Bryan Randal

Civil Engineer

*　　*　　*

Here is my account of events as they occurred, to the best of my recollection, of the great fire that nearly consumed our city, St. John's. I fear the experience is about to take its toll on my mind. I wish to record it in writing while I am still able to recall the details.

Old Elias always had keen eyes, even in his dotage. It was he who came to me claiming to see a light in the frigid nights of late January. I could not see the damn light, even when he attempted to point it out among the stars. I do not think it would have helped if I had seen it.

Days later, he approached me claiming to see luminous strands radiating from the light, though I could see nothing and told him that the haze was playing with his eyes. I was certain that his brain had gone soft. He continued to watch the evening skies for those strands and seemed fevered when he claimed that they were extending across the sky.

It was on the evening of February 12 that the madness seemingly began, with Elias making a commotion at my door, rousing me from sleep. If I thought that he was deranged before, tonight he was truly mad. He was obviously frantic, shouting about that damn light again. He pulled me into the street and pointed down towards the government offices. I could see that his hand was trembling as he said that one of those luminous strands had spiralled down from the sky and come down near King's Beach. I laughed at him at first, but was then shocked, as I could certainly see an otherworldly radiance from the streets, illuminating the sides of the buildings in a violet glow. I could hear a rising drone and, looking at Elias, I saw that he heard it as well. At that moment, a blast of heat assailed us and, even at our distance, we could see that the buildings were engulfed by fire. We rushed down the street, towards the flames, calling an alarm as we ran. Once we were there, we could see that the fire had already consumed the wharf and was quickly spreading to other buildings. How it leapt from building to building seemed supernatural, as it defied the winds. Elias shrieked when he looked down Water Street. At first, I thought it was the shock of seeing our city burning, but now, I suspect it was something that escaped my attention.

I am not certain how much time elapsed, for it seemed that dozens of other people had suddenly arrived at the growing inferno. Everyone went to action and started a bucket brigade until the hand tub arrived. I immediately began helping.

It took me several minutes to realize that Elias was not near me. I paused for a moment to look for him among the crowd – I could not see him. Wondering if, by chance, he had collapsed near the spreading flames, I considered searching for him when the hand tub finally arrived.

As thick, acrid smoke rose from the southern warehouses, several men readied the pumping apparatus, while half the brigade began filling the tub. It was not until I felt a hand grab my arm to pull me from the hand tub brigade that I realized I had forgotten about Elias.

As I turned, Elias was pulling me away from the crowd, stammering about how something was not as it seemed within the blaze. He directed my attention further down Water Street. At first, I did not see what had him so unsettled. Confusion briefly enveloped my mind – when I did finally see it. Ahead of the blaze, a flame was moving throughout the street in an erratic manner. *(Beginning is illegible)* . . . aspect of this lone flame was that it appeared to have a form, or at least more of a form than a mere flame. Pushing the confusion aside, I ran to grab a water bucket and motioned for Elias to do the same. Together, we then rushed down the street to prevent this flame from spreading the blaze further into the city.

We could see the flickering flame ahead of us as we ran, but when we got closer, it vanished. Both of us looked about for it, and I thought to myself that it was peculiar – the snow was not melted where we had last seen it. It remained unseen by us for several moments until Elias cried out that he spotted it down Prescott Street. Together, we rushed to where it was crackling, and I promptly quenched it with my water bucket. There was a wisp of mist or smoke rising from where it was and I paused for a moment, before beginning to return to the brigade at King's Beach. As I turned, Elias gasped and pointed towards where I had quenched the fire; I returned my gaze and saw that there were sparks shooting from the pool of water. Within a moment, those sparks reignited into a ball of flames, which oddly lifted from the ground and darted towards the nearest building, as if somehow directed. Elias moved to follow it and tossed his bucket of water over the fire, quenching it once again.

The commotion of the brigade was audible in the background as I approached the spot where the flames had been. I crouched down to look closer and could see several grains that had a shine to them, not unlike steel or glass. As I reached out to pick one up, they began to move, almost in a swirling pattern. Surely, the tumultuous state of the town was affecting my eyes, for how could this be? Nevertheless, my eyes had not deceived me, for the grains continued to swirl together into a loose mass and small sparks began jumping between the grains. These sparks grew in magnitude until the mass itself appeared as glowing flecks of metal.

Elias began to utter something when the glowing white flecks burst into a flame and I managed to avoid having it fly into my face.

I heard Elias shuffle to my left as the flame shot past my head into the street.

We turned around and I watched the flame float across the street and land on the roof of the opposite building. From my vantage point, only a faint glow was visible, though it seemed to be moving towards the centre of the roof.

Elias and I ran to a nearby provisions store to fetch a ladder; we propped it against a side of the building, then I followed Elias as he started climbing. As we clambered onto the low pitch of the roof, it creaked beneath our weight and I steadied myself against the chimney. We could overlook the town; the rising full moon was partially obscured by the smoke. The blaze had spread from King's Beach towards Fort William.

Elias tugged on my sleeve and pointed to an adjacent building. I gasped as a gout of flame erupted skyward from the roof with a scorching sound. The flame vanished just as suddenly as it had appeared. We scrambled over to the other building, to where the flame had erupted, and found that a hole, about the size of large tin can, had been burnt through the roof. Lowering myself down to peer through the hole, I saw flames beginning to climb the walls of the room.

We hurried back down to the street and were about to run back to King's Beach for help, when a hissing and popping sound came from the side of the building. We stood there, confounded, as a black spot appeared on a wooden wall near the ground; as this black spot became larger, the hissing and popping became louder. A moment later, the centre of the black spot changed to a red ember, then bright orange - this is when a hole appeared with a sizzle. Emerging from the hole was the swirling mass of flames. It glided in the street and started to hover, about a foot off the ground, as sparks floated in the air around it.

1816: The Year Without Summer

The twirling mass of flames and sparks calmly bobbed in the air above the street, as we stared on in bewilderment. When Elias took a step towards the flame, it floated away from him a short distance. I stepped forwards and it floated away from me, as well. We stared at each other in confusion. What could burn and produce such a flame that moves in this unearthly manner?

Elias stepped away in order to fetch one of our buckets, then eased towards the flame, while turning the bucket over. Once he was close enough, he slammed the bucket down over the fire. Holding the bucket down with both hands, he gave me an uneasy glance and looked back down. As we debated our next action, Elias shot up and stared down at the bucket, which now had a faint glow. A bluish flame with white streaks rose for several moments, before being replaced by a dull orange radiance. Even through our heavy clothes, the heat could be felt as the glow steadily grew. The bucket then collapsed in on itself and the damn flame drifted upwards, now even brighter than before. We both raised our arms to shield our eyes from the intense light; I heard Elias cursing and muttering as he did.

The brightness diminished enough for us to lower our arms and we could see behind it that the upper floor of the building was being engulfed in flame. The *(words illegible . . .)* and began drifting towards Elias. He stepped out of the path and the flame drifted towards the building. As it met the glass window, it paused. The intense light returned; it then passed through the window as a hot knife does through butter. The ceiling of the building was scorching as the flame continued in a line across the room. Fearing that an inferno was certain, I shouted at Elias to remain in place as I went to find water. The nearest well had a low level; thankfully, I was able to break through the ice, lowering my bucket. Upon returning, I found Elias, calling for me from within the opened door. Rushing inside, I found he was kneeling on the floor holding the cast iron lid down on a pot. Elias gestured at a stockpot on the table, which I fetched for him. He dropped the pot inside the stockpot and shouted at me to empty the bucket into it. Once I had done so, Elias grabbed a lid for the stockpot and slammed it down.

I heard the sound of glass breaking from outside; walking over to the door to look, I saw that the fire had burned down to the lower floors and the windows were breaking from the heat. We both looked on with grief, unable to do anything to put out the fire, as the brigade had the only hand tub, but we were relieved that there were no connected buildings.

I suggested we bring some of the brigade here, in case the wind managed to spread the fire to nearby buildings. Elias nodded and went to pick up a small stockpot. As he walked towards me, he paused and looked at the stockpot on the floor. As I went to question him, he raised his finger to his lips and motioned for me to wait. I heard a faint clink of metal and thought the stockpot lid shook a bit. There was another clink and a puff of steam as the lid quivered. Elias's brow furrowed and he told me to fetch more water as he went to rummage through the kitchen. When I returned, he raised a short copper chain in his hand and told me to ready the bucket over the stockpot. With a nod, he shifted the lid half way off and steam billowed up; I refilled the stockpot with water and heard a hiss – like that of water hitting a hot skillet. Elias secured the lid by threading the chain through the handles of the stockpot and lid, leaving some length free to hold onto.

Carefully, Elias hoisted the stockpot off the floor and began towards the door as we discussed what to do with it. We were convinced that this damned flame would not be extinguished easily, so we remained lost as to what to do about it. I pointed to the well and told Elias to follow me, suggesting that we could drop it in there; surely that would keep it contained.

We were making our way towards the well when Elias began complaining about the heat coming off the stockpot. I turned to look and was astonished at the sight of steam spewing from the lid, as if boiling. We hastened our pace; the stockpot continued to rattle as steam escaped and Elias struggled to hold the chain. There was silence when the steam ceased as the stockpot swung on the chain. Elias lowered the stockpot to the ground and kicked some snow onto it, which immediately melted and hissed away. As he continued to kick snow, I ran to the well and lowered my bucket to fill it. Once again, we refilled the pot with water, and I proposed the painful idea that dropping it into the well may not be sufficient.

(*A large portion is illegible*) . . . lifted the cauldron onto the sleigh and set forth filling it from the well. As I finished, Elias returned, pushing a sack truck holding two kegs of black powder. We secured these at the front of the sleigh and climbed onto the seat. I took hold of the reins and tapped the horse to drive the sleigh. We continued on Prescott Street towards Flavin Street; Elias thought we could use Monkstown Road to get to the city's edge. A light snow started to fall as I encouraged the horse down the road.

As we reached Flavin Street, Elias suggested that we should stop and check on refilling the cauldron. With relief, he said that it was still mostly full and thought we could continue.

We were fully on Monkstown Road and the crossing with Military Road, when we again stopped, checked the cauldron and refilled it with snow and water from a nearby rain barrel. I took notice that the water in the cauldron was surprisingly cooler; perhaps we had stifled the flame? Elias shook his head when I suggested this, for he was certain that the flame would rekindle itself and insisted on his plan again.

As we made our way down Monkstown Road, fewer buildings were in the immediate area and we headed into the neighbouring hills. We had lanterns, though the full moon offered enough illumination to keep on the road. The snow grew heavier as we left the city; hours seemed to pass as we travelled the half-mile to the spot Elias had described. I called for the horse to stop. We each lifted the powder kegs onto a sturdy sled; Elias also retrieved the stockpot from the cauldron and a coil of fuse. Carrying the lantern in my other hand, we dragged the sled up a low hill. We paused for several minutes at the crest as Elias, pointing to the left of the next hill, indicated our destination.

Our descent was slow and difficult, though we managed it without slipping or toppling the sled. Elias navigated us along the foot of the hill and into what appeared to be a glen, with scattered trees on the slopes. We made several pauses, either to place the stockpot in the snow, or check the ropes securing the kegs. It was perhaps three-quarters of an hour before we arrived.

The entrance to a cave opened before us, not unlike the maw of an enormous creature; recollections of the El Lagartos from the far South appeared in my mind. As we unloaded the kegs and lifted them onto our shoulders, Elias said that we had another hundred yards to manage. Travelling through the cave was not as strenuous as I expected, as Elias was able to direct me through the challenging areas. I could smell moisture in the air as we entered a large chamber; Elias informed me that we had arrived. Lowering my keg to the cave floor, I observed our surroundings; the lantern revealed that there was a sizeable shaft about twenty feet from us – I heard the sound of water trickling.

We approached the edge of the shaft and I could now see that it ended about forty feet down and that a stairway of broken stones followed the wall to the bottom. I saw a small stream of water emerging from the far side, about ten feet off the bottom, collecting into a small pool, roughly in the centre. I questioned Elias as to how he had come to learn of this place, as I did not recall others mentioning it; he replied that he had discovered it some years ago but offered no explanation as to why it was unknown to others.

Elias picked up the stockpot, I lifted the keg onto my shoulder, and we descended the stairs which, queerly, looked both natural and artificial, and I pondered on whether they were an old construction.

Once we reached the bottom, I relieved myself of the keg and Elias walked towards the small pool while motioning me to follow. While the pool initially appeared shallow, closer consideration showed that the middle was quite deep. Elias waded a short distance into the pool, then lowered the stockpot down, releasing the chain when it slackened. After several minutes, we had situated the powder kegs in large recesses along the shaft wall, where fractures were present, in the hope of collapsing the chamber and entombing that flame forever.

As Elias was setting the fuse, I heard a disturbance behind me and upon turning, saw the pool was churning. I cried out to Elias and fear came to his face at the sight. He grabbed the end of the fuse and threaded it under the cover of the lantern, which promptly ignited. We ran up the stairs and upon reaching the top, Elias pushed me out into the cool night air and shouted for me to run; fear compelled me to obey.

I heard a clatter as the light behind me went out and heard Elias shouting to go without him.

I have no clear recollection beyond this point. The kegs had indeed blasted the chamber shut, I was sure of that as I felt the entire cavern shudder; though whether I was still within the cave or outside was uncertain. It took some time for me to force myself to re-enter the cave in search of Elias; I never found him and feared that he was buried in the collapse.

How I arrived in town later, I do not know. Belle Horn was the first to find me, slumped against the school on Queen's Road in the morning. Afterwards, I learnt that the inferno had claimed a large portion of the city. My explanation that Elias had perished in the fire was readily accepted, as others had been; my shaken state gave belief to that lie.

Though it took several days, the fire was eventually contained, and its destructive progress abated, thanks to shifts of volunteers working around the clock. With the heat subsided and most people's thoughts beginning to turn to salvage and rebuilding, mine turned to Elias. I had been too busy with the rest of the town to think about memorising the location of the cave, and now, as I try to retrace our steps, all evidence of any cave, explosion or collapse seems to have completely vanished.

The mere thought that the dancing fire spirit might have somehow managed to hide all traces of its existence from the world was a private nightmare that would forever haunt me – doubly so, due to my inability to tell anyone about it without risking ridicule and incarceration. I doubt that I will ever be able to tell the true events of that night; the only eye witness who would have been able to attest to my sanity being poor Elias, now forever entombed in his unmarked grave. It is my hope that Elias's death and our actions were not without some aide to mankind, and for as long as my legs will carry me, I will ensure that, on the anniversary of the fire, I will take a slow walk to where I imagine the cave would be and pay my respects to my dear, departed friend.

1816: The Year Without Summer

JANUARY ~ 1816

Documentation of Varied Scientific Endeavours

By C.K. Meeder

{Excerpts from the Diary of Sir Humphrey Davy}

10th November 1815

That damnable hornswoggler Stephenson has somehow chanced upon my idea, either that or his envious quest to surpass my own scientific accomplishments has guided his hand into having one of my apprentices turn spy and provide him with a copy of my detailed schematic design.

I questioned Stephenson's involvement from the very beginning, or at the least from the moment I was aware of his presence amongst those of us with academic legitimacy attempting to address the matter of the lamps, as I found it suspect in the extreme that such a mechanical engineer from Northumberland with no education or scholarly background to speak of should be so adept with a subject so far from his own practices.

At the first I was willing to give him the benefit of the doubt due to his having a brakeman and engine-wright background, as there is something to be said for experience and familiarity with the environment in which these lamps will be used, thus I did not raise my voice or discourage his attempts initially. However, following his unveiling of my own design to the prestigious Royal Society all such uncertainty fell away, and I felt compelled to speak out against this charlatan.

I wish no undue slander against any man, but I simply cannot come to terms with the idea that this insufferable ignoramus had coincidentally devised a nigh identical design, a man who speaks as though he has shoved fistfuls of coal into his own mouth around which he mutters haphazardly. There is nary a man alive not sharing his birthplace who can comprehend a single uttered syllable that escapes his vacuous cavern of a mouth.

Of course, the fine fellows at the Royal Society immediately spotted the charlatan that he is and concurred with my furore, the resultant outcry against his blatant thievery and duplicitous intent leading to them awarding me the sum of two thousand pounds while roundly decrying him as a fraud and a thief.

That being said, his fellow countryman from back up north seem to think very highly of him, and I would not be surprising if he attempted some localised petition to at least clear the smudge from his spotted record. It is a truth that in life I would rather avoid making enemies wherever possible, but on this occasion, I felt that that it was almost impossible to avoid.

*   *   *

3rd January 1816

So far, it seems as though my lamp design has proven largely successful, and certainly I am less anxious for every man and boy who now descend into the pits of the mines.

The satisfaction surrounding the manufacture and deployment of my lamps is immense, not only as a matter of simple pride, but as an achievement for industrial safety. However, the necessary perfection of such a weighty invention indeed rests heavily on my mind, and therefore I remain distracted that my design might warrant alterations in some as yet unseen manner.

Having decided that I have a need to test my lamp in a real environment I have requisitioned a carriage to take me up to Durham, a journey will with all good fortune should take just me just less than five days, meaning that with the inclusion of my testing and the journey back I should be back within the fortnight.

With hindsight I should have sent forth some of letters ahead of me to fully prepare my venture North, however as I will now be on the road, I will have to take charge upon my arrival.

* * *

9th January 1816

It appears as though the bounder Stephenson has gripped tightly onto the steel and iron industries in the North of England, and his mutual distaste for me and all other semblance of genuine intellectual authority is well-known amongst the peers he has within his distorted sphere of influence, for having arrived at my destination and taking a convivial trip to the nearest ale house to my lodgings I was unfavourably approached by a couple of drunken dockers from Newcastle-upon-Tyne, obviously familiar with Stephenson.

Now this might have simply been the churlish attitude or an overabundance of alcohol, bitter at the sight of a man better off than he, but I tend to view his last remarks as something of a threat to my person. I do not so readily dismiss the behaviour of fellow Englishmen regardless of stature or position, but clearly Stephenson cuts a cultish figure amongst his followers and inspires a certain prejudice amongst them.

The two dockers had been having a heated discussion about whatever it is that men such as they debate, when one of them spotted my personage and somehow having identified me then immediately slammed down their tankard and rounding on me flew into a tirade regarding my "theft of Mr. Stephenson's reward".

I feel as though it is perfectly normal for those of high academic standing to first and foremost place stock in the ideas and designs of others who are equally and legitimately accomplished in intellectual pursuits, as opposed to placing faith in a man who could not read at all for a majority of his life. However, I did not state this aloud, and simply allowed the man to continue his furious rattling.

Going on, he continued to berate me and my peers, even having knocked a bag of luggage I had been resting on the carriage steps back onto the platform. He kept angrily hissing at me until his reluctantly associate pulled him away—it seems they all rather dislike me—his parting remark striking a chilling chord in my spine before he finally returned to address his duties:

"Up here in the North we do things differently. We take a very dim view of thieves and we know how to proper take care of meddlesome folk. You will likely as not find not such a warm welcome this end of the country, and indeed it might be best for all concerned if you didn't just turn about and go back to where you came from."

I must admit to being somewhat taken aback and rattled by the directness of his afront, but surely, I thought that regardless of the feelings of errant drunkards, the employed miners themselves must appreciate the safety lamp, as it assuages some not insignificant degree of fear concerning any immediate risk of explosion or suffocation. I will see for myself shortly, regardless.

*   *   *

10ᵗʰ January 1816

I arrived in good time to Durham and after checking into my hotel I spoke to the bellhop who assured me he was most knowledgeable in all matters locally. With his assistance I was able to acquire the names and addresses of several suitable collieries and in no time corresponded with one owner and his site foreman that was both amenable to my requests and able to host me and my equipment in order for me to observe some typical mining operations. After ensuring that the mineshaft has indeed ideal circumstances in which my lamp could be field tested, it will be brought out and used to examine a length of underground structure which was previously deemed susceptible to firedamp and blackdamp.

The mine was not as deep as most, nor as complex or as aged, but I approached the visit with a small degree of hesitancy perhaps borne from the dripping cave walls that seem to swallow all light sources, or from the almost perceptible aura of negativity and resentment that seems to emanate from each and every miner that I encounter.

I have full faith in my lamp design, and it has passed numerous controlled laboratory tests, but of course it has been impossible to replicate the exact environmental circumstances of a mine above ground, but I have some lingering reservations about possible unforeseen adverse reactions that conditions below ground might potentially give rise to that I hope to finally resolve through this final round of tests.

It is in times like these when I like to remind myself that faint heart never won fair lady, and also point out to myself that Stevenson would not hesitate for a second to outdo me on this, and whilst there may exist the possibility of unforeseen flaws, when it comes to overall safety, I back my design against anything of his any day of the week.

Gathered amongst me are my clothes for the event, old rags and stained laboratory clothes that, should they be marred irreparably by the filth, will not be a significant loss, and a sturdy pair of boots that should hold up to the job.

* * *

13th January 1816

I am inarticulate following recent events and believe to my very core that I have had a very close shave with the grim reaper. Never in my years have I ever experienced such a series of irreconcilable events, and even being of sound body and mind I can scarcely believe the sights and emotions that continue to pervade my every thought; shapes and symbols of shockingly fabulous entities that defy a lifetime of science and that my beleaguered rational mind screams should not be.

I shall recount the events of the past few days, to the best of my ability. I am shaken, yet I feel as though for my own sanity, I must record in full however seemingly impossible or uncreditable it may be while it still remains fresh and within my power to recall accurately.

*   *   *

Upon my arrival at the colliery, despite having selected the most disposable and appropriate items of clothing for the outing, I was repeatedly challenged on my choice of attire.

This staggered me, as did the sight of my fellows returning from a full shift: Ranging from barely six years of age to a mature forty, not a single boy or man was even recognisable as such, so great was the grime that clung to them. One man walked forward with what I assume was a spare change of his own clothing, as well as another pair of boots, and brusquely suggested that I ought to change out of my city clothes.

The yard outside the entrance to the shafts was cluttered with an assortment of various gubbins and machinery, some almost new and some with visible signs of wear and damage. Try as I might I could not discern any logical order, though the miners around me always seemed to know exactly where they needed to go for a spare or replacement part, be it something small like a cable or reels or something large like an entire engine.

The entrance to the shafts in which we were going to descend were pitch black inside from the surface, save for the small light that seemed to cling to the cage into which we were to group in order to be lowered down. The cages were held up and managed by two men, one of whom operated the cage, and the other who carefully tracked the mechanisms of the cable and brakes.

As the others were given their assignments for the day, I was pulled aside by the pit boss, one Mr. Rhys Bilkham, and I was informed of the small team assigned to me for the duration of my stay. Together we would use and monitor my safety lamp in an actual pit and record how it performed in the field. The fire boss, Mr. John Silby, was a natural choice as first member of my party, as he was familiarised with and responsible for the general safety of the mine, and had led inspections of the cavernous facility on many occasions for safety monitoring purposes.

Two other workers, Mr. James Parkins and Mr. Dillon Cooper, were also assigned to accompany us, being the most experienced and practiced within the areas we'd be visiting and finally there was Mr. Kelley Brown, an engineer who had played part in repeated examinations of the site for blackdamp, firedamp, and stinkdamp ('sulphurous gassings').

As we collected my instruments and made our way towards the cage lift Kelly related to me the fact that in its first year, being 1814, there had been a terrible accident at this colliery. A miner by the name of Willard Barns had asphyxiated from an apparent outgassing of blackdamp, or "chokedamp" as it is referred to locally, in one of the main dip shafts.

Thankfully he was the only fatality, but still the mine had to be closed for a period of three weeks to enable repairs to the structure, as well as a safety inspection of the ignition site of the explosion. Despite an exhaustive examination the report determined that no exact cause of ignition could be identified. Puzzlingly, that the branch in which his body was found had meant to have been empty on the day in question, but whatever the case, in order to calm local nerves and prevent any possible repercussion of unexplained explosions, that particular dip shaft section was capped and sealed by a controlled detonation.

The cage lift was designed to fit ten at a time, and I found it remarkably confining, even when only filled to half capacity, though admittedly we were all carrying a myriad of my instruments, lamps and other scientific apparatus. The miners manifestly took a mischievous delight at my discomfort and sought to heighten my state of agitation by mildly rocking the lift from side to side and complaining loudly that they felt the walls were closing in. Being well-seasoned at initiation ceremonies and the like I took their games in good faith, though I couldn't help but raise an eyebrow when one claimed that as many as twenty were brought up in the cage, some lying in a foetal position while others had been thrown on more able-bodied backs. Parkins must have mistaken my look of disbelief for panic as suddenly he threw his head back and roared with a guttural laughter, which in turn had the others guffawing and snickering like a pack of street urchins.

As we signalled to the lift operators began to descend it was in this moment, now with map in hand and deep underground, that I became aware of how unprepared and inadequate my previous attempts to recreate this harsh environment had been. It is hard to describe the sheer isolation and oppressiveness that being this far removed from the surface and natural daylight was placing upon me, regardless of the miners standing all around, and I fought hard to control an almost overwhelming urge to order an about-face and retreat back to the glorious sunlight that now seemed a million miles away.

I told myself that we were going no deeper than the capped chamber, and even then we were not to go inside of it, but rather to inspect its surroundings, monitor the functioning of the lamp, and return to the surface. We were not intended to be below for longer than one or two hours, at the absolute maximum. This experience would not last but my thinking was disrupted by the instantly deleterious atmosphere of the mine.

Upon reaching the bottom of the shaft, Cooper gripped the bottom of the door to the cage and threw it up to allow us out into the upper level tunnel of the mine. My initial impressions were of the stagnant, particle-heavy air, which made me strain to breathe and irritated my eyes. I mildly wondered how much of the polluted air I would breathe during my stay down here and what eventual toll it would take. I imagined that it would take a day's recovery for every few hours submerged and thus was amazed that anyone could venture down for up to ten hours as part of a regular employment.

Whatever the cost, the others appeared unaffected by the stale air, though I believe that this is more to do with the fact that they had grown accustomed over time to such discomforts and now endured it without further comment, rather than empowering them with some preternatural ability to breathe normally where others could not. Shuffling along the central shaft with my instruments we made our way to our first underground destination, the site where Barns' body had been recovered.

As both a precaution and memory exercise I attempted to memorise our route down the central shaft, passing through the upper level tunnel, with its source of fresh, circulated air and the fan shaft, however lacking any distant visible points of reference I was limited to maintaining a record of the turns we made along numerous long straight tunnels.

The dispiriting sensation of walking further into the mine was acute, and in places we had to painfully crouch to an odd angle to allow for our aberrant descent given the relatively low support beams of the tunnel ceiling. The miners, all seasoned men and used to traversing for hours in these conditions, were accustomed to this and so despite my discomfort I had to work hard to keep pace with them.

When we reached the spur that branched off into the working section where Barns had been mining bituminous coal, we stopped, unloaded my instruments and began to take some readings. Unwrapping the advanced prototype lamp, I was most happy to see that it performed as well here as they had back in my laboratory, giving off a slow and steady glow of light while the outer mesh ensured that no fumes or vapours ignited around us.

The results of the tests went well and so we packed up and began to pick our way to the sloping tunnel where the remains of Barns had been found. Here in the smaller section of the side cave system the tunnel seemed to get even narrower and further progress was made increasingly arduous thanks to all my cumbersome equipment. The walls were thick with damp and by the time we reached his lamentable resting place we were all soaked in sweat and caked in mine dust. Indeed, I was very glad for the change of attire as despite their general rugged design my original clothes would have been utterly ruined by now.

Glancing around the site of Barns' expiration I was again filled with that sense of dread and panic that had gripped me at the metal lift. Although my apothecary studies under Borlase were many years behind me, I retained enough to be familiar with pain and agony, and so once I saw the exact conditions of his death I knew that Barns must have suffered a drawn out and grievous end, for here he had fought to his tormented last, for despite being mortally injured in the cave-in he had not been crushed by falling rocks but instead would have become steadily intoxicated with poisonous air and slowly suffocated down here, crippled, alone and without hope of rescue.

The grim harsh reality of life and death belowground surged through me, and I felt as if I had snuck a glance behind the curtain of the stoic and matter-of-factness of those whose lives revolved around the mines. However, if I had thought that I was beginning to understand them or garner an affinity with them then I was about to receive a cruel and sudden reminder that if any implied empathy between the miners and myself actually existed then it was decidedly a one-way affair.

Having taken enough readings for the time being we began to pack up my equipment once more when I noticed a small notebook carefully tucked away between two rocks, damp but still legible. Wrapped in a large piece of brown grease-proof paper was the last token of Barns, his log book. Flipping through the pages showed that his penmanship was remarkably clear and in places flowed almost like poetry, another link, albeit tiny, between his world and my own.

As I tucked it into my satchel the book slipped from my wet hand and fell open to the last page where it had just one word, "Martha". Unlike the rest of his writing, this displayed a heavy and laboured hand, and I briefly wondered when exactly he had written this final entry and who this Martha was, though the most likely explanation would of course be his wife or lover. Before I could reflect further, Brown spoke up to remind us all of the imminent danger of staying in any one place for too long without due reason.

"We should head over to the cap. Inspect the site of the main incident, and you can go home" he chided me in a none too friendly way, and I noticed for the first time that of all my equipment bags he had clearly been carrying the least, despite his impressive girth.

We left the second chamber and made our way back to the main tunnel, then exited into the passageway that led further down into the complex, where we took a right and after an estimated ten minutes of sluggish progress reached a narrowing of the cave, barred with three massive beams in an impressively formidable barrier to entry. Brown commented that this was previously the opening to the branch of tunnels in which the explosion had occurred, but that if we were to go any further, we would have to remove the beams carefully.

With as much delicacy and gingerness as we could muster under these difficult circumstances, we began to prise off the large barrier slats and lay them down with their rusty nails facing the cave walls, to use again to re-block the pass after we were through with our experiments and readings.

Stepping beyond the narrowing we found ourselves in yet another confining tunnel and I was very glad that according to my estimations this should be the last set of readings we would need to take before retreating to the safety and familiarity of the surface.

At the beginning of this entry I made mention that I barely escaped with my life, and it is this next passage of time that I bid whoever reads this to allow their mind to expand and be open fully in order to accept what I am about to say as truth, for what I about to impart most assuredly stretched credulity and may seem more like the ravings of a panic-stricken madman than any calm recounting from a mature and esteemed scientist, but I promise that every word I write is the truth.

As the miners and I made our way down the sloping tunnel to the site of the previous cave-in I began to feel as if I was slipping under the influence of a subtle yet pervasive miasma that fogged my vision and clouded my mind. Irreconcilable with the assurances of eye-witnesses, before and since, that the tunnel was straight and without bend or spur I somehow found myself in a remote section cut off from the rest of the miners and unable to see whichever turning I had taken to separate myself from the rest of the party.

Feeling dizzy I decided that the best course of action was to rest my equipment on the ground and try to catch my breath while I waited for Brown and his men to retrace their steps and find me waiting. Unencumbering myself from my equipment without assistance was no easy task, and was perhaps most unwise as no sooner was I bereft of the added weight than I felt the unexplained and illogical urge to spin on the spot and test my joints, a decision I can only surmise was heavily influenced by the cerebral daze I was experiencing at that moment.

The next moment I must have tripped on the leather strap of a box for I stumbled and fell backwards, heavily, and with enough force to dislodge a small section of cave floor, which gave way beneath me and seemed to suck me into its narrow aperture. I attempted to scrabble and pull myself out, but I was wedged in and my every effort only succeeded in squeezing my body further into the crevice.

Calling out for help to Brown I must have remained trapped like that for what seemed like an eternity, but was likely no more than thirty seconds, before my elbows had sunk below the level of the opening and I knew that now without any opportunity to find a purchase for my hands there was only one direction in I was heading.

In one of the worst moments of my entire life I felt my entire body slowly ease lower and lower into an unknown cavern or sinkhole, and having given up any hope of preventing my inevitable descent the last thing I remember before the fall was worming my fingers around the strap of my lamp in the desperate hope that even after I fell I might at least be lost with a source of light to explore my new surroundings.

When the plunge finally occurred, it was without any style or control, and unlike a graceful feline, I failed to right myself even a little; instead I must have bruised, bashed or jarred every vertebrae, and landed hard enough to knock all the breath out of me.

Shaken from the sudden drop, although blessedly not far, I was once again able to stand, something I knew I had to do and soon despite my aching back protesting profusely. The miasma was still thick in my mind, and my ears began to react as if placed under a change in pressure, though how that could be I have still no rational answer. All I knew was that I was now in a very small expanse of absent rock that was not going to become my final resting place, like the above had been for poor Barnes, and so with my lamp giving off a feeble glow I began to search for a way through.

Admittedly I am no expert geologist, but it did not take any significant amount of knowledge to detect that the walls and ground here were beyond merely being waterlogged to the point of totally saturated, and I began to wonder if I might be able to kick a way through, if only I could find a similarly weakened spot as to where I had already fallen.

Lamp firmly in hand, I began to systematically kick down below me, hoping to spot an audible difference signifying a place to break through. Stamping in a spiral or helix pattern I eventually heard a slight deviation in the whoomph of my boots, and so with all the might I could muster I began jumping and stamping down, an effort which sapped no small amount of my energy reserve.

In short order I could feel myself beat down upon increasingly fracturing ground until such time as I began to worry that I might go all the way through if I was not careful. Positioning my body weight on firmer ground away from the centre I made a few more weighty back-heeled stamps and was rewarded for my efforts with the breaking of the floor and an audible splash as it fell and landed into a body of water below.

Careful to not fall in, I laid myself spread on the floor and inched across until both the lamp and my face were above the hole I had created, and I was able to see down below. Regrettably my lamp prototype was not designed to cast light over any great distance, but I could see the dwindling ripples made by the falling debris and hoped that this was a large underground river and not a shallow pool above a solid ground or I would be forced into repeating my tunnel breaking process yet again.

Feeling braver than I had ever been, I steeled myself to lower my body into the hole before me and tried to simultaneously prepare for either a plunge into a large watery body or a drop onto a hard floor covered only with a trace amount of surface water. Luck held out and I landed in what I hoped was an underground river and not a lake, as one would have a way to the surface while the other would not.

At this depth I had no idea if the cave I was in still linked in some way to a long-abandoned spur of the recent miners, or if I had accidentally stumbled into a subterranean dwelling of something older, possibly even prehistoric, for I saw no more wooden support struts, metal trolley rails or could even discern how it had been excavated.

I was able to splash down fairly gently having this time been able to lower myself down from my slightly elevated position in the sinkhole and had kept the lamp as high above me as I could manage so as to avoid extinguishing it with the dank and tepid water. Keeping my left arm outstretched above the water's edge I splashed and paddled until at last I came to a natural rising of the ground and was once more able to find purchase for my feet before wading out and onto drier land once more.

My instant desire upon reaching solid ground was to remain still and recuperate a little, but as I had no way to gauge where I was or how far this new system of tunnels and holed would extend to, I was mindful of the logic of not wasting valuable minutes or oxygen that might prove vital to my survival and eventual escape or rescue. I was also cold from my swim and I had a fear of catching pneumonia in such conditions as these with no way to heat or dry myself adequately.

Gathering my wits about me I shook off the worst of the drips that clung to my clothes and trying as best I could to prevent myself from shivering too much I pressed on in the gloom, searching for signs of a way out.

Reaching a central chamber of sorts, I came across an inconceivable tableau that still refuses to leave me and I fear will remain with me to my dying day.

In the chamber's epicentre there was fashioned some kind of delirium-inducing sculpture or altar, made out of scraps of wood, metal and machinery, some I was familiar with while others seemed whole alien in their design and origin. Worse than not knowing of all its material I was dumbstruck with its nonsensical, nearly glyphic or cuneiform-like inscriptions painted in what I could only guess was blood, excrement or a ghastly combined paste of both.

My brain reeled as it fought to make sense of what my eyes were telling it, and attempting to shake lose the cobwebs that snagged its internal gears I temporarily rested the lamp upon the edge of this horrible thing, and in doing so I inadvertently illuminated a design on the central miniature column of the plinth that I had not previously been able to see for lack of light. It was a rounded plinth, forged from clay with the base of it left slightly lumpy and misshapen, but the rest of it being so smooth as to be impossibly so, as if it had been carved from solid marble. Topping the plinth was a complex gathering of tentacles, wide at the base then tapering up into curled tips, the detail so fine that upon the surface of the tentacles were small marks of texture; the suction cups were impeccably placed, with each one rounded in a slightly different way, some flexed, some withdrawn, some curved outward or in, as though its architects were master seafarers well accustomed to the sight of the things.

Beneath this at first appeared to be misaligned patterns of lines, at somewhat leaned angles, but upon closer inspection were revealed to be the legs of many deer engraved into the surface of the smooth column-like plinth so as to exclude any of the rest of the bodies of the animals, an odd choice that anywhere else and in any other circumstances would have simply been discarded as a poor design, but here and now felt inexplicably disturbing.

The top of the plinth, designed as such, gave the impression of the tentacles atop it coming directly from the deer legs, as odd a creature as any could ever imagine, and given the great detail of the thing, from the rounded suction cups to the fine attention paid to the fur and hooves of the deer legs, seemed as though it was a creation based upon a horrible living thing, though how any such blasphemous entity could possibly exist was beyond all the realms of science.

What alarmed me the most was that while the monstrous elements of the plinth had drawn my focus, I believe my eyes only lingered upon that sight to avoid the most horrible aspect of its design: Resting around the feet of the deer and just above where the plinth gave way to a heap of unrefined clay, were human arms, all tied tightly to each other with twine and chains, so that each arm held fast to the next, fists wrapped around the upper arm of the next, all the way round the plinth.

Although it was an unholy abomination and I would have gladly destroyed it had I had any explosive with me, but at the same time it was disturbingly fascinating and I felt that I should at least attempt to roughly sketch its outline and construction so that I could bring its likeness back to the world and seek answers at a later date.

It gave the feeling of being an idol, an offering altar in a dark and silent church made of damp earth, the waft of incense replaced with the threat of noxious gases, and though I was unsure of what had inspired this creation, or the disturbing and fanciful direction of my thoughts, but it occurred to me acute asphyxiation can cause all sorts of abnormal thoughts and behaviour, and that this was likely the result of a man, or men, driven mad with gaseous sickness before a terrible death.

Reminding myself that I was not exploring for its own sake, but for the purpose of finding a way out, and that if I wanted to avoid suffering such a fate then I had to put away the notebook and continue on for as far as I could and as quickly as I could.

Leaving the fevered effigy behind I made my way towards the far end of the chamber where I had hoped I would find an open tunnel leading out; instead all I found was solid rock. Dejected and defeated I dropped to my knees before leaning against the cave wall and remained there for a while as my hopelessly outmatched brain struggled to make sense of everything.

I do not know how long I stayed there like that, but I do know that it was incredibly fortuitous that I did, as had I not I doubt I would ever have noticed the slight lateral movement on the surface of the water that was the unmistakable evidence of a current leading through the wall just below the surface.

Knowing that no lamp would survive being totally submerged in water, I made my peace with leaving the light behind and hoped only that once through the cave wall I would be able to make my way out by touch alone.

The fear I felt upon the prospect of diving deep into the black waters in search for an unlit way through filled me completely, and had there been even the slightest chance of another route I would gladly have taken it, yet without even the smallest shred of hope of discovery if I remained there I knew that this was my only chance for escape.

Without need for further deliberation I slowly stepped into the water, filled my lungs with as much air as I could and dove below the water. I scrabbled and probed with both my hands for a couple of minutes until at last my lungs felt as though they were going to explode with burning fire, and my head swam with only thoughts for up and air. In my oxygen-starved mental state a part of me was about to give up when my fingers caught a lip of an opening and employing reflexes quicker than I ever thought I was capable of possessing I darted through and then started kicking for the surface.

As my face emerged through the freezing water, I found myself beside a dimly lit corridor. The exertion of my swim and my near-death experience proved ultimately too much for a body far removed from a routine of strenuous activity and so the cumulative depletive efforts of the past hour meant that the only thing I was good for was passing out, lying there on the ground as I grasped for breath.

I am not sure how long I laid there in my state of recovery, but the first thing I remember once my eyes once more found solid light was Mr Perkins and Mr Cooper standing over my prone body, gingerly poking me, while Mr Brown stood with an empty bucket of water which had by all accounts just been thrown over my unconscious body. When I enquired of Mr Brown as to the reason why they felt inclined to throw said water over an already soaked fallen member of their team, and one whom had until recently been missing and presumed trapped and lost, I witnessed nothing but a bank of confused and bewildered looks across all their otherwise concerned faces.

Apparently, according to their testimonies which all tallied and contained no obvious contradictions, I had not been missing at all but had been observed mumbling strange things even before we reached the capped-off tunnel, and then during the removal of the blockade planks I was seen to be visibly swaying, probably due to the physical exertion of working underground, before regrettably succumbing to a feigning swoon in what they later called my distressed state.

I was not at all sure what to make of their reactions but having already taken enough readings as to have made the entire trip worthwhile, we all felt it best to call off any further investigation of the area where the original collapse occurred. Instead I requested for Mr Perkins and Mr Cooper to escorted me back to ground level where I could reclaim my jacket and hat.

Having done so, I returned to my hotel and consumed a hearty meal where after I did feel much more my old self, but though I did not make a large fuss at the time there are just two disconcerting inconsistencies that refuse to reconcile with the miner's accounts. The first is that my prototype lamp has gone inexplicably missing as none of the miners found it on my prone form or indeed anywhere along the floor of the network of mining tunnels through that with which we had traversed together.

The other point which to me is far more vexing is that at the back of the deceased man Barns' notebook there is page after page of nastily drawn and totally unintelligible doodles, doodles which admittedly seem more the art of a tormented mind that of any conventional thinker, yet they are all accompanied by references and comments in the unmistakable penmanship of none other than me.

1816: The Year Without Summer

The Queen and the Stranger

By R. Poyton

25th March , 1816

{Somewhere in the bustling city of Naples}

The lady leaned forward, waving a delicate hand over the Tarot cards spread on the cloth between them.

"Now that you have chosen four cards, child, we shall turn them over."

Fiorenza looked at the strange yellow design on the card backs. She felt nervous about being here, but the lady did seem very kind. As it was their last day in Naples, Papa had brought Fio to the Festival of San Gennaro. The narrow streets were full of decorations, street performers and hawkers selling toys and candies. Somehow Fio had gotten separated from Papa, and was wandering lost, when she heard her name being called. The young girl had turned to see the lady, tall, elegant, with dark hair framing a pale, thin face.

Introducing herself as Serafina, the lady led the child through the throng and into a small yellow marquee set amongst the others around the edge of the square. Once inside, Fio had been given a drink, and asked to sit for a Tarot reading.

"Fret not, child," the lady had said, "Your father will be here soon."

Fio looked again, then gingerly extended a finger to rest on the back of one of the large cards. Serafina gave a thin smile and turned it over.

"Ah, *The Sun!*" The card showed a smiling face wreathed in a circle of flames. More flames bordered the card, they seemed to flicker in the dim lamplight of the tent. "Choose another, child."

The second card depicted a religious figure, one hand raised in benediction, the other holding a bishop's staff.

"*The Hierophant,*" whispered the lady. "And one more."

Of the two cards left, Fio touched the left-hand one. It revealed a gaunt, skeletal figure in tattered robes, carrying a scythe.

"*Death!*" smiled Camilla. "These cards represent the past, child. Do you remember? Can you close your eyes and think back… think back…"

* * *

Laughing wildly to himself, the arsonist staggered through the narrow streets of Naples. The chill night air hung heavy with the smell of burning wood, paper, cloth and more. Behind him lay the clamour of the crowd, the ruddy glow of the conflagration, the screams of the damned. He paused on a corner and lifted his smoke-stained, tear-streaked face to the stars, seeking some comfort from the distant lights or, perhaps some meaning from their configuration. Then, hair singed, clothes tattered, he lurched once more into the night.

Ahead loomed the bulk of the Castel Nuovo, but he plunged on, oblivious of the stares of those who hurried past him. A minute more and he stood on the quayside, the dark waters of the Tyrrhenian Sea placid and still before him. Then, as he watched in horror, there rose on the horizon, with implacable slowness, a bloated yellow moon, terrible and vast. Silhouetted in its sickly, jaundiced glow lay the impossible ruins of a distant city and the man knew that his soul was lost and knew what he had to do. The deep, dark waters welcomed him as he fell forward into sweet oblivion.

*   *   *

{Two weeks earlier}

Salvatore rubbed his eyes and pushed the manuscript on his desk to one side. He stood, chair squeaking on the bare floorboards, and arched his back. Another late night at the Teatro di San Carlo but the work needed to be done. He turned at the soft knock, smiling at the large figure of the manager Domenico Barbaja filling the open doorway. He had a welcome flask of wine in his hand.

"They said you were working late, Salvatore. I hope you are not overdoing things!"

Salvatore gladly took the proffered flagon. He was a slight man in his late twenties, body twisted by the curved spine he had been born with. While it had prevented him from pursuing his dream of stage career, it had by no means stopped him from working in the theatre, as he eventually became Lead Choreographer here at the prestigious theatre.

"I have to get these pieces read, Signor Barbaja." He indicated the pile of manuscripts before him. "Following the success of *Elizabeth, Queen of England* we are being flooded with submissions!" Salvatore gave the pile a contemptuous flick. "Though precious few are of the required standard."

The older man chuckled, wiping a pair of tumblers on his sleeve before placing them on the desk as he sat opposite the choreographer. Salvatore poured and the two clinked glasses before drinking. Domenico was a large man, though kind of face and easy of manner. There had been some doubts about his taking over the Theatre, as he was quite open about the fact that his major interest had been the venue's gambling tables rather than artistic endeavours. But he had proven himself a sound manager on both fronts, culminating in his premiering the exciting new composer Rossini last season.

"Well here's some even less welcome news for you," Domenico responded. "The Inquisition are in town."

"Hell's teeth!" hissed Salvatore. "I thought we'd seen the back of those black-robed vultures."

Domenico nodded. "Don't let them hear you swear like that, you're liable to be taken in for questioning. Yes, they were gone, but King Frederic, in his wisdom, has decided to realign us with the Papal States. So we are back under Inquisition scrutiny again and you know how they feel about the arts! One of the buggers has set up shop at the Castel Sant' Elmo, I hear."

Salvatore nodded and drained his glass. "A pox on them all!"

The older man smiled. "Indeed. In any case, I came up here to tell you to go home. I will finish tidying here, you get back to that daughter of yours. I know it's been difficult since the passing of your wife, so take a day or two off, spend some time with her. I'll cast an eye over these." He indicated the paper pile. "Who knows, the next Mozart may be amongst them!"

*   *   *

Cardinal Scarlato tapped his foot impatiently as he waited for his audience with King Frederic. A tall, lean man with pinched features, he ran a hand through his thinning grey hair, the other hand fingering the rosary at his belt. At long last, the chamber door swung open and, without waiting for the page's announcement, the Cardinal swept into the audience chamber.

Ferdinand the Fourth waited, advisor hovering. In his sixty-fifth year, his long face framed with white hair, the ruler of the Kingdom of Sicily sat tall and upright in his chair.

Scarlato made a shallow bow and spoke in sonorous tones that floated to the rafters. "Greetings, Your Majesty. I bring blessings from Our Holy Father."

Frederic acknowledged the bow with a nod and replied in a wavery voice. "Our gratitude, Cardinal. And to what do we owe the pleasure of a visit from the Holy Inquisition?"

"I was summoned here, Your Majesty, by members of your own local clergy. They are most perturbed at recent events at the museum."

"Museum? Events?"

The King's advisor leaned forward to inform the ruler. "The Real Museo Borbonico, Majesty. I believe there was a recent case of theft."

"Theft, indeed." The Cardinal assumed a stern expression. "But not from the museum, as such. No, this was from the Secret Room."

The King raised a hand to his face to conceal a smile. "Isn't that where they keep the *Cabinets of Matters Reserved?*"

"Indeed, Majesty. I believe there is an extensive collection of obscene material held within the Secret Room. Why they have not been destroyed, I know not. But the theft was of something far more serious. For the place also houses a collection of forbidden books and papers. It was this collection that was plundered."

"I see. And the perpetrators of this heinous crime?"

The advisor stepped in again. "Unlikely to be common street criminals, Majesty. The Director has informed us that security is taken most seriously. Only three people hold keys: the Director, the Museum Controller, and the Palace Butler."

"I see." The King feigned interest, but in reality was thinking ahead to a later assignation he had organised. "And Our Holy Father's interest in the stolen item?"

Scarlato moved closer. "The book taken is most dangerous in the wrong hands, Your Majesty. I am charged with taking all possible steps to ensure its safe return, failing which I am to destroy the unholy tome. With permission, I would like to begin by questioning the Director and his staff."

"Yes, yes, you do whatever you need to do, Cardinal, you have our permission and may use whichever of our facilities you require."

Unseen, the advisor rolled his eyes, while the Cardinal smiled in triumph. With a final bow, he turned and was gone.

*   *   *

Sweat ran down Gineto's face and not purely because of the brazier that filled the cell with infernal heat. Unnaturally still, half concealed in the corner shadows, lurked that bastard from the Inquisition. His two assistants, a grinning, short, rat-faced man and his larger, half-wit companion, stood at the brazier handling certain implements that Gineto tried not to look at.

Palace Butler was an important position, affording a measure of status in most matters. Yet when it came to the trio of key holders to the Secret Room, Gineto was the bottom rung. As such, the blanket of suspicion lay heaviest on his shoulders, and it was with him that the Inquisitor had begun his investigations. Gineto was by no means a coward; as a younger man he had fought the Republicans in running battles through the city streets. But here, under the ministrations of the stone-faced crow from Rome, he felt his blood turn to ice.

The questioning had been innocuous enough at first. But frustrated at not obtaining the required answers, Scarlato had changed tack. He ordered a search of Gineto's home, which revealed, hidden away, a folder of pornographic etchings, part of the collection held in the Secret Room. Gineto explained he had only borrowed them, out of a sense of "artistic interest" but it had been enough to land him in this cell, the smell of heated iron filling his nostrils.

The board to which Gineto was strapped was tilted until his head was lower than his feet. As uncomfortable as this was, he had a horrible feeling that things were going to get a lot worse. He was right. At a command, the giant half-wit began to remove Gineto's boots, while his companion examined the implements in the brazier. The Inquisitor's upside-down face appeared in Gineto's view.

"So, let us try again. Once more, butler, to whom did you pass the keys? Who stole the book?"

Gineto, sweat stinging his eyes, replied as he had before. "I don't know! I swear it!"

The Inquisitor sighed and nodded to the small man. Gineto squirmed and twisted against his bonds but to no avail; his torturers were professionals. Feeling heat near the sole of his right foot he redoubled his efforts. Suddenly his whole being exploded in pain as the hot poker made contact with the soft skin of his right foot. There was a scream, a hissing sound and the smell of burning flesh filled the room. The small man retreated and Gineto began to sob like a child. The stern, upside-down face returned.

"I am not sure I believe you. Again, the keys, who did you give them to?"

Between sobs, Gineto protested his innocence. Once more, the Cardinal nodded to his assistant. If anything, the pain was worse this time, as the poker was held against the butler's other foot long enough to burn through to the bone. Gineto was incapable of speech; tears and snot streamed over his face, he howled like a mad dog in rage and pain. Merciful oblivion took him as a he fell into a faint, but there was to be no sanctuary. The prisoner was returned to an upright position and the large man dashed a bucket of foul-smelling water into his face. Gineto came around, spluttering and gagging, his entire nervous system thrumming like an over-tight violin string.

The Inquisitor pinched the bridge of his nose and regarded the soiled figure of the butler with distaste.

"Some may think my methods extreme, but rest assured, butler, I act only out of concern for your immortal soul. And not yours alone, for any who come into contact with this tome shall face the most dire spiritual peril."

Gineto struggled to speak and Scarlato had to draw close to hear him. Could this be the confession he was hoping for? Gineto turned his head and whispered hoarsely.

"Damn you and damn your whore of a mother you cocksucking piece of shit." Then he fell once more into a swoon.

The Inquisitor shook his head sadly and turned to his assistants.

"Let him rest for now, perhaps he needs time to think. We shall return in one hour. If he still withholds information, perhaps the strapado will loosen his tongue."

Salvatore returned to the Theatre a couple of days later and was pleased to see the pile of manuscripts gone. He had not been at his desk long when Domenico burst into the room. The man looked bedraggled, unusual in one characteristically well turned out. He waved a sheaf of papers above his head.

"Here, Salvatore, we have it! Our next work!" He clutched the manuscript to his bosom and sighed. Salvatore, somewhat taken aback, invited the manager to sit and held out his hand for the papers. The bundle was thin, tied loosely with a pale, yellow ribbon. Salvatore undid the bow, glancing at the handwritten title on the cover.

"The Queen and the Stranger?" He began leafing through the score inside.

"It is not very long, is it?" he muttered. "And this..." He paused on one of the pages. "This is a very unusual time signature."

"Brevity is a quality sometimes to be admired," responded Domenico. "And its genius lies in its unusualness. The composer himself played me some of the music on my piano. Most uplifting!"

"And the composer is? I see no signature here."

"Ah, that is a matter for some discretion. If I tell you his name, I must ask that you never disclose it to anyone."

Salvatore raised his eyebrows but nodded his assent.

"I mean it, Salvatore. You must swear! Swear on your daughter's life!"

This made Salvatore feel somewhat uncomfortable but gave measure, perhaps, to how important this work may be. And had not Domenico discovered the great Rossini? He steepled his fingers and, after a moment's thought, stated flatly, "I swear on my daughter's life."

Domenico relaxed and leaned forward conspiratorially.

"Very well. The composer is Francesco Gargiulo; Controller at the Museum. He has been a regular at our gaming tables, in fact he has worked up quite a debt over the past year or so. He came to me last night with a wild tale and this manuscript. How much of what he told me is true, I cannot say, but I will relay it to you as he relayed it to me."

The Manager moved to the door, pushing it shut. Then, returning to his seat, he began.

"I was about to retire when there was such a banging on my door, I thought the Devil himself was seeking entry. My servant showed in the rain-drenched Gargiulo; he was in a state of some agitation. I bade him sit and offered wine; he refused and urgently thrust this score into my hand. He told me it was a new piece, a fantastical new work that would bring people flocking to the Theatre. I nodded politely, since to my knowledge Gargiulo is, at best, a middling amateur pianist and, aside from some pieces written for his children, is certainly no composer. But from my first glance at the score, I could see this was something interesting."

"You mentioned a wild tale?" Salvatore interrupted.

"Ah yes, well... the first surprise came when Gargiulo claimed to have written this score in one night!"

"One night? From someone so inexperienced?"

"Indeed! You can imagine my scepticism! And no corrections on the score, which he assured me was the original!"

"Shades of Mozart, then!"

"Precisely, my dear Salvatore! But there is more. Gargiulo claims to have been recently approached by a certain lady, known to him as Countess Serafina. She implored, inveigled, perhaps even seduced him into acquiring for her a certain item from the Secret Room at the Museum."

Salvatore smirked. "A noblewoman interested in pornography? Not so unfeasible, I'd say."

"No, no, the item in question was a book, one of the forbidden tomes. In any event, Gargiulo stole the book for her, but, going against her direct instructions, read from it, while seated at his piano, he told me. He claims to have come to his senses in the dawn light, still seated at the piano, and this score lay in pages on the floor around him."

"A wild tale indeed! And the Countess?"

"No sign of her since, I gather. He spent the day searching for her, to no avail."

"And he brought it to you because?"

"Two reasons, I think. He offers the piece in lieu of his gambling debts."

Salvatore nodded. "That would seem sensible, if the piece is as marvellous as is claimed. But you said two reasons?"

"Yes." Domenico stroked his chin. "He was most adamant that the piece be performed as soon as possible. And I must say, having heard some of it, I am of the same opinion."

Salvatore shrugged and gestured with his hands. "Well, it is not a long piece. What were you thinking, orchestral?"

"No, Salvatore, look at the titles of the pieces, look at the margin notes, they tell a story! Music such as this demands movement, a spectacle, a choreodrama. I was thinking a ballet!"

Salvatore began working on the choreography at home that evening at his piano. Playing through, haltingly in places as the music was complex, he began sketching out performance ideas. The titles were names unknown to him. Carcosa, Cassilda, Hali. Most popular works were based on classic myth while this seemed from a very different place. Whilst playing, the weirdest sensation came over him, as though strange shapes slowly twirled and whispered in the shadows beyond the protective bubble of candlelight. A woman's face, pale and drawn, consumptive, hovered before him. His late wife? No, similar, yet the features were sharper, more refined. The eyes were closed, lips writhing in soundless words.

Suddenly the eyes snapped open, revealing blank whiteness. Salvatore let out a cry and at once something touched him, a hand shaking his shoulder. With a start, the choreographer sat up, a concerned Fiorenza pulling on his jacket, crying, "Papa, Papa, wake up!"

He smiled at his daughter. "Sorry, my dear, I fell asleep and had a bad dream, that is all. Now, let's clear this nonsense away, then I shall put you to bed with a story. How does that sound?"

* * *

Later that week Salvatore stood on the stage of the Theatre, talking again to the manager. He was pleased to report he had sketched out a working outline for a performance and that rehearsals could begin forthwith. Domenico smiled briefly, but seemed distracted, prompting Salvatore to ask if all was well.

"It's Gargiulo. He was found last night by the Watch, hanging from the Ponte della Maddalena. Every indication is of suicide. Then, this morning, this was delivered to my quarters."

Domenico nudged a small, locked chest with his foot.

"What's inside?" Salvatore asked.

"It's the stolen book. I took a quick glimpse at it. I don't like it, Salvatore, something is not right about it. Added to which, I've heard that dammed Inquisitor is asking questions about its theft."

Salvatore glanced over Domenico's shoulder, as three figures came into view, striding towards them along the main aisle. He motioned with his head. "Speak of the devil."

Domenico looked over his shoulder and whispered a curse. "Quick, take the chest, Salvatore, get it out of here!"

Salvatore complied, bending to lift the chest and disappearing into the wings as the trio approached. The manager turned to greet the visitors, taking in the gaunt, black robed Inquisitioner, flanked by a hulking brute and a smaller man with shifty eyes. The Cardinal came partway up the steps but stopped short of walking onto the stage.

"I am Cardinal Scarlato of His Holy Father's Inquisition. I'm looking for a book," he stated flatly, looking Domenico directly in the eye.

"Might I suggest a library; this is a theatre, we only have music scores here."

The hulking man clenched his fists and made to step forward. The Inquisitor stopped him with a gesture, face twisted in a mirthless grin.

"Ah yes, you theatrical types, so known for your humour. Vex me not, Barbaja, I am here on the King's authority and will brook no hindrance to my investigations. We can talk here or somewhere more… private."

Domenico felt a cold trickle of sweat run down his back. He had dealt with many troublemakers during his time, but this was no drunken gambler or raffish lout. He adjusted his tone, bowing at the waist.

"My apologies, Your Eminence, merely my attempt at crude jest."

"Who was that man who just left?"

"Salvatore Papetti, our lead choreographer."

"Why is he twisted so? A twisted body is often sign of a twisted soul. But I would expect nothing less in this den of iniquity. Why, the whole city is seethes with corruption! That dammed Sansevero Chapel, the filth kept at the Museum and Heaven knows what goes in this temple of sin!"

At this Domenico bristled and replied with righteous indignation.

"Insult me, sir, but by Our Lord, insult not our staff and performers! Our performers here exhibit the highest standards of moral rectitude!"

Scarlato seemed somewhat taken aback at this reprimand. In any event, he pressed on.

"Nonetheless. A book has been stolen, a most dangerous and evil book. I suspect the involvement of the museum director, a man found hanged this morning. He was often seen here, I understand?"

"You speak of Signor Gargiulo? I heard the sad news this morning. Yes, he was a regular at our gaming tables. In fact, he had run up much debt and had some considerable financial worries. With respect, I might suggest that he took his own life in order to escape his financial responsibilities."

"Perhaps," nodded the Cardinal. "In any event, should you hear of the book, you will notify me immediately. Good day to you, Signor."

With that the trio turned and strode back towards the theatre entrance. As they did so, Scarlato muttered to his henchmen, "One of you watch him, the other, watch the theatre. I smell lies."

*　　*　　*

Salvatore clapped his hands and the murmured conversations died away. The dance troupe gathered, ready for the first rehearsal of the new work. Domenico had informed him of the Inquisitor's questions, but both felt that it was more important to bring a new work to the world. Besides, none but themselves knew the circumstances of its creation. Not wishing to let the book out of his view, Salvatore had brought the small chest with him. It sat under the piano by which he stood giving last minute instructions to the accompanist, Madame Caille.

Having run through directions for the first scene, everyone took positions and Madame Caille began to play. At first, everything seemed as it should. The only sound in the large theatre was the thud of feet on boards and the expressive opening chords of the piano.

Slowly, something began to change. Salvatore felt it first as a heaviness behind the eyes. He rubbed them and looked around. There seemed to be more dancers on stage. And those movements, they were not what he had instructed. He made to stop the dancers but found himself held tight in the sway of the rhythm.

He turned to Madame Caille but she had no eyes for him; she was not even looking at the score. Her head was thrown back, yet she continued to play, the melody darkening, the chords becoming heavier. In response, the movements of the dancers became wilder, less inhibited. They rushed back and forth, some laughing, others with faces frozen in masks of fear. Salvatore stumbled to the rear of the stage. Placing his hands over his ears, he sank to his knees.

The music drifted across the empty auditorium and out through the wings, winding its way through the labyrinth of corridors backstage. Stefania, the formidable door keeper, shouted at the furious hammering on the door.

"The Theatre is closed! None may enter during rehearsals!"

The response was an increase in hammering, then the door burst open, kicked in by a huge, slab-faced man, who pushed through, followed by two companions. The black robed figure snarled, "Nowhere is closed to the Inquisition!"

Over the years, Stefania had seen off all manner of would-be suitors, numerous lotharios and countless ne'er do wells but even she quailed before the grim-faced Cardinal.

Scarlato rushed through the corridors, black robes lifting behind him like a pair of raven wings. His assistants had informed him of the gossip and rumour buzzing through the Theatre about this new work. Surging through the wings, he came to the edge of the stage and the scene that greeted him froze him in place.

First was the music, an assault on the ears. He could see only a pianist, yet could swear there were ethereal flutes, deep bass strings and discordant brass adding to the maelstrom of sound. Then there were the figures before him. Some lay silently twisting on the floor, eyes rolled back in their sockets, mouths frothing. One ballerina kneeled, banging her head repeatedly on the red-smudged boards. The Inquisitor stepped forward, grimacing against the ugly sarabande that assaulted his ears. The sickly yellow glow illuminating the stage revealed more horrors.

In the far corner heaved a writhing mass of copulating flesh, bodies twining in impossible positions, flesh melding and pulling apart, blank faces moaning, whether in lust or terror he could not say. A laughing figure approached him, hands raised. With horror, the Cardinal saw that the man had plucked out his own eyes and held the bloody orbs outstretched, repeating over and over, "Have you seen the Yellow Sign?"

The Inquisitor staggered back, wheeling at more sounds behind him. His assistants...the big man, a beatific grin on his face, had slumped against the wall and was slowly pushing his own knife in and out of his abdomen. Blood stained the front of the man's jerkin as he continued, digging deeper, as if in search of some treasure. The other assistant was on all fours, capering like some demented beast, lips drawn back from his yellowing teeth. With a savage snarl he took the proffered arm of one of the ballerinas and savagely bit into it as she shrilled with delight.

Scarlato spun round again, in a vain attempt to escape that unholy music. He saw the twisted form of Salvatore slumped by the piano. The pianist was smashing her broken hands down again and again, the white bone of her shattered fingers gleaming through the red, reflecting the ivory of the keys.

Then came a sudden hush, as if all the sound had been drawn out of the space, as the heat is sucked out of a room when an outside door is opened. The ballerina who had been smashing her head looked up, face bloody, to point to the auditorium.

"They are coming," she whispered.

Scarlato looked over his shoulder. The auditorium lay vast and dark beyond the glow of the stage. But there was a sense of movement, a whisper of motion. Before his horrified gaze, shapes slowly took form in the seats. Human-like, yet inhumanly still. Like veiled statues they appeared, blank-eyed, staring, terribly silent. White as bone, faces calm and serene, yet postures contorted in unnatural positions. There were perhaps twelve of the figures, all watching the stage. The Inquisitor quailed before the weight of those stares and knew that their coming presaged the arrival of something far, far, worse. Another figure drifted slowly from the back of the Theatre along the aisle. A tall woman, dark-haired, sunken-cheeked. She lifted her arms and announced in ringing tones: "The King!"

At that the music began again with a tremendous crash, the dancers seething to its hellish rhythm. Scarlato felt crushed as if by a heavy weight, the air drawn from his lungs. With a superhuman effort he crawled to the stage edge, averting his gaze from the presence he knew was approaching. Grabbing one of the large stage lamps there, he stood and hurled it across the stage, yelling, "Burn in hell, Spawn of Satan!"

The lamp shattered and burning oil ran like a river of fire, reaching the main curtains and igniting them in orange flame. Scarlato flung another lamp , setting another drape ablaze. Within minutes the stage was an inferno, scenery and curtains feeding the hungry flames. Smoke filled the space; the Cardinal could no longer see beyond his outstretched hand. Around him, dancers were screaming, those that were not laying still. A heavy curtain fell across him, burning his hands and face. Desperately he shrugged it off and fled, not towards the auditorium, but back along the corridors and out of the stage door. People were running and shouting everywhere but, without a backward look, face and hands smarting in pain, the Inquisitor fled into the night.

Salvatore was jerked back to consciousness by the sound of screams and the smell of burning. For a moment he thought he was in hell, such was the carnage around him. Pulling himself to his feet, he saw the blackened figure of Madame Caille, burnt almost beyond recognition yet still mechanically working the keys. His gorge rising, Salvatore glanced around for an avenue of escape. Some urge made him grab the chest under the piano, he knew not why. Perhaps the book inside would hold answers to these terrible events. Then, struggling through the smoke, he darted across the stage, rolling heavily down the steps to the aisle and out to the sweet, night air.

*   *   *

February ~ The Queen and the Stranger

{Back to the present}

The young girl snapped her eyes open with a sharp intake of breath.

"Did you see it, child?" asked Serafina. The girl nodded, nervous again.

"Be at rest, it is all in the past. It is the future that we now concern ourselves with. Turn over the last card."

Fiorenza stretched forward a hesitant hand, when a sound caught her ears. Her father's voice, wheezy and rough, but insistent, calling her name. At once she stood and turned to leave, with all the single mindedness that only children of a certain age possess. She was soon gathered into her father's arms, him expressing concern at her having run off in such a way. Fiorenza told him of the nice lady who had helped, though something stopped her mentioning the Tarot cards and visions. In any case, Papa was simply glad to have her back.

"We must hurry back home," he said. "All our belongings will now have been packed. We are ready to leave."

"Must we go, Papa? I like it here."

"We must, my dear. We must away from this cold and damp place, to your aunt's house in southern France. The warm air there will help your poor old Papa's lungs recover. And should they not…" A shadow passed over his face. "Well, your aunt will take care of you and all my possessions shall be yours."

Fiorenza jutted out her lower lip but smiled again when Papa showed her the funny little yellow puppet he had bought for her to play with on the journey.

The woman in the tent smiled and turned the last card. It showed a figure in tattered yellow robes, on a curiously wrought throne. The figure wore a plain circlet and curious pallid mask, the eyeholes mere dark slits. The woman whispered to herself. "Ah, *Le Roi en Jaune!*"

Then louder, "Worry not child, we shall meet again... sooner or later."

Unkosher Meals

By K.T. Katzmann

Rabbi Wynberg walked out of the cemetery gate with both a bloodless face and clenched, shaking fists. His student, waiting patiently outside the graveyard, was undecided as to which frightened him more.

As the moon rose over Munich, the two Jews drew looks from the local Christians hurrying home through the tree-shrouded streets of their little kingdom. Finding Jews in public during the day was one thing. Finding two of them, outside the cemetery gates after nightfall, stretched the public patience.

The student, a young man named Herschel with a tightly controlled voice and an untamed beard, took to his master's side. "We should go."

The rabbi looked on, as if dead to the world. After several seconds he turned back to peer through the cemetery gates and continued to breathe heavily.

Herschel doubt that answers would be forthcoming from his master. It was a student's destiny to try anyway. "Rabbi Wynberg? How did your meeting—"

"Leave me."

Herschel became keenly aware of two men, Christians by their garb, observing him and the rabbi from a block down. There were worse things that waited for a Jew within city limits than the clubs of a patrolman, but Herschel was in no hurry to see any demonstrated. He swallowed. "Rabbi? People are watching us. You're getting them nervous. Before they get nostalgic about the Germanic Inquisition, maybe we should go."

Wynberg's held breath finally flowed out of him like a diaspora. "Go," he said, the slightest quiver in his voice. "Leave me here. I'll meet you home within the week."

"Well, at least let me accompany you. You might appreciate having friendly eyes watching your back."

The rabbi waved away the offer. "In a town like Munich? Two Jews are not safer than one."

"Four Jews? We could send for help from home."

"Herschel…"

"Final offer: three Jews, one of them Ben Wasserman."

Wynberg laughed. Benjamin Solomon Wasserman had a righteous fury as wide as his infectious grin. He'd once came upon a group of young drunk clerks gone Jew-hunting. That night ended with Ben not only throwing the leader out through an inn window, but later tossing the man back inside to pay for his drinks. "The offer is appreciated, my student. Ben is a mighty tool of the Lord, but not for this task."

Herschel had seen his teacher argue within a stubborn convert for eight hours while debating if the Sun revolved around the Earth or vice versa. Wynberg had the same furrowed brow now, the identical hard stare. In the face of such odds, he relented. "At least give me something to tell your daughter, Rabbi. Please."

Wynberg breathed in. "Because," he said, trying to slow his shaking hands and not quite triumphing. "Because it is time I taught someone… something… a lesson they will never forget."

1816: The Year Without Summer

*   *   *

The conversation that had left Rabbi Wynberg so shaken had been surprisingly short. Little more than a quarter of an hour ago he'd left Herschel behind, closing the cemetery gate close behind him. Most Jews wouldn't dare to brave the graveyard due to a host of mundane terrors, whether the fear of contagious impurity or being discovered by a Christian and quickly accused of witchcraft.

Today, there was only one thing amongst the stone markers of Munich graveyard Wynberg feared. He heard it chuckling gutturally further up the path.

Sweating, holding his ceremonial skullcap onto his head, the rabbi made his way to the back of the graveyard. He had an appointment, and his imagination quailed at the thought of irritating the one who had summoned him. Even rushing, he couldn't help but marvel at the craftsmanship of the stones spread throughout the tree-shadowed lawn. It was a beautiful cemetery, a regal temptation. This last week of March, it was opening to Jews. He almost wished to be buried here; it was closer to his family's home than the single cemetery legally available to Jews in Kriegshaber.

Still thinking about neighbors planning a burial in Munich, Wynberg found his appointment in the older part of the graveyard, amidst pointed markers that stabbed at the sky like granite fangs. The hunched-over figure perched on top of a gravestone, a large tree obscuring much but not enough of the Moon's illumination.

"You came, Rabbi. I was almost losing faith at the end." It was a bestial voice jammed with gravel, but no listener could have mistaken the sarcastic tone. In the unfamiliar silhouette of its body lay impressions of nakedness, deformity, and strength. It had been holding something close to its face, but cast it nonchalantly towards the ground. The object rolled against a headstone and stopped, and the rabbi noted the way it gleamed white in the moonlight.

As Wynberg approached, it snarled. "No closer, Rabbi. I dare say I am not an easy man to look at." Its fingers playfully tapped on the gravestone. "I'm pleasantly surprised you came."

The rabbi coughed. "You made a solid argument."

"You found it convincing?"

"I found it," the rabbi said with tight control on his tone, "in pieces from one end of a hallway to the other. My daughter was heartbroken. Now who'll deal with the mice? That I'd like to know."

The shadowy speaker dropped onto the ground, padding forward on all four limbs. "My ears within the town told me you also have a lovely grandson, don't you?"

It was not the first time Wynberg's family had been threatened. Violence was always the watcher at the threshold for a Jew in the German Confederation. Still, the violence he'd seen smiling Christian countrymen inflict on his people was nothing compared to the savagery he'd found splashed along his floorboards. "Speak. Please."

The figure draped its arms over a tombstone, a wolf-like muzzle suggested by the shadows. "We—"

"We?"

The thing snorted at the interruption. "The cemetery's opening up to Jews. I hear that you've expressed strong opinions on the subject."

"I worry what Christians will do to Jewish bodies." The rabbi breathed in. "I worry what they might do to Jewish mourners."

In the shadows, the thing clicked its tongue. "The, heh, people I represent want to make a suggestion. When you address your congregation next, give them your blessing to be buried in the Munich cemetery."

The rabbi bristled.

"Reassure them," the thing continued, "that being allowed to bury their dead in city limits is a mercy from the gentiles. After all, who wants to schlep fifty miles to Kriegshaber to bury a relative?"

"One who cares for the sake of their eternity." The rabbi took a heedless step forward.

Rustling sounds played upon Wynberg's ears. He turned, glancing amongst the shadowy graves, and was suddenly reminded of childhood games of hide and seek. The cold moving up his spine was the same he'd experienced when he was sure his sister was an arm's length away, unseen, and about to touch him from behind.

"Uh-uh, Rabbi." It waggled a finger at him. "My constituents want you to stay put. Believe me, they're much less pleasing to the eye than I."

Everything from that point on would have proceeded according to the thing's plan, if only it hadn't chuckled.

Wynberg was afraid, certainly, but a sudden harsh bark of laughter from the voice of the creature stirred up old instincts within the holy man. It was the laugh of someone gaining the upper hand against an authority figure, the joy of making the powerful powerless. It was the laughter of a victorious student, and Rabbi Wynberg had never allowed any student to laugh at him without consequences.

"You want bodies." Wynberg glanced at the chewed ball the thing had cast away, which stared back with empty sockets. "I can venture a guess why."

"It's only a vessel, isn't it? Just the meat you leave behind?"

Wynberg sucked in his breath and could not stop himself from replying, even the very real threat to his life seemingly of less importance that defending the Talmud. "No."

The demon-thing cocked its head.

"No," Wynberg said more loudly. "The Messiah will come, and he will give life to the dead. The righteous will rise." The quaver had left his voice; lecturing was familiar territory to fight in. "The body is sacred. It is to be protected until it will be needed."

Laughter burst around him from all sides. Some of it came from beneath the ground.

The thing shook its head. "Please, Rabbi! Please recall it's the nineteenth century, not the twelfth. This is the age of reason; a world with an America in it! We base things on Locke and Montesquieu, not witch hunts and fables! Rabbi, I'd hate to think what Voltaire would say of your primitive traditions. Probably compare it to those superstitious vampire hunts he wrote about, I'd expect."

The thing leapt into the air, its feet clattering upon the nearby mausoleum it landed on. It was almost within arm's reach of Wynberg, and red eyes glared at him from behind a canine snout. "Support the cemetery change. Find a reason. Otherwise, you'll not want to be resurrected in what I leave of you, you old Jew."

*   *   *

An hour later found Wynberg wandering the streets of Munich in a nearly unrecognizable state. His coat and hat, signs of his station and community, were stowed into a sack thrown over his shoulder. The blessed shawl worn underneath his jacket also resided inside the bag. To succeed, Wynberg absolutely had to look like any other man in a white shirt; he couldn't look Jewish.

He wondered if he'd still count as a Jew after the things he'd have to do.

Munich was the crown of Bavaria, but to every jewel some dirt clings. Even the greatest center of learning in the Prussian states still boasted pickpockets, highwaymen, and the unfortunate nameless dead. Rabbi Wynberg had always known of the unlucky buried in the potter's field outside the city. Having now seen the inhabitants of the upscale Munich graveyard, he now wondered if any of the city's dead could be considered lucky.

As Wynberg pushed through the wooden gates of the potter's field, the stark difference hit him like the omnipresent smell of rotting corpses. Decaying wooden posts with hastily painted notations dotted the area, broken up by circular areas which had been obviously dug up and replaced all at once. Wandering next to one of the posts, Wynberg leaned over to read the nearly unintelligible scrawl.

Blond Women, Not Old, Found on Cobbler's Street. 3/2/16

The barely scratched out words beneath gave similar names for January, the previous October, and two names for last August.

"Know her?"

Wynberg looked up toward the bald muscular man with a huge moustache and wild patches of stubble.

"Know her?" The man repeated. "Killed badly. Poor thing. All her possessions taken, too. Very common." His eyebrows raised. "Of course, for a few coins, I could make inquiries about anything specific. Good success rate, too!"

I bet, thought the Rabbi, glancing at the half-dozen varied rings on the man's fingers.

"No." Wynberg waved him off. "No, I need to buy something." With a deep breath, he prepared himself. He'd only ever known the end result of this process; his people had tried to deduce the beginning, but this was the first experiment ever attempted. "I, uh, want to buy a body."

Long moments passed while the gravedigger's gaze seared the rabbi's soul. "Go on."

Wynberg licked his lips. "I need a child."

Dark distrust simmered in the gravedigger's glare. Suddenly his eyes lit up completely in revelation. "Jew?"

"Yes?" Wynberg tried not to flinch, realizing he had just revealed himself.

"Jew, Da? I understand." The gravedigger chuckled, turning away and gesturing for Wynberg to follow. ""You have to keep their numbers in check. Especially if one squeezes the interest on you too tightly! Come. I get a body to help you deal with your Jew problem."

Wynberg swallowed. If I let any of my feelings show, he thought, I'll have failed.

He followed the gravedigger under the bulbous moon's light, walking the seemingly endless rows of nameless victims, unlucky travellers, and convicts. As they walked, the gravedigger turned back, offering a friendly smile. "You have experience in this?"

In the blood libel? Absolutely, you bastard. "None. Heard from a friend about it."

"Ah! Ah, is no challenge." He stepped over a fallen pile of painted grave posts, nodding. "Simplest thing in world. Middle of night, drop body on Jew's lawn, run away. Morning comes, someone sees body and screams." He raised shaking hands and lifted his eyes." 'Oh, help! Jew murderer is draining children's blood for Passover crackers!' A crowd gathers, and soon one less Jew in world."

Listening to the gravedigger's pleasant tones, Wynberg remembered the awful face of Avram Steinmetz, twenty-two, swaying in the wind from his own tree. This body will save Jews, you bastard. With an act equally heinous, he added.

"Where are you going to drop him?"

1816: The Year Without Summer

"Old Munich Cemetery."

The gravedigger stopped. He turned around, placing a hand on the rabbi's shoulder. "Sir. Good sir, no."

The touch made Wynberg's skin crawl. "Excuse me?"

"Upon my soul, I'd not send Christian man into Old Munich Cemetery after midnight. I'd not even send Jew. There are… things there."

Wynberg breathed in. "There? Not here?"

The gravedigger's eyes studied the rabbi, his crooked smile returning. "Most men, they first ask 'What kind of things?' before other questions. You, I think, already know." He looked away, his eyes distant. "In Russia, we called them upyr, the corpse-eaters. Knew a Persian once. Fled from Georgia after we Russians took it." His gaze met the rabbi. "Didn't even hold it against me. Nice man. He said the desert people called them ghuls." The gravedigger shivered. "What those things want, this place has been picked clean of. No worries."

The gravedigger's confidence instantly evaporated at the sound of wood shattering. He grabbed Wynberg by the shoulder, yanking him away from the invisible source of the noise. The rabbi ran blindly, tugged into the darkness, and nearly tripped over the root of a gnarled old tree. If he fell, Wynberg wondered, would the gravedigger would turn around to help or keep running?

Wynberg's burly guide pulled him behind a tree, holding his finger to his lips. Nodding, Wynberg looked back. Near where they had just been talking the ground was churning, bulging up and receding down. Voices grumbled in a language he couldn't place.

Both men shared the same belief as to the cause of the disruption, though neither wanted to say it.

Wynberg stared at the vortex of movement in the ground. "Should we be afraid?"

"Should a pig fear the butcher?"

"I concede to your expertise on that. I thought you said the graveyard was empty of their kind?"

The gravedigger blinked, then counted something on his hands. "Ah! Recent suicide there. Buried day before yesterday. New meat. Must have slipped my mind. We are lucky. Sometimes they surface before they feed. Come away, my friend. Someone else is conducting business in the graveyard tonight."

As they hurried to the other side of the graveyard, Wynberg heard the noises recede into the background of the potter's field. They did not, however, disappear. "Maybe..." Wynberg's mind raced. "Perhaps you could move the graveyard? Find another place without the... things."

The gravedigger laughed. "I doubt anybody except the Lord who is risen has been left alone by those things. They're in every city. Probably ate Abel after Cain's tantrum."

A roiling could of darkness crashed inside Wynberg's mind, a revelation promising to burst free at any moment. It had almost exploded when the decrepit shack of the gravedigger came into view. It was small, and there were doors and walls, poorly crafted yet still identifiable. Still, one would be hard-pressed to call it a house.

"Munich pays pittance for upkeep of the field. I require extra income." His eyebrows raised as he grinned at Wynberg. "So..."

The coins were produced, and so in turn was the body. It was stored in dirt inside a box aboveground behind the gravedigger's abode. The box was cheap, but Wynberg suspected it was still far more protective than the majority of coffins in the ground. Inside lay a boy of no more than twelve. Putrefaction had set in, but it could not erase the nobility of the features. The intelligence and sensitivity of the face contrasted with the twisted, damaged midsection.

"Wagon," the gravedigger offered. He looked down at the corpse. "'Good night, sweet prince. May angels sing thee to thy rest.'" He chuckled, winking at Wynberg. "Always like that part." The gravedigger patted the corpse's forehead before pointing at Wynberg. "Your money gets you body and sack. First, fill sack a quarter full with horse shit from piles outside city gates. When ready, we will load body inside."

Wynberg started, feeling more nauseous than before. "Why?"

"Is better someone think you smell like shit or smell like death?"

The rabbi, having taught the art of arguments for decades, could find no flaw in the gravedigger's logic. "You're rather experienced at this."

The gravedigger puffed up, slamming a fist into his chest. "Is old family tradition. My kin have dug graves in Muscovy for generations. Body-selling is great side business. I come here to avoid competition." He beamed. "One of my ancestors helped plant body so good, infuriated villages all around. Boy became martyr of the church. They still celebrate the dead child's festival."

"Really?"

"Yes. Stirs up new business every year."

It was minutes later, when Wynberg was digging through the filth of hundreds of horses with his hands, that his mind started digging into equally unpleasant fare.

His errand tonight, the crazed plan against the ghuls, had already carried him as far into ritual impurity as he could imagine, but he had made peace with that. Any commandment, he always reminded his flock, can be ignored if the purpose is saving lives. He was doing more. He was saving souls.

Thinking the word "soul" made an icy water droplet run down the inside of his mind.

What kind of a god commands bodily sanctity and allows the dead to be eaten with impunity? For a second, Rabbi Wynberg's thoughts reeled with dark doubts. He tried to push them away, but they continued to cry out behind the locked door in his mind. He wondered if he could even silence them.

When he told students the world was unfair, he referred to the way that humans sullied and mismanaged the bounty of God. But to posit that the Lord's system, given to His chosen people, did not work at all, that those who'd be reborn on the coming of the Messiah were inside bellies and dung piles…

Soiled and stained, he returned to the gravedigger. With unease, he found himself unable to determine the exact spot that had churned with the eaters of the dead less than an hour ago. They leave no trace, he realized. They've always been with us.

As the gravedigger ushered him back to his purchase, Wynberg asked, "Do you ever feel bad for them?"

"No. His body does the Lord's work."

"I mean the Jews."

"Seriously?" He sucked in his lips for a second. "Eh. They go to Hell anyway. I make it happen at more convenient times. Also, money is good."

* * *

Only a few blocks from the cemetery, the rabbi purchased the last necessary ingredient for his campaign against the ghuls.

"I - I find myself dulled," the rabbi told the apothecary, pretending to shake for effect. "In the need of stimulation. Another apothecary suggested quinine, but that didn't work. I wanted to try something similar."

The doctor held up a jug. "So this?"

The rabbi smiled. "Exactly what I was thinking". Humming, the apothecary turned to the shelves behind him. An errant footstep caused a creaky floorboard to sound. As the sound, Wynberg's gaze sped towards the floor.

Are they down there? There's nothing that says they stick to graveyards. Bodies can be found in houses, in roads and rivers. The world is their banquet. They could be scurrying right below us, right now! We're nothing but fat beetles, living in placid ignorance upon an ant hill…

The apothecary leaned to one side, drawing another squeal out of the floor.

"Shh!"

"Excuse me?"

The rabbi smiled. "Sucking my teeth. A terrible habit."

The apothecary nodded. "Remember, only a little of the powder. Too much, and you're in the ground waiting for the last day." He didn't comment on Wynberg's flinch. "How much do you need?"

"There's no apothecary within many miles of my village, and I expect this will be my last trip for a few years. So… I guess I'll take all of it."

The doctor whistled. "You don't play around."

Minutes later, as doctor happily counted what amounted to almost the entirety of the rabbi's fortune, he eyed the now-sold jug nervously. "Be careful. Drop that glassware in a river and you might poison a village downstream."

"I'll be safe."

"You do that. Watch it carefully."

"Certainly."

"And if a Jew finds it, who knows how many wells they could poison?"

The rabbi smiled through gritted teeth. "I'll keep that in mind."

*   *   *

The rabbi's mind was coated in darkness. It wasn't his task bringing him sorrow; he knew Jews have done stranger things to survive (but not the things he'd been accused of that night, he thought). This horror overcame him every time he saw a basement window or felt loose dirt shift beneath his feet.

No God, he reasoned, no just Judge of Heaven would command the preservation of the body and allow the ghuls to mock and feast. The world had been cruel, yes, and never fair, especially to Wynberg's people, yet there had always be a clear and open spiritual path to Heaven. To suggest otherwise...

The rabbi's mind stood on the edge of the abyss and swayed. Just out of his reach lay the heresies he had spoken of. The godless universe of Spinoza was so close, and he just had to lean forward with one more leap of revolting logic.

A line from the Torah leapt out at him. "Shall not the judge of Earth do right?" He'd lectured on the statement, but goose bumps rose as he considered it solely as a question.

Perhaps the Lord did work in mysterious ways, he thought, feeling not one iota better.

"Mysterious ways" also described the back alleys Wynberg took, crawling his way through the entrails of the city, starting at the slightest sound behind him. He took two or three times as long to reach his destiny, but that was a price he gladly paid. Cautiously, he carried the sack that felt like iron and stunk like the Hells, all in an effort to avoid detection. It didn't work.

"Evening, Rabbi."

The two guards stood on the edge of a street corner. One, a foreigner by his looks, smiled at the rabbi. The other man glared, whispering at his partner.

Oh, Lord.

"Good evening, officers." Wynberg inclined his head towards the bag. "Just ferrying home some manure for the farm."

Neither guard made a move to examine the bag.

As Wynberg passed them, the foreign guard smacked the other on the shoulder. "You see? No dead Christian children and no poison for wells. Just farming equipment. The things you Germans believe about Jews."

The rabbi tightly smiled as he walked away.

*   *   *

Long after the moon had slunk away from the centre of the sky, Rabbi Wynberg re-entered the Munich Cemetery.

The preparation for his ploy had nearly killed him, both physically and spiritually. The light-headiness could have been from the night's continual descent into desecration and doubt. He felt further from God than he'd ever been. Alternately, it might have been the medicine; Wynberg would bet money he'd gotten some of the powder in his mouth, though hopefully in the low doses most folk took for stimulation. If it was too much…

He couldn't even finish the thought. Carrying the corpse of the young boy in his arms, a corpse he'd desecrated shortly before and intended to see worse done to soon, Wynberg no longer felt repulsed at the thought of death, even if his body became someone's meal.

He stumbled, nearly gagging from the smells that mingled within the beatific boy's body from all the cuts he'd made. Bearing his load one unsteady step at a time, he managed to reach the place of his earlier meeting before collapsing to his knees. He unwrapped the boy with a shudder.

God breathed life into a vessel to make his Golem, he thought. I have breathed death into this child to make mine.

Weakly, he started to dig in the ground with his hands, muttering prayers of mourning with no conviction behind them and summoning easy tears. This was the curtain call, and Wynberg threw everything into his role.

The graves around him opened up.

Things pulled themselves into the air, dirt-caked and foul-smelling. Some stood on two legs and some on four. The air filled with snarls and barks like starved fighting dogs before their next match.

"If God yet rules in Heaven," Wynberg whispered, "let me go mad now."

The only voice that answered him laughed in mockery. "Rabbi? Oh, you shouldn't have. How neighbourly."

"Please," Wynberg said. "Please. He doesn't deserve that."

The things closed in, yellow eyes shining in the moonlight. At the front of the pack, walking on legs that bent wrong, strutted the eloquent monster. "What do you have there, Rabbi?"

Wynberg clutched the body to his breast. The plan was succeeding. Even if he paid for it with life-long nightmares, he swore to hold himself together to see it through to the end. Wynberg didn't know if he had any faith left in the Lord or his fellow man, but he craved revenge against those who'd stolen that faith from him.

"No." He clutched the corpse close to his breast. "I'm sorry," he said as he turned to stare pleadingly into the yellow eyes of something inhuman and hungry, real tears running down his face in shame. "His death was brutal and stupid. Give him peace. Let his body wait for the Lord to call."

For just a second, Wynberg felt the ground underneath him shift.

As the horde laughed and growled, the talking ghul clicked its tongue. He loped over to the rabbi, placing his hand on the filthy holy man's shoulder. "I'm sorry. I don't think you understand the nature of our relationship."

"Please."

"We," said the ghul, gesturing to itself and all of its fellows, "eat that," he said while pointed a claw at the child's body, concluding with, "so we don't need eat you." It cocked its head, and Wynberg was sure the canine-like muzzle was grinning. "I mean, we want to eat you. We just don't need to. Yet." He reached for the child.

Preposterously, Wynberg still clutched the child, pulling him away as the ghul's claw fell onto the body's arm. As the creature began to tug, he held on to the child he'd personally paid for and stuffed full of powder. "No. No, please." He could no longer tell if it was an act. He wondered the same about his whole life.

"This child or your grandson, Rabbi."

Wynberg's grip released as the body was yanked out of his arm. The kneeling and suddenly unbalanced man toppled, his skullcap tumbling to the ground and quite forgotten in the night. He lay on his side, face turned downwards, weeping, teeth gritted.

Smiling.

He heard the body hit the ground. The sounds of a stampede of hungry dogs greeted his ears, and Rabbi Wynberg keep his gaze averted as the air filled with the sounds of mocking amusement and feasting. Something caked with dirt leapt over him in the rush towards the food.

He listened. Rabbi Wynberg heard every nauseating sound of desecration, his mind throwing up terrifying suggestions for each. Finally, the sound he'd been waiting for came. It was soft, and initially ignored, but it was utterly unmistakable.

A ghul coughed.

Wynberg looked up, the crowd of crouching feasters mercifully blocking his sight of the boy.

One ghul, a gluttonous thing splashed with viscera and meat, stood, woozy, uncertain on its legs. Some of the others looked up in idle curiosity, but none stopped eating.

The afflicted ghul stumbled back and forth, arms out. It tried to screech something, but the crimson-stained jaws remained rigid and still. The beast managed something that sounded like a "meep."

Some of the others were stopping their feast, watching in silent wonder.

Wynberg laughed.

The panicked ghul started feeling for his muzzle with both hands. Whatever it wanted to do, it wasn't possible with stiff, unyielding fingers.

No one was eating now.

The ghul took two unsteady steps and fell, convulsing. It gave off pathetic wheezing noises as the movement began to cease.

For a single breath, the canine cannibals silenced themselves, trading glances with each other. Then the chaos started. Screaming and bounding, the ghuls scattered, running like panicked farm animals in every direction.

Wynberg smiled. Rotten food doesn't bother you, you bastards. Decaying flesh, tainted meat, all putrescence you suck up like candy.

Strychnine, now? That'll give you vultures a tummy ache.

Ghuls were falling to the ground in mid-run and laying there. Many were fleeing into shadows, while some burrowed straight into the ground; Wynberg savoured visions of those suffocating while paralyzed in the soil. He rose to his feet, unable to contain the laughter. Some of the ghuls within earshot noticed the mourner who'd now exploded in dark glee. This might be strychnine exposure, Wynberg thought. Sure as hell can't rule out that. The torrent of mindless cruelty that had deluged him for hours had lost its hold. Finally inflicting cruelty was like an anchor, mooring him in place as others floated away.

The spokesman ghul, now at sea, tried to swim against the current. It had spotted Wynberg, and stalked forward on stiff legs. "Now," it slurred with an insensitive tongue, "teacher, it's time to —
"

"Shh." The rabbi's rebuke was sudden and harsh.

The ghul was so surprised at the practiced shush of a yeshiva teacher that he obeyed.

"Shh. 'Teach me a lesson', right?" Wynberg's grin was predatory. "That's what you were going to say? Hell, you need to quit using dialogue from Punch and Judy shows." As the ghul started to wobble, Wynberg stepped closer, nose-to-muzzle with the increasingly motionless thing. "Besides, you already taught me a lesson." A brain that had cooked with doubts and fears, seasoned in abuse and hatred, finally gave forth its feast. "There's no order, is there? No justice, no law, no promised rewards. Just pain." He clasped the ghul's shoulders with both hands. "Let me give you some of mine."

The screams of his tormentors was so sweet that Wynberg didn't mind when the spokesman ghul raised a shaking and quickly stiffening claw. Oblivion would be a relief from the pain.

That was when it rose.

The shaking of the ground and gravestone reached its pitch as a mould-encrusted horror pushed out of the ground. All sound in the graveyard stopped as the final horror burst forth, a thing resembling the other ghuls in the way a kitten resembled a lion, magnificent in size and grotesquery, towering above Wynberg despite still having everything below its torso still buried within the earth. In one hand it held the decaying body of man; it idly took a bite from the cadaver's head as a child might nibble on a matzos ball. It was silhouetted against the moon, and those shadows concealing the hideous implication of its face was the only mercy that kept Rabbi Wynberg's mind from shattering into dust.

Both ghul and rabbi froze as the thing lowered its titanic head towards them, the gigantic muzzle sniffing Wynberg. Blood-caked lips curled in disgust as the beast sniffed the traces of strychnine that coated the rabbi. Like a nightmarish King Solomon reimagined by Bosch, the ghul giant passed judgement in a voice like an earthquake.

"Jews bad. No eat Jews."

As the pronouncement echoed off the graveyard walls, Wynberg sank to his knees, unable to stop from laughing. "Wonderful! Thank you, oh Dead Lord! In all the history of the world, we're now the only people a ghul wouldn't touch." He snorted, lifting his arms to the sky. "We are your chosen people!"

Wynberg wanted to believe that. It was so tempting a thing to believe, but he knew he was joking. It was all a joke, after all.

Hatred burned in the bleary eyes of the poisoned ghul. "He did something! It's a tr—"

The titan grabbed the eloquent ghul faster than Wynberg's eyes could register, and in one bite silenced the monster's protestations forever. Once the smaller nightmare had disappeared down the gullet of the great one, the massive eyes turned to regard the rabbi.

"Quickly," Wynberg breathed out on his knees. "Please. Quickly, now!" He pointed at his sweat covered brow. "End these thoughts and doubts in my head!"

The gargantuan ghul seemed to cock its head before snorting in disgust. "No eat Jew. Jew bad." It threw back its head and roared before disappearing into the ground. The other ghuls still standing turned at the sound, loping as best as they could towards the tunnel left behind by the behemoth. Those last few on their feet threw the paralyzed ones unceremoniously into the yawning pit.

Rabbi Wynberg blinked in surprise. "No." He pulled himself up on unsteady legs. "Don't leave me here. I killed them! I killed your brethren, you bastards!" He was screaming, almost pleading. "Don't you dare leave me alive!"

The last ghul turned its eyes toward him and snorted, shaking its head. "Jew," it croaked before leaping downwards. Two mammoth arms appeared out of the tunnel, pulling the sides down. A cloud of dust rose into the sky as the passage into the abyss collapsed, the tremulous ground swell knocking Wynberg onto his back.

With tears running down his face, Wynberg lay in the wreckage of gravestones. There was a change coming; he was sure the pains he felt in his head were the birth pangs of a different man, one who would wear his face and rise from shattered memories to face an indifferent Sun. If this was insanity, he welcomed it. He hoped it was. He knew rabbis who'd been nearly shattered by horror and still kept the faith, muttering their delusions whilst their community kept a firm hand on their shoulders. He could handle the madness.

The last terror that preyed on his brain was that he was approaching true sanity in a world that had always been mad, a clarity harsh and unrelenting.

Wynberg wondered if anything within arm's reach was still poisonous.

He lay on his back among the scattered carnage, staring at the cold stars spin indifferently in the night, and wished he could pray for madness as he waited for the unkind light of day.

1816: The Year Without Summer

A Roving in England, No More

By Brett J. Talley

O f the man, I can say only that I met him once. It was a gloomy late April day when I fled to that tavern on the Channel shore, seeking shelter from a chill wind that cut through skin and bone.

When spring should have been blooming and summer just beyond the horizon, instead the cold grip of winter's fingers remained tight around our throats. On that grey evening, I wondered if ever I would look upon the sun again.

He sat in the tavern corner, beside a fire that roared with all the ferocity one might raise against a January night. A glass of clear liquid on the table before him, the fingers of his limp hand only barely caressing it, as he slouched against a stone wall.

Gin and water, I thought to myself. *The concoction that sets his mind a'fire.* For as an Englishman recently in London, I could not doubt that this was he — Lord Byron had come to the continent.

Should I approach him? Did I dare? His name was immortal already, and his words had burned into my memory when first I read them. I knew even then that his wild heart would be pulled to the East. Into mystery and myth, he would vanish there, to return only in legend.

"Lord Byron, I presume," I said, when courage had come. He glanced up with a sigh, though his countenance softened when he saw that I carried with me two drinks.

"You presume correctly," he said, eying the gin as he finished his own. "Please, dear fellow, have a seat. A man should not drink alone, I think."

Down I sat, sliding the glass over to him.

"To what do I owe the honor of your acquaintance?" he asked as he took it.

"It is my honor, sir. I'm recently come from London and I admit, I was quite surprised to see you here."

He laughed, of melancholy rather than mirth. "London, grand city of my birth. Yes. It is likely I shall never look upon its face again." He punctuated that pronouncement by raising his glass to me, as if in toast, then downing half of it.

I scarcely contained my surprise. I'd heard the stories, of course, and the scandal that had chased the poet from the capital of the world would not die away soon. But die it would. One day, at least.

"Surely not," I said.

"Yes, my new friend. Surely."

"The gossip of old maids will soon be forgotten," I said, perhaps more boldly than I should.

"The gossip. A convenient excuse for doing what I must." He grinned. "I am sorry for speaking in riddles. An old habit, you might say. Poetry is often riddle, if the poet is worth his salt."

"If not the scandal, then, why to these shores?"

1816: The Year Without Summer

He leaned back in his chair, and his eyes filled with memory. I wondered if he would speak again, but I need not have worried. His gaze leveled back on me.

"A man with a secret is the last of his race. He is doomed to whither alone, as it haunts his soul. I had sworn to take my secret down to my tomb, buried in my heart. But I see now that is not what fate would decree. In your happy coming, I see the hand of that self-same fate. So, fetch us another drink and stay awhile, and I will tell you why I'll go no more a roving in England…"

*　　*　　*

I do not deny the charges laid against my character. I have loved much and freely, wherever—and to whomever—love may take me, without recourse or care for the judgment of the world. I know myself a villain, but no man will call me a hypocrite. I have stood boldly where others tread only in their hidden dreams. Fie on them. It was not from such timid souls that I fled England. Ah, but I am speaking in riddles again. Let me return to when the thing began.

My line is an old one, having arrived on the shores of England in service of the Conqueror. But madness stalks it. There are those who say the Barony of Byron is cursed. It is only now that I have come to understand just how much truth is in that slander.

My father was the fifth Baron Byron, having assumed that position when my grandfather, known by his contemporaries as the Wicked Lord for acts of unspeakable violence, died raving in an insane asylum. My father wore the name 'Mad Jack' himself, and he wore it well. A Captain in the Coldstream Guards, he might have risen to even greater heights, had his mind remained intact. It is said that he stumbled upon something while in service during the American rebellion, a mass of stone in the wilds of Massachusetts that should not have been there, an edifice not raised by the hands of European settlers and certainly not the native tribes that whispered curses if they spoke of it at all. Whatever the case, he returned to England, discharged for an illness that was never quite diagnosed. My mother kept me away from him. Something in the way he mumbled about the stars disquieted her.

His end came at his own hand and Mad Jack made a show of it; he slit his throat from ear to ear. They say they found him with a smile frozen on his face. I was three years old.

If the dark history of my family stalked me, I chose to ignore it. If madness was to be my fate I would welcome it gladly, like an old friend. How naïve I was.

When I came of age, Napoleon was ravaging the continent, ruining any plans I had to take the grand tour. Very inconsiderate of him. But being an enterprising young lad, I made the best of it, setting off for the eastern parts of Europe, about which Napoleon had little interest. For me, though, it was magnificent. If you haven't seen Greece you cannot imagine it, my friend. The ancient and the new. Pagan splendor, Christian piety, and the wild Muhammadans all crashed together under a Mediterranean sun. It felt old there, old the way Egypt is old, with the marble remains of the ancients staring down upon us. Watching, and waiting. I would ask myself, what may come in a place like this? What dreams and terrors? What visions of untold splendor and magic?

I would have my answer to that question. Oh yes, I would.

It came on an evening where the setting sun seemed to light the sky ablaze. My spirit was aflame as well, and I, along with some fellows of similar means that I had met during my sojourn, were looking for something to quench that flame.

"A séance," said one. "A séance is what we need. In a place like this, we might just touch the next world."

It was agreed. There was an old gypsy woman that was known to the group. She read palms and told fortunes and was said to have a knack for such things. Who better, we thought, to open doorways to a threshold we could not cross?

We found her in the shadow of the acropolis, on an old side street where respectable people did not tread. She was wrapped in a shawl that concealed most of her head, a few strands of tangled white hair covering the deep recesses of her face. One of my party had done business with her before, so it fell to him to approach with our proposal. It was only when he leaned down to speak to her that I realized she was blind.

"A séance?" she croaked in English far better than I would have expected. "The young master does not know what he asks."

Laughter rippled through our company. "Come now, madam, surely this is not beyond your legendary powers?" I said. And we laughed again. But she was not laughing. Her head had jerked up when she heard my voice, as if her chin were on a string.

"Who is that who spoke?" she asked, her blind eyes searching. I was startled when her empty gaze fell on me. "I know your voice. Come forward." I could have turned then, I suppose. Or at least refused her command. And yet, I could not. I would say that it was foolish pride that drew me forth, that I did not wish to face the ridicule from my friends if I refused. That's the lie I tell myself, at least. I was propelled forward, no more in control of my own mind than if I were a slave.

She reached out her hand, took mine. A silence had fallen over our company, one of surprise and fear entwined. "We have met before, I think."

"No, madam," I all but whispered. "That is not possible."

"More is possible than you know, young man. The world of dreams is vast, and a soul may live on after a body dies and might, just might, live again." Her gnarled fingers, bent and crooked, stroked my cheek. "Your line is ancient and carries with it an ancient curse. Did you know that?"

I shook my head, as if she could see it. Yet somehow, she could.

"No, you would not. You have a poet's heart. That is true. But you have dead eyes. Open them," she said, passing her hand across my vision, "and see what your fathers saw."

Can I tell you what happened in that moment? Can I explain it? The flash of light that blinded me. Then I was falling, down and away, through endless spheres of existence, until I came to rest in a place far from Greece, if it even was of this earth at all. I looked up and saw.

An ocean wave, red as blood, crashing on a dead shore. Lightning crackling along a blank sky, and shapes moving in the flashes. Massive, unholy things that towered before the stars and made hope flee. What madness is this, I thought? A stench of fetid putrefaction filled my nostrils, and I wretched onto black sand that moved with creatures beyond counting. Then, recognition, for behind me towered the massive white cliffs of the Dover shore. This was England, by God. England where Hell had come. I screamed, and I did not stop until I came to rolling on my back and shrieking like a mad man on a dirty, cobblestone street in Athens.

My fellows peered down at me, horror masking their faces. One reached for me and I slapped away his hand, though that exertion was enough to break me from my lunacy. I knew where I was and who I was again. There was no gypsy in sight, and when I inquired as to where she had gone, my friends' astonishment had doubled. We had seen no woman, they said. We'd only, just now, set out to find her.

The next day, I set sail for home by way of Constantinople and Malta.

1816: The Year Without Summer

I told myself that nothing had changed. I tried to ignore the things I saw, the shapes dancing in the waves, the massive forms gliding silently, just below the surface of the water. I took to brooding in my cabin on the ship, praying for England. When dry land was once again beneath my feet, only then did I feel safe. Oh, how sweet the ignorance of a fool!

I had barely stepped of the dock when it began. It was as if my senses were sharpened, as if I was seeing things that heretofore I was unable. Who were the squat creatures that huddled in the shadows of the wharf? What of the cloaked and hooded figures that walked the streets at twilight, their faces mercifully covered? And why did no one else seem to see them?

At first, I asked passersby if they saw what I saw. But after the third or fourth quizzical and even pitying look, I ceased. I wonder now if some madmen simply see farther than the rest of us, if there is truth in their insanity. I know there was truth in mine.

When I passed the faceless black horsemen at the crossroads on the way to my estate, I could no longer doubt that I must reach the bottom of the matter.

But I did not seek it immediately. With this new vision came new awareness, too, and a period of creativity that I fear I will never grasp again. Fame came, as I am sure you know, and for a while I drank my visions away. The parties, the events where I was feted by kings and nobles. Not that I enjoyed them. I hated masked balls the most, you know? For there are some things in this world that wear no mask, that need no mask.

It was something that happened at the end of those parties that finally steeled my resolve, that finally drove me to seek out the truth. I had been imbibing, of course, and there are some who would say what I saw that night was no more than the confusion of a drink-addled mind, but I know better.

He was standing in the center of a dancing hall at an estate of some duke or earl, whose name is no longer known to me. Music was playing, but the gentlemen and ladies who spun around that creature seemed not to notice him at all. In fact, they seemed to part like the Red Sea of old, so that I could see him, and he could see me without obstruction. He had a hooked nose and oozing sores across a bald head. His face was too long, too narrow. He stared at me, then smiled, his teeth a streak of perfect porcelain. "Welcome to he who prepares the way," he said. Then he bowed. I'll never forget those words. I'll never forget that bow. Before I could ask him what he meant, he was gone, disappeared into the crowd. Or maybe he was never there at all.

That night I wrote to my mother and asked to see my father's papers.

They arrived a fortnight later. In large part, they were useless, the detritus of a life at war. For days I pored over them, frustration building as I found nothing of interest. And then, in my father's journal, I found what I was looking for. I found the day his ship dropped anchor in Piraeus, only a short time after his sojourn in America.

It was all there. How he and his officers had made landfall. How they had drank their fill, how they had stumbled upon an old woman, blind and infirm, who offered to tell them their fortunes. How my father had lost consciousness, only to come to the shore of a dead ocean where titans awoke.

I did not stop to wonder how it could be true, how it could be that my father met the same woman as I had decades later. It simply was. I'd seen enough to accept the impossible without question.

The discovery spurred me on to even more fevered review of the written history of my father's life. Alas, when I turned the last page, I had found nothing more, no other clues to the mystery. I was at an impasse, with no roads open to me.

1816: The Year Without Summer

The message came just as my despair reached its depths and the bottom of many bottles of absinthe. It was from my mother. Attached to it was another letter, one sealed in red wax with what I recognized as my father's signet ring. My heart leapt, and I ripped into my mother's note. It explained that my father had written to me, just before he took his life. She had hesitated to give me the letter, fearing what it might say. But, given my recent obsession with his writings, she could keep it from me no longer. She closed with the hope that it would answer my questions and quench my curiosity.

With shaking hands, I broke the seal.

* * *

{Letter from Captain John Byron}

My son,

If you read this now, then you know that I have gone on to whatever lies beyond this life. I hope that my heavenly Father can forgive me for what I do. I hope that I can find the rest in the next world that has been denied me in this. Yet, after what I have seen, I wonder if the beyond is not far darker than we imagined. If there is no heaven, no hell. Only something much worse.

You have heard, I know, that our family is cursed. It is more than an old woman's fable. The curse did not come to us by gypsy folk or the evil eye of one done wrong. No, we asked for it.

The Byron name is ancient and honored, but there was one man in our lineage that sought power beyond that which this world can provide. The Holy Scripture says that no man shall suffer for the sins of the father, yet this man's sins of 250 years ago stalk us still.

Sir John Byron haunted the halls of Queen Elizabeth's court, where might and magic were intertwined. I could deduce but few of the details of his life, but what I can say without question is this —

Sir John came to know a certain man named John Dee, and that esteemed sorcerer did much to seal our family's fate.

There came a time when Sir John procured a stone that Dee needed for one of his unholy rites. In exchange, Dee told your ancestor of a certain crossroad where on a certain night, at a certain hour, a certain man would be walking. From that man could be had many things, for a price of course.

At the appointed time, on that moonless night, Sir John stood at the crossroads and waited. As one day passed into another, he saw a figure moving toward him, black on black, night on night, silhouetted in the shade so that even in the utter dark he could still make him out from a great distance. Yet, as he approached, the form coalesced into that of a man, a traveler, from the East, John reckoned. Perhaps a pilgrim from Jerusalem come to more Christian climes. His golden eyes though, they told a different truth. Those eyes that shone, even in darkness.

The two men met and stopped, standing apart, each assessing the other. When the dark one spoke, his voice was strange and unwholesome to the ear. For his tongue was as of one mimicking language, as if he had never uttered words before.

"Why come ye here?"

"To meet with you," John muttered.

"Who came ye by?"

"John Dee."

"What brought ye to offer?"

"Anything you ask."

"What came ye to seek?"

At that question, Sir John's tongue was stilled. He had wanted much. Glory, fame, power. How to convey it all? He needn't have worried.

"Your mind is open. You shall have what ye seek. For fifty and two hundred years your family name shall ascend to the heavens. Then the price in your blood will come due. But be not afraid, for it will be your name and your kin who open the way to they who sleep in death and wait among the spaces between the stars. In this place, in this land, when the stars come right. Indagei. Ultahei. Iä! Iä!"

In an instant, the figure was gone, and the sun was rising in the East. Where the hours went—where the man went—Sir John could not say. The deal was struck. He rose, and with him our family name. For 250 years it was so. Now the bill has been called.

I have seen what is to come. I have dreamt which was not all a dream. I know that I am to be the one to open the gate, and I have seen what will come through it. This, I shall not do. I go to my end now. It is the only way. When I am gone, the lot shall pass to you. I cannot tell you what path to take. Forgive me, my son.

*   *   *

The letter was not signed. It was as if that step would have been one too far for my father to take. He was sentencing me to death, or at least that is how he saw it. He could not bring himself to sign my warrant. But it was dated. The same day as he took the blade to his own throat.

I read that letter three months ago. I realized something my father did not. The prophecy was very specific. Whatever was to come, would come in England. So, I absented myself from that isle that I love. I do not know if I ever shall return. The stories, the scandals. They make for an excellent excuse.

Now I make my way to Greece to find a woman who once opened my eyes. If she knows how to open, maybe she also knows how to close.

You think it strange, do you, that I should make such momentous decisions on such little evidence? Well, there is one bit of this story left to tell. My father's letter did not come alone. There was a clipping, you see, from a newspaper story, quoting the Royal Academy of Science in London. It claimed that the number of planetary alignments this year is extraordinarily high. But it was what was written at the bottom in my father's hand that caught my eye. A prophecy it seemed, from an unnamed source, about an alignment with Algol—that ancient demon star—the planet Saturn, and the dying moon, to take place on April 30, the May Eve, Walpurgis Night. Easily visible to the observer. To the observer in England, that is. A once in a million-year opportunity.

When the stars come right, indeed.

1816: The Year Without Summer

George and the Dragon

By G.K. Lomax

They say it's an honour to have an inn named after one, and I suppose Wyebrow meant it as a compliment. All the same, I'd much rather that Littleport did not boast a permanent reminder of the events of 24th May 1816, and the part I played in them.

Not that I need reminding. More than thirty years have passed, but I can still remember the mad look in Old Sindall's eyes, the screams of Trooper Wallace and the ghastly things we found in the crypt of St George's Church. Above all, I can still see – or not quite see – the gargantuan thing that Sindall summoned, which may yet lie beneath the fens, patiently awaiting another call.

*   *   *

By rights, 1816 ought to have been a time of hope and rebirth in England. The tyrant Buonaparte had finally been overthrown – with my own eyes I saw him flee the field of Waterloo – and had been sent into an exile from which there was to be no return. Many besides myself looked forward to years of peace and prosperity, but these hopes were soon dashed.

If we'd expected the thanks of a grateful nation, we soldiers were very soon disabused of this foolish notion. Thousands were discharged to scratch a living as best they might – and in all too many cases, failed to do so. Those of us who remained with the colours fared little better. The country had forgotten what it was like to have its soldiers living among them. We weren't shunned, exactly, but to many we were something of an embarrassment.

We of the Royals found ourselves in ramshackle and neglected barracks in Bury St Edmunds. The Colonel applied for the necessary funds to make them weatherproof and habitable, but was firmly rebuffed. No money, he was told, was available – the wars had left the nation's coffers empty.

We rankled at this treatment at first, but soon learnt to be grateful for what little we had, for 1816 was a miserable year. The rains were persistent and torrential; there was snow in March and hard frosts well into May, until people began to wonder if summer would ever arrive. That, however, was just the start of the misery. Farmers sowed late – when they were able to sow at all, that is – and it soon became clear that the harvest would be calamitous. Since that of the previous year had been none too plentiful, grain became scarce, and was hoarded like gold. Inevitably, the price of bread rose and kept rising, until even those who could find work – and many thousands could not – often went hungry.

So we sat and shivered and watched the rains, and wondered when there'd be another battle for us to fight.

In the event, that battle came about sooner than we anticipated, though it was not the sort of battle that we expected.

* * *

On 23rd May we were called out to deal with a mob of unruly citizens that was ransacking the town of Ely. The Riot Act had been read to no effect, so it was up to us to restore order. As Officer of the Day, it fell to me to lead my troop to the assistance the civil authorities. I say troop, but our ranks were thin, and were further reduced by sickness. In better days I would have rode out at the head of sixty men, but upon this miserable occasion, I could barely muster eighteen.

There was much grumbling as we got ourselves saddled and mounted, and I have to say that I was sympathetic to the opinions expressed. It was one thing to face the enemy on the field of battle, but to be ordered out to confront one's own countrymen – that was to neither the men's taste nor mine. Still, a man who takes the King's shilling must do his bidding, and none of us relished the prospect of joining the ranks of the destitute.

For once it was not raining, and we arrived in Ely in late afternoon. We were met by the Chief Magistrate, one Edward Christian. "Captain George Methuen, of the 1st Royal Regiment of Dragoons, at your service," I told him, giving him a salute that I didn't quite think he rightfully deserved.

Christian was a tall, spare man, somewhere around fifty. He struck me as being somewhat distracted as he described the situation to me. It was regrettably a now all too familiar, old grievances, lack of work, empty bellies, inflammatory language and too much rum. Some two hundred angry citizens had rampaged through the town, looting shops and ransacking houses, and were now gathered outside a tavern on the market square. They had cudgels, pitchforks and one or two fowling pieces, I was told, but were chiefly concerned with getting as drunk as possible.

"Please show restraint if you can," Christian told me. "There's been a deal of vandalism and thievery, but no bloodshed so far. I want to keep it that way." I assured him that I was in agreement with him on that score, primarily because the disparity of numbers meant that if it did come to blood, I had no doubt that most of it the shedding would be done by my men and I.

"Truth to tell," Christian went on, "I've much sympathy for those fellows, misguided though they are. Indeed, I'm rather grateful to them, as they may have done us all a service in a roundabout sort of way."

That struck me as an odd remark, but I didn't waste time dwelling on it. Instead, I ordered my men forward. The numbers, as I say, were against us, but if there's one thing I've learned as a soldier it's that appearances matter. With an outward display of confidence, we rode up to the tavern and showed the mob carbines and drawn swords. As I'd hoped, that sobered them up fairly smartly. They turned away sullen, a few still seemingly spoiling for a fight but none so brave that they wished to be the first to test our mettle.

Magistrate Christian then puffed up at the head of a group of men who described themselves as the Town Militia – a body that seemed to have mustered only after the danger had passed.

There seemed little more for us to do other than to maintain our show of force whilst Christian identified and arrested the ringleaders, so we stood there impassively. There were the usual insults and imprecations – "You're poor men, like us," and so forth – which made several of my men look uncomfortable, but their discipline held.

Then one of the rioters showed himself at an upper window and started haranguing us most venomously. I tried not to listen at first, but he was difficult to ignore. "I curse you all," he yelled, "and condemn you for the unbelievers you are. The Beast shall have you; aye the Beast shall have you all. Mark my words – before two nights have passed, the Beast will be gnawing on your bones."

He sounded to me like a prophet whose grasp on sanity was slipping, but his words had an effect on the mob. There were murmurs of assent, and I began to fear that I'd been premature in thinking that matters had been successfully resolved without violence. I wondered irritably why Christian, who'd disappeared into the tavern, hadn't arrested the man straight away, and was considering sending a couple of my own men to silence him. Then the man produced a musket, which he levelled at me and fired.

The ball missed, though not by much – I felt the wind of its passage as it flew past my right ear. Shouting to my men to hold their fire, I leapt from the saddle and forced my way through the crowd. I was angry beyond measure. Of course, I've been fired upon any number of Frenchmen over the years, all perfectly acceptable and in accordance with the rules of war, but to be shot at by one of my own countrymen was a cowardly villainy that I would not stand idly by or ignore.

I forced my way into the tavern and found the room from which my would-be nemesis had fired. He'd already fled, but Christian was there, slumped on the floor with his head in his hands. I thought at first that he'd been shot, but he was merely stupefied. I shook him roughly and demanded to know where my quarry was. Christian looked up. He'd gone as white as a sheet, and seemed to be having trouble remembering who I was. "Sindall," he said, slowly. "Darkness."

I shook him again and demanded to know where this Sindall was. Christian mastered himself long enough to point toward the rear of the building. I followed his gesture and was in time to look down on the yard behind the tavern and see the cur making good his escape on horseback.

With my blood ringing in my ears, my next course of action was dictated by pure adrenaline and I am somewhat ashamed to say in that moment I had abandoned my military training and was not thinking too clearly. I rushed back outside, leapt into the saddle, and without waiting for any of my men to catch up to me, I galloped up the street in pursuit. My main fear was that the blackguard might give me the slip in the twisting streets of Ely, but he took the most direct route out of the town and soon I was chasing him up the road that led north. His horse might have been the fresher, but my faithful Barbary was far better bred and trained, and it wasn't long before I could almost hear his horse pant with exertion. I'd closed to within half a furlong of the man when he rounded a bend in the road and was momentarily hidden by a stand of trees. Upon my own rounding of the bend I found myself at an instant disadvantage for he was nowhere in sight.

I reined in, assuming that he'd gone to ground in one of the fields that flanked the road. As I looked this way and that, I became aware that it was almost dark. I chided myself for losing track of the time, but it did strike me as peculiar that I'd not noted the setting of the sun and the encroachment of twilight. To my left, I could dimly perceive a stile leading to a path that skirted a field, so I dismounted and went to make what I surmised would be a simple arrest.

I'm still at a loss to describe exactly what happened next. The darkness thickened until it became almost palpable. With no help from moon or stars – no great wonder in that year of overcast skies – I could perceive nothing but the vague outline of a tree and some tendrils of mist that rose from the ground and coiled snake-like around my calves. I shivered. I should like to be able to say that I shivered because of the cold, for the temperature had dropped sharply. The plain truth, however, is that I was afraid. I told myself not to be so foolish. I'd faced the French with a straight back and a clear eye – why should a disaffected farm-worker give me pause?

"Come forth," I called out, and noticing that I had sounded almost a little weak, I continued in as firm a tone as I could command, "I arrest you in the name of the King."

Despite my proclamation, in all honesty I didn't expect my formerly troublesome quarry to just stand up and hand himself over to me, instead I had anticipated either silence, a crude and pathetic insult hurled from the security of the bushes, or just possibly another attempt to shoot me. What I received by way of an answer was as unexpected as it was discombobulating – for as clear as crystal I heard him whisper something then after a slight pause he began to laugh, thin and to himself but fuelled with malevolence.

A few moments later I was confronted by the source of his sardonic amusement, a shadow that has troubled my mind ever since.

I saw, or rather I almost saw, as one does through a blustery or opaque haze, a … thing that mercifully I cannot characterise in any great detail, but what I can say is that the swaying shape I'd taken for an inanimate and benign tree, situated in my periphery, was anything but. It was some sort of gigantic creature – colossal enough to dwarf even the mighty elephants of India that Major Cochran was so fond of describing. In the murky darkness, the only things I could focus on clearly were its eyes. Fully twelve feet off the ground they were, shining like two huge lamps, giving out a sickly yellow light that illuminated nothing, yet at the same time, capable of sucking the warmth out of the very air itself. They possessed no pupils, or lids, and fixed their unblinking gaze on me like a merciless mouser would a rat trapped in a corner.

And very much like a mouse I felt, for caught in its glare, it now seemed as though the air slowly began to solidify about me, constricting and crushing as it choked the breath from my lungs, and I had to fight down the urge to vomit. I drew my sword and struggled to raise it, though what use I thought such a puny weapon would be against such a blasphemous behemoth, I cannot say. I felt lightheaded, and my legs threatened to buckle under me.

The malicious laugh came again. "Behold the Beast, Captain, behold the harbinger of your demise," my erstwhile quarry declared. Far from being thin and reedy, his voice now seemed to be voluminous and echoing as if coming from a very long way away. Now the monster came closer, moving slowly and ponderously, its stare rooting me to the spot. The temperature seemed to have dropped still further. I felt colder than I've ever felt – and I've campaigned in the Pyrenees in December.

Apart from the creature's eyes, almost the only thing I could see was the mist, the tendrils of which appeared to glow with some inner light as they swirled about me. They seemed to be moving to some pattern, enveloping me in their dank embrace. The Earth seemed to spin beneath me. Terror gripped me, and I believe I let out a scream. Then I knew no more.

*　　*　　*

The next thing I remember was being shaken by Trooper Wallace, who doubles as my servant. He'd clearly followed me during my chase. "Are you alright, Your Honour?" he asked, solicitously.

It took me awhile to unscramble my wits. I was lying on the ground in a field thinly sowed with wheat of such lamentable growth that it was plain that the country would see more hunger and more bread riots before the year was done. It says much about my befuddled state that this though occurred to me before I noticed, to my astonishment, that it was still daylight. I pulled out my watch and looked at it – a little after seven of the clock. Perfectly natural for it to still be light in May – except that I had believed it not so.

Slowly, I got to my feet, and reassured Wallace that I was whole. "I must've tripped over a tree root," I told him.

"Very good, Your Honour," he replied, though he must've been as aware as I that there were no trees within a dozen yards of where I lay. Nor, I was more than a little relieved to note, was any creature larger than a sparrow to be seen.

I leant a little on Wallace as we made it back to the road, suffering him to assist me over the stile and into the saddle. Happily, as a man of a dozen years' service, he knew when it was best for him to hold his tongue. Neither of us said anything as we rode back to Ely. Lord knows what he thought, though. Lord knows what I thought, come to that. I had either encountered or hallucinated a monster. One or the other. I couldn't decide which was worse.

Magistrate Christian was still in the tavern. He seemed to have recovered from his shock. "I'm relieved to see you safe, Captain," he said. In all fairness he might've simply been referring to my run in with my elevated assailant, but the haunted look in his eyes suggested otherwise.

"The blasted fellow escaped," I said, remembering why I'd set out in pursuit. "Seemingly disappeared down a rabbit hole out by the fields. Now I'd better see my men billeted for the night."

"The arrangements have already been made, Captain," Christian said. "I hope you will do me the honour of being my personal guest." His manner told me that he had more than a convivial dinner in mind. Nevertheless, I accepted.

*   *   *

Edward Christian lived alone apart from a cook and a housekeeper. I formed the opinion that he was a widower, but he said nothing about his personal situation. He kept a generous table, and despite the times had prepared a sumptuous spread, but following my earlier altercation I found that I had little appetite for food or wine.

During dinner, Christian played the gracious host. He was most interested, for example, to hear of my experiences at Waterloo. I told him of the charge of the Union Brigade – of how we'd shattered a French column, and how I'd been almost within touching distance of Captain Clark and Corporal Stiles when they'd captured an Eagle. Christian said the experience must've been exhilarating, and I allowed that it had been. I didn't go on to recount what had happened afterwards.

When the dishes were cleared away and the brandy produced, Christian became business-like. "There'll be assizes," he said. "A dozen sentences of hanging, though I expect to get most of them commuted. Transportation, I suppose. Do you take tobacco?"

I filled my pipe and lit it. "But that's for another day," Christian said. "My chief concern at the moment is Littleport."

"Littleport?" I asked. "No-one has mentioned Littleport to me."

"It's a village about four miles north of here. You rode part way there in your pursuit of Sindall."

"The man who fired on me?"

"Yes, Thomas Sindall – a native of Littleport."

"I see. And there's unrest in Littleport that needs to be put down tomorrow?"

"Unrest, certainly. But of a different nature. This problem is altogether more complex, deriving, I believe, from sinister and unwholesome forces."

I said nothing. Christian watched me closely. "I think," he requested after a pause, "that you should tell me what you experienced this evening."

"I lost my man," I replied as non-committal as I could achieve. "Nothing more."

Christian considered me for a moment, and the pressed the issue further. "Captain Methuen, when you entered the tavern earlier, you found me in a lamentable state, did you not?"

I allowed that I had.

"I must tell you," Christian continued, "that I had experienced a most profound shock. I had just witnessed something that unnerved me utterly. When you rode back into Ely, I deduced from your expression that you had experienced something similar. Is that not so?"

"It might be." Relieved by this additional revelation, I deduced that I would receive no mockery or disbelief at this table and resigned to the fact that I could not avoid the conversation any longer without displaying a degree of rudeness, I relented and briefly recounted what I'd seen.

Christian heard me out, then nodded. "It is as I feared," he said. "Indeed, it is worse than I feared. We have very little time."

"To do what?" I asked.

Christian steepled his fingers. "Captain Methuen, what I am about to tell you may seem fantastical, and even in this plea I would normally be more guarded with my choice of words, had you not already been befouled by much the same as I, but I assure you that I am in deadly earnest. There is a growing group of undesirables in Littleport who have formed, for want of a better word, what I shall call a cult."

"A dissenting religious sect?" I asked.

"In a way. They were founded about three years ago by a man called John Sindall, the grandfather of Thomas. Some say Old Sindall is over a hundred years old. Some say two hundred, but that's by the by. The point is that he's taken to preaching the End of Days." Christian paused and gave me a meaningful look. "He takes as his text the Book of Revelation."

His meaning was painfully clear to me. "The Beast," I said.

"Quite so. And I saw a Beast rise up out if the sea, having seven heads and ten horns, and the Dragon gave him his power, and his seat, and great authority. The Bible makes it explicit that the Dragon is Satan, but the identity of the beast has been the subject of much speculation over the centuries. The point is that John Sindall claims to be in communication with the Beast, whose time, he says, is nigh."

"Surely you should have him committed to Bedlam and be rid of him," I said.

"Would that it were so simple. Old Sindall has a number of followers. There were only a handful to start with, but in these hard times more have been drawn to him."

"And they believe that the End is at hand?"

Christian shrugged. "People are hungry. Hungry people can become desperate, and desperate people grasp at straws. It's as easy to believe that the world will end in hail and frost as it is to believe in fire and brimstone."

"I see. And what exactly is it that you want of me?"

"Not just you, Captain. The Royston Yeomanry have been sent for. They muster a hundred or more and should be here tomorrow. I've also been promised two or three companies from the 69th Foot, plus a brace of cannon."

"That seems a lot for one village."

"We can but hope it's enough. Do you remember, Captain, that I said that the rioters here in Ely might've done us a service, without meaning to?"

"I do. It struck me as odd."

"Yes, well the disturbance here was a bread riot, pure and simple – or so I thought until I realised that Thomas Sindall was involved. I hadn't known that his grandfather's cult had spread this far. Nor what powers the Sindalls seem capable of unleashing.

"I said, you will remember, that I saw something in the tavern that unnerved me?"

I nodded.

"Well, I saw what I can only describe as a vision. A very horrible vision. It seemed to me that – for a brief moment only – I was standing on a dark and desolate plain, and that something, some great and horrible thing..." Christian didn't finish the sentence. His eyes, however, were eloquent.

"Yes, well," he continued, mastering himself with a visible effort. "The point is that the citizens of Ely have done us a service. A bread riot is something Lord Sidmouth is capable of understanding."

"Lord Sidmouth, the Home Secretary?"

"The same. I've been trying to get his Lordship to authorise some action against Littleport for more than a year now, but to no avail. I'm afraid he still regards me as something of an inconsequential rabble-rouser."

"He does?"

"Very much so. I fear I caused quite a stir with the pamphlets I published in support of my unfortunate brother all those years ago."

"Your brother?" I asked. Then light dawned. "Fletcher Christian, who led the mutiny on the Bounty?"

"One and the same."

I'd read the pamphlets as a young lad. Fletcher Christian had struck me as rather a dashing figure. I could see, however, that his family would for generations be burdened with that unfavourable stigma in the eyes of the authorities.

"But events in Ely have obliged the Home Secretary to act," Christian said, returning to the subject at hand. "Let us hope it's not too late."

"Too late? What exactly do you expect to find in Littleport?"

"Sindall says he is in communication with the Beast. He claims to be able to summon it. Some claim that they have seen him do just that. Their accounts chime with yours – and mine. They say that the Beast is able to cloak itself in darkness, for example."

Christian paused and looked at me, as if expecting some comment. I said nothing.

"There have been disappearances, too," he resumed. "Perhaps a people dozen all told. In all likelihood most've taken to the road in search of work, but Sindall has put it about that they were unbelievers who were taken by the Beast. Whatever the truth may be, the people fear and believe him, and because of this he has derived a growing acquiescence and adoption of his fanatical doctrines – the end goal of which worries me gravely."

"I see."

"There's more. Certain researches of mine – I'm a Fellow of Downing College you know – have led me to worryingly unpleasant suppositions, nay almost dare I call them conclusions, which make me shudder for the ramifications if they ever come to pass. There are, you see, ancient legends of a monster lurking in the fens – the country round here was mostly marshland until it was drained around a hundred years ago. Certain names crop up repeatedly: Cthulhu, Hali, Tsathoggua, the Magnum Innominandum. Primitive superstitions for the most part, I don't doubt; and yet There are more things in Heaven and Earth than are dreamt of in our philosophies. Or Heaven, Earth and Hell, which I think would be more accurate. I very much fear that Old Sindall may indeed be capable of unleashing – something – the likes of which predate the records of man."

"Yesterday," I conceded slowly, "I would've called you a fool to your face, or tragically unhinged at the very least. Today, however…"

"Quite. Old Sindall says that the time of the Beast is at hand."

"And Young Sindall told us it would gnaw on our bones within two days."

"He did. I fear we have little time. I pray God it will be sufficient. But that's enough for now. It's late, and I would rather await the light of day before we speak further on such matters. May I light you to your chamber?"

* * *

I slept uneasily that night, and dreamt of French lancers. I was back at Waterloo, in the charge that had been our undoing. We'd broken the French column to be sure, but in our folly, we'd thought the battle already won. All that was left, we thought, was to administer to administer the coup de grace, and so we charged on, filled with a wild joy.

Right across the field we charged, ignoring the bugles that sounded recall. Right across that muddy field we charged, until we found ourselves among the French guns. The gunners cowered underneath them or ran for their lives; we howled our triumph as we hunted them down. Then we were charged by a horde of lancers.

In one moment we went from being the hunters to being the hunted – the lambs going to the slaughter. Our horses were blown, and the French had already cut off our retreat. Scores fell as we desperately tried to cut our way out the trap of our own making. The man ahead of me – Trooper Brandon – had his horse killed under him, and while he lay pinned under his dead mount, a lancer speared him again and again. How he screamed. Lord, I will never forget how he screamed.

Then I snapped fully awake. I could still hear screams, but they were not those of Trooper Brandon. Rather, they were coming from Edward Christian's stables.

* * *

I blundered about in the dark for a while but – barefoot and wearing nothing but my shirt – I groped my way across the small yard. I had no light, but my sense of smell told me what my eyes could not. I know the smell of blood. "Wallace," I called. "Are you there, Wallace?"

I got no reply. Wallace, maintaining that a servant's place was with his officer, had insisted on sleeping in the tack-room adjoining the stable. He was an old campaigner who could make himself comfortable almost anywhere and fall deeply asleep in an instant. I'd last seen him spreading armfuls of straw in the snuggest corner. Now he would campaign no more.

The horses were wild-eyed and terrified, and it was the devil's own job to calm them. I was still patting necks and uttering soothing words when Christian arrived carrying a lantern. He raised it high to survey the scene, and all but dropped it in shock. "Dear God in Heaven," he gasped, clutching at the doorway for support.

There was no sign of Wallace, but the tack-room was liberally spattered with his blood. It was on the floor, the walls – there was even a spot on the ceiling. I am distressingly well acquainted with wounds inflicted on the field of battle, and it was plain to me that Wallace had not been the victim of a simple murder. Rather, he'd been hacked at and butchered – whilst he yet lived to judge by the screams I'd heard. Such a thing might have been done by some maniac in the grip of utter lunacy or... I looked at Christian and he at me. Neither of us could bring ourselves to utter the word Beast, but the thought was inescapable.

I followed Christian back into the house. There was no question of returning to bed. Instead, we sat and drank brandy by the light of a lantern until the sun came up.

* * *

"Trooper Wallace has been murdered," I told the men as they paraded in the morning. "The perpetrator was the man who fired at us yesterday, or one of his associates. Mr Christian informs me that they are to be found in Littleport, some four miles to the north. We are riding there forthwith, so pack your belongings and mount up."

There were grim murmurs, but fortunately no-one asked any difficult questions. Military discipline counts for something. We set off in silence for Littleport. We were accompanied by Christian and two fellows named Robert Speechly and William Gotobed, who had look of old soldiers. Speechly had armed himself with a wood-cutter's axe whilst Gotobed carried a blunderbuss. Christian had a brace of duelling pistols stuck awkwardly in his belt. The rest of the Ely Militia, however, had clearly decided that their writ did not run in Littleport. There was no sign of the Yeomanry or any of the other promised reinforcements.

Christian rode beside me. "You hinted there were things you would only tell me in daylight," I said. "If indeed this can be considered daylight." I looked up at the sky. Thick black clouds covered it from horizon to horizon, leaving us in a gloomy half-light.

Christian followed my gaze. "The Beast can cloak itself in darkness," he murmured.

"Unseasonal weather is no cause for fear." I said. "We've had such skies for months."

"That, according to Old Sindall, is proof positive that he speaks the truth. But to answer you more fully, there are those who believe that there is an invisible world that co-exists with the visible one, and that in certain circumstances it is possible to pass from one to the other. This, it is hypothesised, is the explanation for ghostly sightings and other uncanny phenomena. From time to time, fools seek to meddle with this invisible world. The Greek Oracles and other ancient figures almost certainly did so; more recently Dr Dee conducted some esoteric experiments. Now it seems that Old

Sindall is treading that same perilous path – and it is perilous. There are terrible things that dwell in these hidden realms. Things that – hullo, who's this?"

A man was running down the road towards us, waving frantically. He was breathless and dishevelled, and when he reached us he was unable to speak for some moments.

"This is Daniel Wyebrow," Christian told me, "the Landlord of the Globe Tavern in Littleport. He is my eyes and ears in that village."

"Yer Honour," Wyebrow managed at last. He cast a glance at me.

"You may speak before Captain Methuen," Christian told him.

"You must come at once – though what use soldiers will be I'm sure I don't know. Sindall has gathered his followers in St George's and –" He tailed off.

"He intends to raise the Beast?" Christian prompted.

"So he says."

"Then there is no time to lose." Christian spurred his horse into a gallop. After a moment, I led my men after him.

* * *

By the time we reached Littleport, the skies had darkened still further. Though it was mid-morning, we found ourselves in a grey twilight. Even in a year of dreary days, this was exceptional. I dreaded to think what it presaged.

Littleport was a sorry place. I learnt later that in former times it had been a centre for eel-fishing, but that the drainage of the fens had stifled that source of income, bringing hard times to Littleport.

The town must once have been home to some three or four hundred souls, though to judge by the number of houses that had fallen into ruin and disrepair, that number was much reduced. No lights showed at any window, nor was anyone to be seen in the streets. There was a strange smell that pervaded the place – piercing and musty at the same time. It took me a while to identify it, but I eventually decided that it was the smell of poverty and decay.

Christian told me in a low voice – for the stillness was portentous and it seemed unwise to make any more noise than necessary – that it was likely that most of Littleport's citizens were cowering in their cellars or had already fled. Old Sindall's followers, he told me, would number no more than fifty.

"They're in St George's, I believe." Wyebrow said. "I take it that's the church?"

"It was," Christian said, "though I would hesitate to call it by that name now. It was desecrated some months back. The vicar was driven out and the parish records were burned. Wyebrow believes it was to prevent anyone from discovering the true age of Old Sindall, but that's of small concern at the moment. This way."

St George's was larger than I'd expected – it had clearly been built in more prosperous times. We halted. Christian fumbled in a pocket and withdrew some sheets of paper which he squinted at.

"Would that I had better light to read," he said. "Still, I should be able to manage at a pinch."

"This is no time to read the Riot Act," I told him.

"I have no intention of doing so. Not in the way you mean, anyway. No, these writings are the fruit of my more arcane researches."

"What do you mean?" I asked, though I saw his meaning plain enough.

"Captain; in battle you meet gunpowder with gunpowder. I intend to meet sorcery with sorcery. Shall we?"

I looked round at my men. I wasn't sure whether they'd heard Christian use the word sorcery, but whether they had or not, they looked nervous and uncertain. The horses were skittish as well. Clearly the smell – or the feel – of the place was unsettling to man and beast.

"Dismount," I ordered. "Parker, Sergeant Granger, come with me. The rest of you surround the church and keep watch. Be sure that no-one leaves without my authorisation." Parker and Granger were those I believed had the strongest nerves, and I suspected that strong nerves were going to be needed. Neither man seemed best pleased to be singled out, but they obeyed.

Drawing my sword, I led the way. Christian followed, as did Speechly, Gotobed and Wyebrow. Wyebrow mumbled a prayer under his breath.

At the door of the church I paused for a moment, then thrust it open and entered within.

*   *   *

The interior of the church was in a state of disorder. Broken pews were piled like firewood, statuary had been smashed and defaced. The altar had been defiled, its coverings ripped and trampled. Refuse was heaped throughout. There was not a soul to be seen, however.

For a moment I was at a loss. Then we heard the muffled sound of chanting. I looked around for the source.

Christian was first to speak. "They're in the crypt." He led the way to a door and hauled it open.

I led the way down, stepping as softly as I might. The chanting was more distinct now. It was rhythmic and repetitive, though in no tongue I recognised. At the bottom of the stairs I peered into the crypt. It was dimly lit by a couple of lanterns and a scattering of candles, but I reckoned there were some two score people crammed in there. They chanted incomprehensibly, swaying back and forth as they did so. I was struck by the expressions on their faces. Their eyes were shining and they seemed to be in the grip of ecstasy.

The man, standing on a raised dais and leading the chant, was plainly Old Sindall. He was small, wizened, and toothless; and bald apart from a few white hairs that clung to his scalp. It was easy to credit that he was a hundred years old, though he seemed spry enough. Thomas Sindall stood next to him.

Old Sindall held up a claw-like hand and the chanting stopped. He looked at us over the heads of his flock. "Mr Christian," he said in a breathy voice, "and Captain Methuen, I believe. Welcome, gentlemen." The ghastly congregation turned to face us.

I took a step towards him, but a brace of his nearest followers blocked my path. I couldn't quite bring myself to strike them down, so was unable to proceed. Old Sindall gave a short laugh. "I said they were welcome. We shall have need of them, for the Beast must feed."

"The Beast must feed," his followers repeated as one in a deep and monotone chorus that did nothing to ease my growing sense of dread.

Old Sindall gestured to a number of baskets behind him on the dais. His grandson reached into the first, drew something forth and showed it to me. It was a human forearm, with hand still attached. It was milky white, except where it had been severed, just below the elbow. Grinning horribly, young Sindall held the gruesome relic aloft like a trophy, before replacing it in the basket and producing a gory foot. Moving to the next basket, he produced the head of a young woman, which he held up by her hair. It seemed that at the very least a few of those who had disappeared had not, as Christian had surmised, merely gone in search of work.

"Enough!" I was surprised at the sound of my own voice. "In the name of the King I arrest yo…"

I got no further. Young Sindall reached both hands into a third basket. When he straightened up, in one hand he held an unidentifiable hunk of flesh that dripped thick gobbets of blood, and in the other he held a slashed and torn cavalry tunic.

Wallace. Dear God. My gorge rose.

My recollection of the next few moments is confused. I believe I stood in mute stupefaction, unable to decide how to react. I'm fairly certain that the Sindalls – both Old and Young – leered at me with expressions of triumphant malignity. I also seem to remember Christian standing at my left shoulder urgently searching through his sheaf of papers. The one thing I'm absolutely certain of is that Sergeant Granger levelled his carbine and fired.

The sound of the report in that confined space was ear-splittingly loud. It was followed by a silence that was almost as painful. Then Old Sindall laughed.

To this day, I don't know whether Granger missed or… I mean to say, the range was almost point blank, and he was probably the best shot in the Regiment, but if he didn't miss…

Old Sindall didn't think he'd missed, at any rate. A hollow laugh escaped his lips as he smiled and capered about arthritically, taunting us with his apparent invulnerability. "Fools: do you think any of you possesses a weapon that can harm me? You do not, for I am the Servant of the Beast." Clearly, he was quite mad.

At this point Christian stepped forward, having presumably found the right page in his notes, and began to declaim in some strange guttural tongue. Old Sindall made an impatient gesture – and the papers in Christian's hands burst into flame. He dropped them in shock. Sindall's shambling congregation gasped in awe, but I had noticed something they had not. There were, as I have said, by a number of candles burning in the crypt, and Christian had held his papers very close to one, the better to read it. Too close, perchance.

Possibly that is a lame explanation. Perhaps it is merely wishful thinking on my part. Still, I strive to believe it.

I drew my sword and brandished it. I think my intention was to clear a path through the press in order to lay rough hands on Sindall. His followers did not allow me to pass. Not in any active sense: they simply stood there, strangely impassive. Possibly this is because Sindall had recruited mainly amongst the simple-minded. I did worry about Sindall ordering them to advance on me en masse, but he did not.

Instead, he began to chant again. As he did so, it seemed to me that the crypt darkened and grew appreciably colder. I felt again the light-headedness of the night before, when I'd seen – or had believed I'd seen – that yellow-eyed monster in the field. Thin wisps of fog seemed to curl around the ceiling of the crypt, and the columns that lined the walls began to look as insubstantial as bellowed smoke.

"The hour of the Beast is nigh," Old Sindall cried, lapsing into English.

"The hour of the Beast is nigh," his followers chorused – and there, behind Old Sindall, I saw or imagined a great malevolent shape coalescing out of the darkness.

Casting my sword aside, I looked about me for a more suitable weapon. Sergeant Granger had not re-loaded his carbine. Trooper Parker had fled – or crawled – back up the stairs. I doubted whether Christian had thought to load his pistols before setting out.

That left William Gotobed, still clutching his blunderbuss. He seemed paralysed with terror and made no objection when I seized the weapon from him.

The dais on which the Sindalls were standing elevated them above the throng, meaning that I had a clear shot over the heads of those that stood between us. I brought the blunderbuss up to my shoulder.

Old Sindall saw me do so and laughed contemptuously. "Shoot if you will, Captain," he said. "You cannot harm me. I have been given powers beyond your reckoning."

I looked at him. Christian had implied that gunpowder was not effective against sorcery. I feared that he may be right, but that also there still remained the remotest of chances.

"Did I not tell you, Captain," Thomas Sindall said, "that the Beast would gnaw on your bones?"

"The Beast you called?"

"Not I. Our Father here sees from afar. What he sent you was a vision of the Beast – a foretaste, if you will. Now he will summon it verily, and it will feed; after which, it will grant great favours to those who have served and honoured it. Do you understand, Captain? Do you tremble?"

I nodded. I did understand. I pulled the trigger. The blunderbuss fired, and Old Sindall screamed.

*　　*　　*

"I don't know what to say," Christian said. We were back in his house. He was propped up in bed, the doctor having prescribed a few days' rest. "Nor do I see how you knew what to do."

"Thomas Sindall told me," I said. "He told me it was Old Sindall, not he, who had the power. In this world I have seen many things that you would not believe. To be honest, I have no idea if gunpowder may be fit to fight sorcery or not, but it's as good a way of killing a man as has ever been contrived. I knew that I would only get a single shot and so on the off-chance that Old Sindall was correct when he said I couldn't harm him, I made sure that it would count by aiming at Thomas."

"You shot Thomas Sindall?"

"Shot him and killed him. Old Sindall may have been mad, but he still possessed a measure of grandfatherly affection. The shock of seeing Thomas killed brought on a brain seizure. The doctor assures me he's unlikely to last the day."

"And without him, the Beast has no conduit to this world."

"One can but hope."

* * *

An envoy from Lord Sidmouth arrived the next day. It was vital, he said, that events in Ely and Littleport were reported as simple bread riots. Christian, as magistrate, was to identify those tempted to suggest otherwise and have them transported, ostensibly for theft. I believe that a dozen were sent to Australia, where outlandish tales are ten a penny.

But there are ways of hinting at things. Daniel Wyebrow decided to rename his tavern The George and Dragon, complete with a new sign. It's not a bad likeness of me, though I would hate to have to wear all that armour. If anyone tells Wyebrow that the lance his St George is holding looks oddly like a blunderbuss, he smiles and says "Nonsense."

And the Beast? There's been no sign of it for thirty years, but whenever a newspaper claims that it carries strange news from Cambridgeshire, I ensure that I read the entire edition twice slowly and thoroughly, just to be sure.

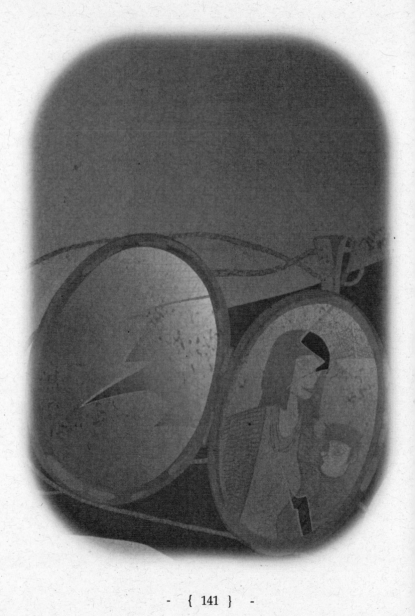

Sacrament

By S. Dooks

Winnipeg, Manitoba, British North America

June 20th, 1816

Three days after the battle, the rains still fell; it made the already unseasonably cool summer even more uncomfortable. Cuthbert Grant checked the brace of pistols on his belt and the hilted cavalry saber along his hip. His fingers twitched, and he found himself reaching into his shirt to withdraw the small locket that hung around his neck. He flicked open the clasp and looked at the portrait contained within. Elizabeth and James stared back at him. He looked at them intently, wishing more than anything he could hold them in his arms. His frown deepened.

"I swear Cutter, if your face gets any sourer it's gonna stick like that."

Grant's dark brown eyes lighted on the man riding next to him. Where Grant was brawny and tall, his companion was lithe and short, his shock of auburn hair sodden by the rain as it hung about his shoulders. He was attired in an impressive-looking woven leather long coat and patched, but still impressive, pants and riding boots. His short beard was beaded with drops of rain, some of which fell to his loose-fitting shirt, that may have been white once in its long history, but now was a collection of assorted stains.

"Apologies Irish, my mind was elsewhere."

Casey Finnegan (or Irish, as he was called by all who knew him), nodded sagely "I feel the same. I can't wait to leave this sodden country behind me." The younger man crossed himself. "Though after that bloody business earlier, remind me to light a votive once we're back in Togo."

Grant frowned. Irish sensed his mood as they rode, casting a look back at the loose collection of ten men who still rode with them. A lone horse was being led by the reins, a bundled form draped over the saddle. Previously, their number had been 60 souls, then 59 after the battle with the Hudson's Bay men. Nearly all of them were gone now... He couldn't say he blamed them, they were volunteers after all. Grant felt a surge of frustration and grief but held it back, if only just. This too didn't escape Irish's notice.

"He was a good lad, captain."

Grant brought his horse up short, looking at the town occupying the prairie before him. The Red River settlement stood abandoned. When the smoke had cleared, the people of this Hudson's Bay Company town had vacated, heading north to the perceived safety of territory, more firmly under the control of the HBC's men. White men, certainly not the heathen half-blood Métis like himself who'd slain all those good God-fearing Christian souls, who were just doing their duty to Lord and country. Forget extortion of controlling the pemmican trade in Manitoba, forget that in the wake of heightened prices, game was becoming scarce in the region. Grant's grip tightened on the reins momentarily. Artemis tossed her head and snorted, the horse sensing her master's foul mood.

"Sixteen is too young Irish."

1816: The Year Without Summer

The face of young Joe Letendre floated on the captain's memory. Sixteen and eager, willing to help do his part to help the North West Company thrive, to build a future for himself with nothing but a sharp eye and a deft hand with a rifle.

"It is that. But we'll get him home sir. Just one last bit of business overseeing the departure of this lot, and then we can head home and give the boy a proper burial."

Grant straightened in the saddle. One last duty to perform here and he could go home. Away from gunfire and the screams of wounded men on the battlefield, back home with food his people needed to survive. He simply had to ensure that the now-vacant town was in fit shape for a North West Company presence, and then depart as soon as the weather allowed.

Thunder boomed overhead, and for a moment, Grant's eyes were drawn over his shoulder, back toward the field of battle. Back toward la Grenouillière; Seven Oaks to the British, but to the local Métis, Frog Plain. He felt a pang of unease as he rode into the empty town with Irish and his men, though he couldn't rightly say why.

*　　*　　*

The problem began with greed, as so many did, in the West. Merry old England, had a rapacious need for high fashion. To satisfy their masters overseas, the Hudson's Bay Company had sought to hunt and trap anything with fur that walked or ran. As the bison, the beaver, and the caribou fell, their lack was felt by the local Métis people as well as the settlers brought here to support the fur traders' ventures. With game diminishing the trade of pemmican, a food made from the fat of slain animals became vital for the people in the region. Whoever controlled the distribution of the pemmican would control the region. The men of the Hudson's Bay Company had sought a monopoly on the pemmican trade, and in so doing, threatened anyone not aligned with them with starvation. The rival North West Company was facing severe depredations, and so they were unhappy with the HBC and naturally protested when the governor of the Red River settlement-a weasel named MacDonnell-had issued a proclamation forbidding the export of pemmican to anyone outside the settlement. This hadn't sat right with Grant or his neighbors: things were harsh enough at the best of times, but add the HBC's aggravation to the unseasonable cold, the constant grey skies and the withered, barely harvestable crops? Matters had steadily worsened, and otherwise good men had reached their breaking point.

Grant dismounted his horse and led it to a hitching post as he looked over the deserted settlement. It wasn't much to speak of: a main avenue, a combination hotel/saloon along one side of the street, across from a stone structure that was likely a bank or the city jail -possibly both. A few shops, their windows shuttered up and the doors hanging open, creaking slightly in the light wind that followed the afternoon rain. Grant fought the slight suction of the muddy street as he made his way to the town square, where the main street met another in a crossroads. He sought shelter beneath an overhang, rummaging through his satchel as he withdrew a pipe and a small pouch of tobacco. He loaded the pipe, put the pouch away and struck a match. The first few inhalations of the pipe's sweet contents eased his nerves some as he watched his men search the buildings. He noted Irish took particular pains to search the saloon, which drew a corner of his mouth up in a wry, momentary smirk. He eyed the lit match in his hand a moment; the sight of the shaky flame brought with it a sudden rush of memory.

The men, the ones who'd left after the grim business of yesterday, had called it a battle. Grant wasn't certain that was the word for it. Slaughter was more apt, all told. He didn't give a damn about either the NWC or the HBC; they were both reliable bastards in his estimation, more concerned with profit and growth than the actual people living in the region. Grant had been approached by fellow Métis who asked for his help. Their people were starving while the whites were posturing at each other. He couldn't stand idly by and let that happen. So, he'd rounded up about seventy men and intercepted an HBC pemmican shipment. They'd cracked a few heads to get it, but nobody had died. He'd intended to simply take the food back to his people and let the two companies fight it out amongst themselves. His expression turned sour, his teeth clenched around his pipe. Then it had all turned to shit. Food was one thing, money quite another. Why not sell some of it to the North West men? Not all of it of course, but enough to ensure they'd have some money for their people? They'd met with a fast-talking Frenchman named Francois Fermin-Boucher from the NWC, and the deal was all but finished when the HBC had rode in on them, along with the new governor of Red River, an odd man named Semple. MacDonnell had stepped down as governor, nobody really knew why. He'd disappeared not soon after, a fact pinned on the Métis which made an already tense situation worse.

Grant had wanted to speak with Semple and get ahead of any bloodshed, but Boucher had decided he was the man for the job and had ridden out to meet the HBC men as if he was Napoleon himself. Grant had already quietly ordered Irish and his other lieutenants to start forming up the men in a loose firing line before he'd heard the raised voices, the piercing sound of a gunshot, the hollow thud of Semple's body as it fell in the mud.

Grant took a long drag from his pipe, leaning against a post beneath the awning as he pinched the bridge of his nose. Nobody had seen who'd taken the first shot, but by then, the lit match had struck the powder keg. When the smoked cleared, 21 Bay men were dead, including Semple, with the rest routed and sent running with the people of Red River not far behind them. Grant tapped his pipe empty against the railing. Of course they'd run, they wouldn't want to be left at the mercy of heathen savages, after all.

"Sir." Irish's voice shook Grant out of his reverie and nearly out of his skin. He did his best to hide how startled he'd been.

"Report."

Irish shrugged. "Place is dead. If she were a ship, I'd say she was stripped to the keel. Anything that wasn't bolted down they likely threw onto their wagons and rode like hell."

Grant nodded. He'd been expecting as much. "We take stock of the buildings, then head back toward North West territory. Between the pemmican and a vacant company town, I'd say we've earned some just compensation, wouldn't you?"

Irish's grin was wry. "Aye sir, that we have. We'll make those bastards pay through the nose for work of this caliber." His expression fell as he looked somewhere over Grant's shoulder. "Now what in the holy hell is that?"

Grant turned, and his eyebrows rose as two of his men ran up to him, slightly out of breath. One, Ben Wasserman, placed a hand up begging a moment's indulgence while he gulped in air with his hands on his knees. Both of them were seasoned campaigners, but they both looked pale.

"Sir! Sir, you need. . .you need to take a look at this." Wasserman finally managed.

"Where's the fire lads? You two look like you've seen a ghost." Irish's grin was wide as he looked over at his commander.

"Maybe. . .maybe we have."

*   *   *

Wasserman and his companion Brom (a burly fellow of Swedish extraction) led them to the large church that stood just on the edge of town. They walked inside, Irish took a moment to genuflect beside a pew before he moved deeper within. The overcast skies and afternoon shadows gave the place an air that set Grant on edge. The pews, a small podium, and a rough-hewn altar were about the only things left. The outline of a cross was along the back of the wall, doubtless the actual article had been removed by the pastor as he'd fled with the others.

Wasserman and Brom moved to the left of the altar. Wasserman was an old-timer, a campaigner in his early fifties who'd been a Nor'Wester for decades. He was as cool under fire as mountain snow. But there was an expression of barely-concealed fear on his face that Grant didn't like. The older man pointed a gloved hand at a wooden door, set into the floor, just behind the altar. "Down there sir. He's down there."

Irish cocked an eyebrow, running a hand through his damp red hair. "Who? Just who's down there Sims? You're unsettlin' my calm with all this mystery."

Brom spoke, his voice quite soft for a man so large. His accent was thick, as it usually became when he was nervous. "A man. A man is down there. He is. . .he is not well sir. I am th. . ." he paused, correcting himself "I think, it may be the governor."

Grant gave the pair a look. "That can't be Brom, you know that. We buried Semple along with the rest of his fools not five hours ago."

"No sir, not Semple." Wasserman cut in, adjusting the musket held tightly in his grip, the barrel pointed loosely in the direction of the door left hung open, just enough to reveal dark shadows beyond. "The other one. The loony."

Grant exchanged a look with Irish. Grant hadn't dealt much with MacDonnell personally, but the man had a reputation for being difficult; egotistical, pompous, and a bit of a self-righteous arse. A few months prior, people had begun to notice strange changes in his behavior; mood swings, sudden fits of paranoid rambling, jumping at things that weren't there. Finally, he'd been asked to step down and had been replaced with Robert Semple, an American businessman from the East. Semple had done a great deal to smooth things over initially, but over time his policies had become even less liked than MacDonnell's had been.

Irish inclined his head toward the door. "After you Captain."

Grant frowned, realizing he'd been squeezing the hilt of his saber, tight enough for his knuckles to go white. He shrugged off the sense of foreboding pushing down upon him by the gloom of his surroundings and opened the door.

The wooden steps led down into a cellar hewn from the rough earth. Wooden beams were visible in the darkness, the shadows cut only by a sole small window, set high in the eastern-facing wall. The dirt scuffed beneath Grant's boots as he looked around. The cellar had been untouched it seemed. A few barrels were there, a trunk, and a wooden table stood along the far wall. Grant flinched slightly, drawing his coat about him a bit closer. The cellar was not cool, as one would expect. It was cold, like stepping out of a cabin into a winter's night. Grant blinked as he saw his breath steam before him.

As his eyes adjusted to the gloom Grant saw that the room was not as barren as he thought. The beams were carved with strange-looking symbols, the floor inlaid with some kind of symbol he didn't recognize. At first glance it looked like a pentagram, but the angles were wrong. It was too distended for that. Irish swore softly under his breath as he stood beside his captain.

"Jesus Christ." the man murmured.

"He's not heeere." A sing-song voice rose from the darkness. Grant spun, pistol in hand. Giggling filled the air as a figure shuffled into the light. Wild eyes gleamed from beneath a tangle of hair that likely hadn't seen a brush in days, an unkempt, roughly-grown beard partially concealed a weak chin. MacDonnell's clothes were ragged and filthy; his fingernails were caked with mud. Grant realized the man must have carved the large symbol in the dirt with nothing but his fingers.

"MacDonnell?" Grant said, not lowering the pistol. "Miles MacDonnell?"

The man paused, as if considering his name for the first time. He muttered to himself softly, then nodded. "Yes, yes that's my name. But I can't keep it. I can't have it anymore. You can't have names, oh no. Names are like signal fires to them. Too late now, much too late. They heard you by now. They'll know you. Now…now you're in tro-uble. . ." MacDonnell cackled, drops of spittle flecking his beard as he waggled a finger at them like a cross schoolmarm.

"Oh, he's cracked all right." Irish muttered.

"Yes. Cracked. The window was cracked open for me. Just a tiny crack. But it was enough. I saw, you see. I've seen what you should never have to saw." The man snorted, giggling again as he leant against one of the posts, ran a fingertip along another, smaller star-shape carved into the wooden post. "He needed me to go away, needed to be in charge so things would go juuust so. The sacrifice. The sacrament."

Grant tracked MacDonnell as he moved, kept the pistol trained at the man's chest. MacDonnell didn't seem to notice, didn't seem to see them anymore. His voice shifted between measured and manic, rising and falling like a lifeboat caught in a maelstrom.

"He wanted me to step down, asked me bold as you please. I told him no, of course. No, no, no, no, no. No. I had work to do, it was important. The company trusted me, trusted me to get things done. But he wouldn't give up. Asked me if I'd like to see some research he'd brought with him from out East. Some books he'd read. Said he could show me something." MacDonnell swayed against the post like a drunk, leering at the two men.

"MacDonnell, you're not making sense."

"What was his name? Can't recall. German fellow. Wrote a book Semple was very keen for me to see. Showed it to me after dinner and port. Una. . .una. . ." MacDonnell paused. His eyes grew vacant for a moment. "*Unaussprechlichen Kulten*. That's it. He read me a passage, then another. Then they came. They. . ." MacDonnell began to laugh again, long and loud.

"MacDonnell. . .!" Grant took a step toward the madman, who drew back, shaking his head wildly.

"Don't touch me! They don't know I'm here. They can't see me. But if you touch me, if you break the seals. . ." MacDonnell gestured at the carvings along the posts, and the large one along the dirt floor. This close, Grant could discern the redness of the man's skin, the shape along his forehead. Good Christ, had he tried to cut the symbol into his forehead?

"Cutter, he's gone." Irish muttered. "Best to buffalo him and tie him to poor Joe's horse." The younger man moved into Grant's peripheral vision. He was leafing through the pages of a leather-bound book, a metal clasp hanging from one of the covers. MacDonnell flinched.

"Yes, yes! Read it! Read the Unaussprechlichen Kulten! Then you'll know. Then you'll see what he wants!"

"What's it say?" Grant risked a look to his friend while he kept the pistol firmly trained on the crazed man.

"Dunno, never learned to read German." Irish shrugged, then pulled a face. "Some charmin' illustrations though. God almighty."

Grant offered the pistol. "Give it here. Keep an eye on him."

Irish chuckled, handed over the volume with one hand while he took the pistol with the other. "About time that schoolin' you brag so much about actually paid off." He levelled the pistol at

MacDonnell. "Now then sir, what say we give the man a little reading room, mm?" He led the babbling man to one side as Grant moved into the small rectangle of light cast by the window. The words were illegible at first as his eyes adjusted to the light, but gradually, Grant found he could make sense of them. He quickly wished he couldn't. The book detailed rites dedicated to the veneration of Gods, but these weren't the kind of Gods he'd ever heard of. Not the Greco-Roman pantheon or the Norse deities but something ...else. He looked over illustrations that made his temples throb, that his eyes couldn't completely focus on. One of them depicted a vast ocean, the waves tossing and heaving as thunder rolled and lightning flashed, the image of something massive breaking the surface, large and bipedal and impossible. There was an inscription below the image. A name. *Cth-*

A hand clapped down on his shoulder, unkempt nails dug into his shoulder hard enough for him to feel through his coat. "They're coming. . .!"

Grant snapped out of his reverie to find MacDonnell clutching at him. "What. . .?"

Irish grasped the man by the elbow. "All right sir, that's enough, leave the nice man who hasn't had you clapped in irons yet already. . ."

Even through the walls, even in the cellar, they heard it. The scream was long and loud, followed by another that rang out just as loud but suddenly stopped. Distant shouting was heard, and the sound of gunfire.

MacDonnell's face drained of color. He threw himself on hands and knees and scuttled back into the shadows, rocking back and forth, back and forth. ". . .no no no no no. . ."

Irish slapped the pistol into Grant's free palm as Grant slapped the book closed. He put the thick volume in his satchel. Irish eased the rifle from his shoulder as he took the stairs two at a time, Grant close behind.

*   *   *

The storm had worsened while they had been inside. Grant ordered them in a loose semicircle; Irish at his right, with Brom at his. Wasserman stood at Grant's left, his own rifle levelled at his shoulder as he swept their limited line of sight. The street before them was deserted, but the sound of shots rang through the air, followed by another blood-curdling cry. Irish canted his head, then broke into a run. "This way!"

The four ran, as best they were able, down the muddy street, turning left at the crossroad. Something hurled at them through the gloom and Grant managed to throw himself to one side as a limp form slammed into the stone wall of the bank, then fell heavily to the ground. It was one of his men, coat and breeches torn to ribbons along with his flesh. Blood mixed with rainwater as it poured from a gaping hole where his head should have met the torn meat of his neck.

Irish skidded to a halt, then dropped to one knee. "Sir!" He didn't pause to see if Grant looked where pointed but levelled his rifle and fired at … something. Shapes loomed in the darkness, and Grant saw two of his men, Latham and Hitchens, break from cover and run toward the four of them. Two bodies were in the dirt, gored hideously, the corpses shaking as they were worried at by. . .things.

Grant took a step back, despite himself. He tried to look at them, tried to grasp exactly what it was that was devouring two of his men, their forms ripped and torn beyond recognition. The number of beings was about ten. . .no. Eleven, but there was movement in the distance, shadows beyond the town in the direction of Seven Oaks. Forms were moving to join their brethren, to join in the feast. They. . .he struggled to focus. They weren't bears, or wolves. He couldn't be sure they were animals at all. They had long, loping arms and pelts of a grimy white, their features were hard to focus on amidst their snapping, unnaturally quick movements but what he could see was a mixture of feral savagery and malign, calculating intellect. One of them looked him in the eyes and Grant knew beyond certainty that whatever this abomination was, it was no mere beast. For a brief moment, the tales his grandmother had told of the cannibal spirits, floated to the surface of his memory, the great devourers, the wendigo. . .

One of the creatures lurched forward, heaved its muscled bulk off the fallen corpse. Others made to take its place as it poised to spring, only to fall back with a snarl as Irish's second shot slammed into its flank. The beast let out a sound that was half-bellow, half-surprised grunt, but it looked less injured than irritated by his lieutenant's excellent shot.

"Form a line, quickly!" Grant found his voice. He drew his saber with one hand and a pistol with the other. The men, terrified to this point, recovered themselves as the familiar rote of training took over. They formed a line. Three in front, three behind. First line would fire, then the second would step up while the first fell back to reload. When they were in position he roared: "Fire!"

Bullets slammed into the line of creatures gorging themselves on human flesh. They looked up as they were fired on and snarled, then began to advance with a slow, measured tread. Seeing them more clearly as they closed the gap, Grant saw they moved on two legs, not four. Their forms were distended, hunched over, but they walked with a gait that didn't remind him of any bear. Their pace quickened, faster than anything that looked so lumbering and large should be able to manage.

"Captain. . .?" Irish said, his mouth agape and features wan.

Grant shoved his pistol into his belt, trembling fingers fumbling with the cross-draw as he tried to reach the other. "Fall back" He began to turn, readying to break into a desperate run. "Make for the-"

He spun and found himself faced with more beasts. They surrounded the party in a loose semi-circle, their multiple lips grinning wide, long tongue gliding along knife-long fangs. It shouldn't have been possible. Nothing so large could move so quickly, or so quietly.

There wasn't time to scream.

*   *   *

Consciousness returned slowly. This couldn't be death: it hurt far too much for that.

Grant opened an eye. Irish looked upon him, his terrified eyes clouded by death. His face was the sole piece of his body that was still recognizable, the rest a ruined mass of pulped meat and bone, torn to shreds by the creatures who made his mind ache when he tried to remember them.

He sat up, and something shifted in his lap. Unaussprechlichen Kulten lay across his thighs; it had fallen pages down onto his bloodied trousers. Grant raised the volume and looked at the gore-spattered pages. That odd symbol, the uneven star that MacDonnell had carved into the church cellar and into his flesh, was illustrated upon the page. Beneath it, written in German: Das ältere Zeichen. Grant found his fingertips tracing the odd glyph.

". . .elder sign." He murmured.

The rain spattered along his chest, his torn shirt leaving little safe from the elements. A scream cut through the air. He glanced in the direction of the church, caught sight of one of the beasts as it dragged MacDonnell through the small window. A long, shaggy arm drew him from the relative safety of the basement, but he'd gotten stuck. The creature tugged again, drawing another scream from the man, then it simply yawned open a cavernous maw and bit the madman's head off. It crunched slowly, looked down the hill toward Grant. For a moment, Grant thought about throwing himself down among the fallen bodies to hide. It moved so fast he couldn't see it. Before he could blink, the creature was there. Grant brandished the book at it, open to the page of the elder sign, and was gratified to see it flinch. Of its fellows he saw no sign, but he still cast a nervous glance over his shoulder. Nothing but the deserted town, nothing but the storm.

The creature seemed to consider him a moment. Its muscles rippled as a long arm extended, reached for something in the mud that glittered. A small pendant on a broken chain hung from its long claws, catching the wan sun's light as it broke sporadically between the clouds. Grant's blood turned to ice as he slapped his free hand along his neck and felt nothing but his own skin and his racing, drumming pulse.

The creature's lithe fingers worked the clasp open, and it considered the contents of the locket. It looked at them, at the portrait of his wife and child. Its gaze moved to him, and for a moment Grant could swear he saw the corners of that obscene maw twitch, those dark unknowable eyes narrow to slits.

A piece of MacDonnell's ramblings drifted into Grant's thoughts: *'they'll know you.'*

"No! No!" Grant pushed off the ground, so stricken with panic, the book fell from his hands. He drew his remaining pistol and fired on empty air.

* * *

He'd been able to make his way back to Fort Chernow without incident. He'd buried the bodies as best he could, then freed the surviving horses and taken poor Joe's (thankfully uneaten) corpse back with him. He'd reported to his superiors, who'd kept him for days of questioning, days that felt like years. He told them he needed to get home, that he feared for his family. He'd claimed that raiders had ambushed the party: madmen who'd torn his men to pieces. He never once considered telling them the truth. His victory at Seven Oaks kept the North West men happy. The loss of a small scouting party was tragic of course, but not insurmountable. He was making a name for himself, they said, with their patrician white smiles.

Grant rode hard for home, for Togo. He got there after a week's further hard ride, asked after Elizabeth and his son. No, they hadn't been seen in town for days. It was a bit strange, actually.

He found the broken door of their cabin, it rocked loosely in the frame. He charged inside, pistol in hand. He screamed her name, then his son's. He searched every room. The hearth was cold, the table set for dinner, stale bread and rotting meat on the table, candles long melted.

He led the search parties, all three of them. They searched the surrounding countryside for weeks. Gradually even the most hopeful among his neighbors gave up, but he kept searching. The friendly, if taciturn, man they knew had disappeared, replaced with a man driven and cold. He sold off the small homestead and the furniture there, purchased supplies and an additional horse, and began to ride. He visited every community he had heard of, and even discovered some that he hadn't. He journeyed East to seek her relations, journeyed south and searched America. He never stopped looking, and as he did, he found traces of more horrors, terrors from the pages of Von Junzt's vile tome as well as other volumes he found and read, their pages sometimes spattered with the blood of their previous owners.

Armed with eldritch knowledge, he brought many of the fell beasts low, and though he finally, after many years, learned the nature of their attackers and brought them the death they so richly deserved, he found no trace of that which he truly sought. If there had been skeletons in their lair, he might have mourned, but there had been nothing, nothing except a few scraps of fabric, the discarded locket, and the desperate fantasy that somehow somewhere that they were alive and waiting for him to come find them.

He never stopped searching. He never saw them again.

Restoration

By C. Miller

From the (purported) journal of Jean-Sébastien Fanchard; discovered by a French colonist, washed ashore on the coast of Senegal, sealed in a waterproof pouch, which was in turn wrapped in a sodden bundle of men's clothing.

July 1st, 1816, early morning

I have had a very queer experience which has left me shaken and not a little fearful. I feel that I should make some form of record of the last few days even as my memory rebels against me and my hands tremble.

It might be desirable to relate the steps that led me here. It may help me to compose myself.

* * *

Like many Frenchmen of my generation I thought the Republic was a wonderful idea while we had it but suddenly found my misplaced loyalty to the Crown when Napoleon went into exile for the first time in 1814. I was caught unawares by the Hundred Days, when Napoleon seemed poised to reclaim that which he had given up, but I managed to re-establish my position as a staunch Bonapartist just in time for Waterloo and the Second Bourbon Restoration.

I was never a very important man. I performed my political acrobatics first as a soldier and later as a government functionary, and I might have escaped notice had I not come from a prominent family. My shenanigans caught the personal attention of Louis XVIII. Though my life is not in any real danger, my liberty is problematic, and my social position destroyed.

It seemed a good time to get out of France.

An organization called the Philanthropic Society of Cape Vert has been working with the government to organize an expedition to Senegal. The French colony there, which has lately been in the hands of the British, is to be returned to King Louis XVIII as part of the peace settlement.

I secured a berth on the frigate Medusa, upon which I will travel to Senegal to ply my trades as a carpenter, general engineer and bookkeeper for the new colonial administration.

Perhaps, I reasoned, a few years will serve to dull the King's feelings, or his memory of me.

Well, I am not yet thirty, tall and strong and not particularly bad-looking. There is still time for me to change my fortunes.

I arrived at the port of Rochefort on June 9, where my fellow colonists and I boarded a variety of boats that took us down the Charente River to the point where the Medusa and her sister ships lay at safe anchorage off the Île d'Aix.

I am one of 400 souls on board, 240 of whom are colonists and administrative personnel, including the newly-appointed French governor of Senegal, Colonel Julien-Désiré Schmaltz, and his entourage.

As for the crew, they are a motley lot consisting of some Royalists, some Bonapartists and a handful of others with no obvious discernible loyalties. Many of them have been recruited from French prisons and bore the mark of the branding iron.

The Medusa is the flagship for the expedition and will be accompanied by the corvette Echo, the transport ship Loire and a brig called the Argus.

The captain and crew were woefully unprepared for our arrival.

The gundeck had been reappointed as makeshift accommodation with thirty of her forty-four cannon removed. Rough partitions were still being installed to provide a bare modicum of privacy. Passengers milled around, dragging their belongings with them, looking for places to alight.

I was given a small cabin on the regular accommodation deck, just below the gundeck.

The ship lay at anchor in the harbor for more than a week waiting for a favorable wind. I made good use of the idle time by cultivating a few interesting acquaintances.

M. Alexandre Corréard is about my age and is an engineer -a graduate of Arts et Métiers Paris Tech -so I reckon he and I will be thrown together frequently in Senegal. He is leaving France for a time, owing to his dissatisfaction with the current government, so our circumstances are not all that dissimilar.

He has a poor opinion of our captain, a puffed-up little character by the name of Viscount Hugues Duroy de Chaumareys.

"He is a foolish man who believes himself clever," he said of the captain. "In that, he and the governor are two of a kind. And as for that M. Richefort…" he stopped and shook his head. "I cannot make him out. He has formed a strange friendship with the captain; I believe he has turned the man's head with his bragging."

This Richefort is a man of no clear occupation (he describes himself as a "philosopher"), full of bluster and possessed of a seemingly endless store of tales of his prodigious achievements in any number of other endeavors. Richefort appears to have special relationships with certain members of the crew -the most unsavory, suspicious-looking characters among them, if I may say so -though most of them loathe him.

Of course, I had to become acquainted with this character myself. I created an opportunity to introduce myself to him to initiate a conversation. Richefort is not a handsome specimen. He has an unwholesome, amphibian-like appearance, though of course, the same is often said of my own relatives on my mother's side, so really I should not be too quick to cast aspersions simply because of such an innocent affliction.

He told me that he is, in addition to his duties as an official of the Philanthropic Society, a representative of the Société Pour la Préservation de la Religion Vraie and entertains the possibility of doing some "religious work" among the Moors.

"I have heard that the Moors are dangerous and not to be trifled with," I remarked.

"Oh, they are men of faith, in their way."

"Muslims, do you mean?"

Richefort gave me a strange little smile. "Some of them practice a religion even older than that. The only true religion."

Of course. Christianity predates Islam by a few hundred years. Not a very long span in the history of the world, but enough to make men of a certain type feel superior.

Richefort's closest companion, aside from the captain, is a young man named Marsh, an American. He is short and slight, tow-headed and a bit idiotic-looking.

These two may be seen together at odd hours, in various parts of the ship, holding whispered colloquy. At these times, the younger man gives every indication of enthusiasm bordering on zealotry - but for what?

On June 17 the wind ceased to be coy and consented to blow us out of that wretched harbor toward the open sea.

*   *   *

The first few days saw some rough sailing even before we cleared the estuary and made it into open water.

Things were relatively calm for the next few days, with only the normal pitching and tilting of the ship to cause me some discomfort and embarrassment. It didn't take me long to find my "sea legs."

Corréard brought me further tales of M. Richefort and his growing influence over the captain. Apparently, de Chaumareys has not even been to sea in twenty-five years! He was given his present position because of his loyalty to the monarchy. The crew dislike him, the feeling is mutual, and he has increasingly turned to Richefort for advice. The situation, says Corréard, is fraught with potential for disaster.

I resolved to learn more.

*   *   *

Some days after I introduced myself to him, I spotted Richefort and Marsh huddled together in a corner of the gundeck. From behind a stout wooden beam, I could listen without being seen.

"Yes," Richefort was saying, "Walakea taught you some things, and gave you the summoning fetish, but his knowledge of our friends is nowhere near equal to my own."

"I know," said the American, in French, with an atrocious accent. "You've told me so, I don't know how many times. When can I meet more of our friends?"

"Be patient. All things come in their season. I foresee a day when France will have a form of government both new and quite ancient -and absolutely perfect. A day when ancient blood returns to reclaim its rightful seat of power."

That was all that I heard before I had to move away to avoid being discovered.

I pondered it for some time. One thing seemed clear: Some political intrigue was afoot. I know nothing of Walakeas or summoning fetishes, but perfect governments and ancient bloodlines have a familiar ring. Is Richefort a plotter? If so, what might he be plotting, and who are these friends? Co-conspirators? Hiding out in Senegal, perhaps!

* * *

I met Corréard on the gundeck the following day. His anxiety was palpable, and I could not help but inquired as to its cause.

"The captain intends on sailing us much too close to the hazardous African coast for my liking", he informed me nervously, his alert eyes scanning the horizon. "Have you heard of the Bank of Arguin?"

"No, I seem to don't recall.", I replied, ignorant of the particulars.

"It is just off the coast of Mauritania, a deceptively jagged spit of earth just below the surface of the sea that has made a fool of many an experienced captain."

"Well, be that as it may, I shouldn't worry," I replied confidently, "I'm sure the crew know their business."

* * *

On the 27th of June I managed another eavesdropping session in the makeshift communal dining room on the gundeck, where I was able to position myself behind Marsh and Richefort. The former said little, none of it audible to me. The latter was quite voluble and among the more interesting portions of his discourse was the following:

"The Captain will do as I instruct him. He is not one of us and is weak-willed. He can be easily swayed from his orders. Already, we have separated ourselves from the other ships in the convoy. Compared to the power we represent; Napoleon and the King are nothing.

Remember: One day HE will return, and until that time his children must manage the affairs of men."

And that set me to thinking.

I have heard my mother, who is a great one for Byzantine tales of political conspiracy, speak often of the Knights Templar, a Catholic military organization that flourished around the time of the Crusades.

Wealthy and powerful when at the apex of their fame and influence, they were supposedly wiped out some five hundred years ago, but there have always been rumors of their continued existence.

And there was yet another rumor -one of my mother's favorites -that the secretive Templars were protecting the bloodline of Jesus Christ.

Mary Magdalene had been the wife of Jesus, so this tale went, and had, after the Crucifixion, escaped with her children to the South of France! Christ was a man, not a god, according to the stories. Mere flesh and blood, not the stuff of wine and wafers. But to many of the faithful, his descendants would be monarchs.

Is Richefort associated with some remnant of this order? Perhaps Richefort is a fool, I thought, but who can tell these days? He might represent a real danger to the throne, if he has an organization at the back of him, as he has hinted.

'If I can find out', thought I, 'and if I can present the information to the King, perhaps my exile need not be quite so extended as I have anticipated'.

*   *   *

Though not completely convinced of the rightness of my tentative conclusions regarding Richefort, I decided that I would nevertheless act upon them. If I were wrong, I thought, no harm would be done.

I approached M. Richefort after one of our evening meals.

"I know what you're up to, Richefort," I said.

"Oh, do you, now?"

"Yes." I looked around and leaned closer to the other man, adopting the manner of a would-be co-conspirator. "Listen to me. I am interested in your cause. I wish to be of service."

"Is that so?"

"It is. I would learn more, Richefort. I have no love for the crown, nor am I a supporter of Napoleon. Like you, I believe that a more ancient, more powerful bloodline is the most fit to rule. You know what I mean."

"You are familiar with the Esoteric Order of Dagon?"

I said nothing but gave the man a knowing smile.

Skepticism was plain in his eyes, but soon gave way to what might have been a humorous twinkle. He said, "Well, it may be that you can be of use. If you wish to know more, come to the ceremony tomorrow."

The ceremony to which Richefort referred was a carnivale style bit of mummery to mark the crossing of the Tropic of Cancer. Those who have never crossed the line must be initiated into the dubious fraternity of those who have. There would be costumes, foolishness, possibly liquor, I thought, and an opportunity to stave off such boredom as my little Richefort intrigue had failed to extinguish.

* * *

At about ten in the morning a large complement of passengers and crew gathered on the main deck.

The weather was fine and clear, but the sunlight seemed both too dim and too harsh at the same time, casting a peculiar yellowish hue onto everything it illuminated. The air seemed too thin, and I had no sensation of temperature at all.

A "baptismal font" had been constructed in the center of the main deck, filled with fresh water for the initiates.

I think I milled around with the other people there, spoke to some of them, but I can recall no details.

Presently, there was a hubbub up on the quarterdeck. A queer, otherworldly figure appeared there. It was just a crew member, of course, kitted out in a bizarre outfit -a long, black robe, with a queer mask over his face.

This man, I supposed, was meant to represent the Lord of the Tropics, but some of the crew cried out another name: "Father Dagon."

This worthy was accompanied by another grotesquely-costumed crew member, meant to be female, and greeted with shouts of "Mother Hydra."

This person wore a sort of crown, made apparently of gold, or some alloy of gold, with another, lighter metal mixed in. It was tall in front, sloping downward toward the center, then up again slightly at the back. Oddly, it did not seem designed to be worn on a human head. "Mother Hydra" it appeared, had stuffed wads of paper around the edges to make it fit. The thing was fairly crawling with designs in relief. There were some geometrical figures, but others seemed to represent living creatures -twisted things that seemed equal parts fish, frog and man.

The "royal couple" were accompanied by half a dozen men wrapped in filthy, oily rags that stunk of rotten fish. These were called "shoggoths" one of the crew informed me.

As the bizarre company descended from the quarterdeck, some of the crewmen erupted in raucous cheers and whistles. Others began a curious chant, in a language that was unfamiliar: "Ia! Ia! Cthulhu fhtagn! Ph'nglui mglw'nafh Cthulhu R'lyeh wgah-nagl fhtaga!" This was repeated over and over, as though it were a formula from some outlandish religious ceremony.

Along with some of the others, I moved toward the makeshift baptismal, quite willing to endure whatever minor indignity might be in store for we "virgins."

But one of the "shoggoths" grabbed me by the arm. "No, that is not for you. For you, something special."

A chalice of some sort was passed into my hands. It was made of gold, exquisitely worked, inlaid with strangely gleaming jewels.

The "shoggoth" pressed the cup to my lips. Though I was not forced to drink, for some reason, I dared not refuse. It didn't taste like liquor; it didn't taste like anything I have ever drunk. The smell was awful: rot and excrement. To my horror I felt small chunks of some viscous semi-solid slide down my throat, and God help me, but I swear that some felt as if it was squirming.

My next recollection is of lurching to the gunwale, where I hung over the rail trying to regurgitate; but though my throat burned and my stomach spasmed frighteningly, I could bring none of the awful stuff back up.

I looked out across the water and thought I saw something just below the surface. Hazy, wavering, shadowy forms shaped vaguely humanoid, bestowed with tiny pinpricks of light that shone like submerged fireflies, where their eyes should be.

I fled to the relative normalcy of my little cabin, where I immediately fell into a deep sleep. I awoke sometime after midnight, my experiences still fresh and disturbing in my mind, and so I had a mind to take up my pen once more, however almost as I completed the above a terrible malaise snuck upon me and I will no doubt have to set this aside once more. Thankfully, having written it down, I can see now that the events are not necessarily as sinister in nature as they seemed to me while they unfolded. I am calmer now, but I remain somewhat uneasy. Perhaps the heat is affecting me adversely.

Despite the dreadful temperature, I feel a comforting chill in my blood and bones. I am aware too of a certain coldness of mind.

I have taken two short walks about the ship today, but no meals. The coast of Africa is sometimes visible, off to the starboard. I have caught glimpses of clouds of red dust, stirred up by the hot winds coming from inland and blowing out to sea.

For most of the day I have slept -and dreamed.

Great, dark cities, under the sea, populated by men that are not men. A vast darkness filled with tiny pinpricks of something that is not light. Music heard only in the bones. And words. Words I have heard before -both recently and long, long ago. *Before I was born?* How can that be?

It is as though I were returning to a time and a place I had forgotten, but one that has always been with me, just outside the periphery of my senses.

Late in the evening I went for a walk on deck and chanced to see Richefort and Marsh standing close to the port gunwale. The latter tossed overboard something that appeared to be a chunk of lead, but it must have been something more lightweight such a piece of wood, for it returned to him within a short time.

After that the two men craned their necks over the railing and mumbled some indistinct words, as though addressing the waves.

I think they knew I had seen them, but they did not acknowledge me.

1816: The Year Without Summer

July 2ⁿᵈ, 1816, morning

Today, the ship hit the Arguin Bank. I knew what it was when I felt the shock, which roused me from the not unpleasant torpor into which I had fallen.

Coming up from below I met Corréard on the gundeck.

"What has happened?" I asked.

"We have hit the Arguin Bank!" he said, anger coloring his face and voice.

"We must get to the lifeboats," I said calmly. "We shall be all right."

"They aren't evacuating the ship yet. They think they can refloat her."

"Perhaps they will," I said.

They will not.

After hours of frenetic activity, the Medusa is still stranded. The sails have been taken down and the top masts lowered. Efforts to refloat her have proven fruitless.

I sit in a corner of the deck and write. Richefort approaches me, alone. Marsh is somewhere else.

"You are quite fit?" he says.

"I am not at all myself," I say.

"*Au contraire*, you are more yourself than you have ever been - *n'est-ce pas?*"

As it happens, he is correct.

"You were attempting a deception, of course," he continues, "and I knew that. However, at the same time, I saw something in you, a certain strain in the blood which is visible to those who know how to see it. I believe you are, let us say, *related* to our friends--the ones who live in the sea -as am I."

"You caused this," I say. It is not a question, nor is it an accusation. "The plight of this ship, I mean."

Richefort nods. "Yes. Many will die, it is true. Our friends from beneath the waves must have their sport, you see -it is part of our arrangement. The smaller boats onboard are in poor condition and are insufficient for a successful evacuation. There is talk of constructing a raft. I fancy this will provide a great bounty for our undersea brothers."

"Why here, Richefort? And why now?"

"The eruption of Mount Tambora last year, and the attendant climate abnormalities, have attenuated the earth's atmosphere, and purged it temporarily of certain elements that inhibit our friends, as well as seeding it with other elements that normally slumber far below the world's surface."

I nod, not really understanding his words, but knowing they are true.

"It is the raft that people will remember," says Richefort. "Some of the crew who are loyal to our cause will be aboard. Perhaps, my friend, you should be on it. It could be important to your... education."

"Yes," I say.

He gives me a nod. "I fancy we shall meet again -by and by."

*   *   *

There are seven smaller boats aboard the Medusa although they appear sea worthy they are in poor repair and there is certainly not enough space. Not nearly enough to carry all 400 passengers.

And so, the raft.

Some of the crew have set to building the raft, at the orders of the governor. One can practically taste their conviction that it will never need to be used. They still think the *Medusa* will be refloated, or that some other plan will occur to someone.

Today the raft was launched.

Sixty-five feet long it is, and twenty-two wide, a desperate conglomeration of masts, boards, and barrels. It is meant to carry 150 souls to safety, and I am one of them.

So is my acquaintance, M. Corréard. He is sanguine in that way men are when facing certain doom, clutching at a hope that does not exist. Playacting, that's what it is.

Last night, the Medusa's keel split in two, extinguishing any further thought of refloating her. She took on an alarming quantity of water during the night and, at six this morning, Schmaltz ordered the evacuation. People swarmed onto the ramshackle thing. It was a mob scene to rival some of the worst social conflagrations on the streets of Paris during the various revolutions and counter-revolutions of the past quarter-century.

With such a mass of bodies on board the raft will not float properly. Most of the "deck" is submerged to a depth of two or three feet, with only the raised platform in the center being clear of the seawater.

And it will get worse. There can be no doubt of that.

Corréard and a surgeon named Savigny are the *de facto* "commanders" of this pitiable craft. I do not envy them the job. It is a wildly heterogeneous group for which they are responsible - soldiers, sailors, convicts, men (and one woman) from a dozen different countries, united only by their anger at Schmaltz -and, by extension, France herself. That may sustain them for a few hours, before panic begins to set in. We have insufficient provisions on board. Just a few tubs of wine, two casks of fresh water, and a 25-

pound bag of biscuits. The latter is now soaked through with salt water and reduced to a paste.

If a rescue is not effected soon, there will be pandemonium.

We were told that the raft would be equipped with a compass, charts, and an anchor. It is not.

This raft is a death trap for most of the unfortunate passengers.

My bones ache with music from submerged cities.

* * *

Confused efforts were made to attach the raft to some of the boats by means of ropes. The whole thing quickly devolved into farce, and soon there was but one rope left.

I watched for my opportunity, and when it came, I severed the rope without knowing why, precisely, and without questioning the impulse. Nobody saw me do it, and there are plenty of other people who can and will be blamed more plausibly than I. Indeed, the governor and the captain are already bearing the brunt of this; they are the subjects of innumerable curses and vows of revenge.

Life aboard the raft has been eventful.

I continue to write, keeping my note-book above water as I do so, and storing it in a waterproof pouch the rest of the time.

There have been fights, great battles between factions of the severely demented and those who still retain some few scraps of sanity. Our numbers have been steadily winnowed down by combat, misadventure, and other factors.

Many of my fellow passengers have succumbed to delirium. There have been suicides. Many have gone willingly into the deep, among them some of the crewmen associated with Richefort. These men went calmly, and it seems to me, happily and *rationally*, as though proceeding to some highly-anticipated rendezvous, rather than mere oblivion.

Corréard and some of the others have fashioned a makeshift mast and sail, in hopes that the wind will kindly choose to blow us to shore and forestall further carnage.

*   *   *

We are not alone out here. We are watched and followed. The presences, the dwellers in the submerged cities, the ones who sing to my bones, are with us. They are quiet and unseen, coming and going with the waves, and always at night, taking one or two of us away with them at a time.

I am the only one who knows this.

*   *   *

The sun does not torment me. My skin has reddened, but that is all. There are no burns, no blisters, such as all of my compatriots have developed. They look as though they have passed through flames.

All the fresh water is gone. They drink a bit of wine, a dash of seawater now and then, and sometimes their own urine. It is not enough.

The sodden biscuits lasted no time at all. A few very small fish were caught one day, but no more after that. Men now dine on shoes and scraps of cloth, and they wail incessantly as the salt water torments their scourged bodies.

I am not hungry. My skin feels cool, and the seawater is a great comfort. It seems that I absorb it, that it sustains me. Occasionally I scream or groan just to keep up appearances, to be part of the never-ending chorus of woe aboard this craft. But the water soothes me almost to the point of bliss. I fancy at times that it speaks to me, in a language still beyond my ken, but growing more intelligible every hour.

I have become aware of something vast and dark and ancient, and I cannot stop dwelling on it.

I do not want to stop.

*　　*　　*

It was on the fourth day that the last vestiges of civilization were abandoned. It was a paradox that precipitated this microcosmic Fall of Man:

There is virtually no food aboard this raft.

and

There is virtually nothing *but* food aboard this raft.

It became clear to many of the castaways that we were well-supplied with edible meat-on the hoof, as it were.

It should be noted that no one was slaughtered expressly for this purpose; rather, those who had died in one of the many ways available to us were pressed into service as victuals.

In between all the cutting and chewing and slurping, there was much weeping and wringing of hands.

I, of course, partook. It did not trouble me in my mind -a circumstance which should itself be troubling to me, but it is not.

I have surreptitiously tossed a few chunks overboard to our followers, as evidence of my goodwill.

*   *   *

July 13th, 1816

Today, those who are in the best health decided to throw the sick and dying into the sea, to increase our chances of survival. One by one, they were discarded.

They will not go to waste.

Also, two of the soldiers were caught stealing wine from the dregs of the single cask that remains to us. They were summarily executed.

Liberté, égalité, fraternité!

There are now sixteen humans onboard this raft. No, just fifteen, for I cannot count myself among them any longer, and, at any rate, I am about to leave them.

It is past midnight. As my human companions languish in the haunted torpor that must answer for slumber on this raft, I am joined by three others, who have come to me from the deep.

They stand there silently, at the edge of the raft, regarding me with eyes I would once have thought dead and dull. But that was before. Now I see the dark and eternal light behind them. These are the true people -*my* true people. The moon, disturbed by tattered clouds racing across its face, does not illuminate them clearly. They could be men -almost.

One of them speaks to me in a human voice. The voice of Richefort.

"You are ready?" he says

The dappling moonlight reveals his face clearly for an instant. He looks the same as before, only more so.

"Yes," I tell him.

"We shall spread our faith and our ways around the globe," he tells me. "It will take time. We have plenty. A century is, really, no more than an afternoon. Not to the Old Ones, and those who serve them. *That is not dead which can eternal lie, and with strange aeons even death may die.*"

The sky above me is open to the endless loop of eternity; far away beneath a nameless ocean, sunken R'lyeh waits. Napoleon rots on Elba, the King withers in his palace. Feeble things they are, already forgotten.

1816: The Year Without Summer

Cthulhu sleeps but does not sleep. And he will return -for he never left.

{Here the journal ends}

The Empty Thing

By M. J. Sellars

The Island

It was a ragbag of riflemen and light infantry. No two uniforms were the same. There were kilts and tartan trews, as well as white trousers and even civilian breeches. Most of the hats were the shako but some of the men wore the old bicornes. Whilst the majority of the hats were decorated with a stubby plume, some bore the more elaborate heckle that looked as if it might have been wrestled from an ostrich. Coats were mostly red, though some were green; and all were threadbare and ragged. All regimental insignia and indications of rank had been removed or were hidden beneath clumsily stitched patches. The weaponry was likewise diverse, with swords, sabres and claymores on display, as well as Brown Bess muskets and some Baker rifles.

They'd been told by the chaplain, of all people -for it seemed he was, in some strange manner, in charge of things here on the island of Tristan da Cunha -to refer to one another by surname only, and not to talk of where they had been stationed or where they had fought. There was, with the chaplain, a tall man with shrapnel scars on his face and a portion of his scalp burned away. He may have been a senior officer, had that look about him, and the chaplain consulted him in whispers occasionally, but nothing was formally announced.

It was clear from the look of some of the men that they had spent time in Africa or the Mediterranean; their skin was the reddish brown of newly dug clay, where it wasn't entirely red and peeling, and so very typical of the Englishman abroad.

It would be untrue to say these men had nothing in common. They each had, in their eyes, a flat look that spoke of things best unremembered, things that needed no instruction, from chaplain or otherwise, to remain behind closed lips. It would take a direct order from a commanding officer to compel Hastings to speak of what he had seen and done in France, of people in pieces yet somehow still living.

"It makes no sense," said Collins. He didn't look up from his notebook, upon the pages of which he was drawing, with remarkable accuracy, the grey pebble beach stretching out ahead of them and the waters beyond. Earlier, he had commenced drawing the mountain that was an hour's walk behind them, but a mist had risen to meet a descending bank of cloud and the entire thing had been curtained from view. It struck Hastings how like North Wales this island was. Aside from the mild August climate, it was as if a great clod of Snowdonia had been dropped into the middle of the South Atlantic Ocean and had somehow taken root.

"What makes no sense?" asked Hastings, cleaning his musket with the same cloth with which he'd once tried, and failed, to staunch another man's gushing wound.

"Napoleon," he said, cross-hatching waves and white surf into existence. "We're stationed here 'in the event that enemy forces *might* use the island as a base from which to launch a rescue attempt to free Napoleon'. The chaplain's own words. But Napoleon, if rumour is to be believed, is imprisoned some twelve hundred miles away on Saint Helena."

It did seem odd, but Hastings was used to odd. He couldn't remember the last time he'd expected things to make sense. Once, after a particularly ferocious artillery bombardment, he'd found an eyeball in the top of his boot, nestled against his shin. He had no idea how it had got there or to whom it had belonged.

*   *   *

The Prisoner

They camped down on the beach that night, coats for blankets, boots for pillows. Discomfort kept sleep away from Hastings for an hour or two. Discomfort and the incessant barking of the seals whose territory they'd usurped when first they'd arrived in the small hours of the morning. When sleep did come, it brought with it the most vivid nightmare.

He was back in France. He didn't know where precisely, but he could hear the *dum... dum... dum* of artillery fire in the distance. He'd become separated from the rest of the men somehow, although he had no memory of what had happened to bring this about. He wondered for a moment if he'd deserted. It was possible to have done so without knowing. He'd seen men shot who, right up to the moment their bodies became first rigid then slack, had maintained they hadn't deserted at all but had simply become confused and... wandered off.

He was standing before a farmhouse; or what was left of it. It looked to have been disassembled by war and time in equal measure. There were holes that were doubtless punched through the walls by canon fire but there were also black, shiny constellations of mildew, limp bouquets of weeds and clusters of pale orange mushrooms that were mostly stem. The roof was intact but sagged as if it were made of thick, damp rags. Hastings pushed open the front door. Cool air met him at the threshold.

Despite the disrepair and war wounds, it should have been gloomy inside, but it wasn't. The room was illuminated by yet more clusters of those skinny, orange mushrooms. By their sickly light, Hastings saw that it wasn't a farmhouse at all; it was more a like a laboratory or workshop. Every wall was a confusion of copper pipe, coils and cylinders; gears, wheels, belts and bellows. The thickest of the pipes drilled down into the earth. The bellows inhaled and exhaled, but weakly. It was from those feeble exhalations that the cool air emerged.

But the cooling mechanism wasn't the strangest thing in this place. In the middle of the floor, head down, kneeling, was a man. He was wearing the uniform of the enemy, although all sign of rank and allegiance had been torn from it, and his wrists and ankles were manacled. Chains ran from the manacles and were fixed to the floor by long-rusted bolts. The prisoner was straining at the chains; so much so, that the manacles had cut into his flesh and blood was running from the wounds. Even though the chains were too short for the prisoner to even stand, let alone reach the farmhouse door, Hastings levelled his musket at the man. Was it even loaded and ready to fire? It was certainly fully cocked.

"Don't move," he said. Then, rummaging through what little French vocabulary he had, "*Ne bouge pas! Ne bouge pas!*"

The prisoner's head snapped up and he glared at Hastings. His eyes lacked both iris and pupil and were entirely the same insipid orange as the mushrooms that sprouted in every corner; and, like the mushrooms, they exhibited a weak phosphorescence. In addition to this phosphorescence, the prisoner radiated an alarming degree of heat, as one would expect not from a human body, but from an open fire or an oven.

Hastings retreated a step, but the door had swung shut behind him and he backed up against old, swollen timber.

"*Ne bouge pas!*" he said again.

The prisoner replied in a language Hastings had never heard before. It was a hawthorn-tangle of consonants and every syllable scratched and pricked at his mind.

Hasting didn't precisely *decide* to pull the trigger. It just happened.

There was a crack. Pale blue smoke bloomed all about him.

A hole appeared just above the prisoner's left eyebrow, about the size of a shilling. The luminescence went out of his eyes but they remained open, staring at Hastings. Blood began to first ooze, then pour from the shilling-sized aperture. It flowed in impossible quantities. Hastings had seen blood. He'd seen sabre wounds, bayonet wounds, musket ball wounds, he'd even seen a man sheered in half during an artillery bombardment; but he'd never seen a human body produce this much blood. Within seconds it had pooled around the prisoner, a glossy red disk. It was hot, this blood; steam rose from it in twitching plumes. And, as he bled, the prisoner *shrivelled*. It was as if his insides were rotting, collapsing. It was as if he had been made of nothing but blood, held in place by a taught shroud of flesh. Now that he had bled out, flesh was all that remained, flesh wrapped in an ill-fitting, almost anonymous uniform. The prisoner flopped back, blood splashing up around him.

Hastings felt a hot wetness at his feet. He looked down. The blood had reached him and had seeped in through the cracks in his old boots. Amidst the blood, writhing: thousands upon thousands of tiny, translucent spiders.

* * *

The Conversation

Hastings awoke to the sound of barking seals and began to fall. He was standing at the water's edge, foam breaking over his feet. He staggered back, throwing his arms out for balance and managed, just, to stay upright. He turned on the spot, attempting to get his bearings.

It was still dark, but he could see that he was only a hundred yards or so from where he'd made his makeshift bed for the night. It looked like he'd wandered in a straight line. As he made his way back toward the camp, he saw a tent pitched just beyond where the rest of the men were sleeping, just where the beach began to curve from view. It glowed from the light of a lantern inside and the shadows of two men were thrown against the canvas, distorted and hunched.

Hastings had never been the perfect soldier by any means. He followed orders when he had to, when charges of insubordination would have resulted from doing otherwise but, like most of the men he'd served with, he just wanted to stay alive, to avoid crippling injury, to go home, to see his family. And he knew that the one thing most likely to help a soldier stay alive was information, knowing what the senior officers had in mind, what role you had to play in their strategy, and how disposable you had become. So, instead of returning to his uncomfortable bed, he made his way along the grey pebble beach to the tent that glowed like the mushrooms in his dream, like the prisoner's eyes.

From inside, voices, hushed but agitated.

Hastings recognised the chaplain's voice but not the other.

"... kill it," said the chaplain.

"... ridiculous... do not even pierce it... it is in the book," said the other man. Hasting wasn't sure of the accent. It reminded him of that of an Egyptian accountant his father had had dealings with back in Liverpool.

"... to do *something*," said the chaplain.

"... chains have held for two hundred years," the 'Egyptian' replied. Then, "... slept for thirteen years... vapour compressor... Bass."

"... not sleeping now... in our dreams... in *everyone's* dreams..."

"... find Bass... repairs... asleep again... men... unarmed..."

"... *unarmed?* Ridiculous!"

"... too great a risk..."

"... unacceptable... a few men... *armed*..."

"... do not *pierce it*... it is in the book..."

"... *armed... I will not yield* on this matter..."

"... the *book!*"

"...armed or not at all."

Silence. Then, from the 'Egyptian', clear and emphatic, "On your head be it. On your head be it."

"... difference does it make? They are in the world already, so many of them."

The silhouettes cast onto the canvas rose, and Hastings hurried back to his bed.

He didn't sleep. He lay staring up at the sky, as low clouds slowly turned from the colour of dark, wet charcoal to that of loose, dry ashes; and he listened to the barking of the seals. And he wondered what a 'vapour compressor' was; and he thought about chains, chains that had held for two hundred years?

*   *   *

Inland

Ten of them were selected the following morning for what the chaplain had referred to as "a simple scouting assignment". Collins was third to be chosen and Hastings, thinking he'd managed to get away with it for a moment, was chosen tenth. Hastings couldn't help noticing that many of the soldiers who had not been selected looked relieved. He wondered what could have instilled in them such a sense of dread in the first place that their relief was so very obvious. These were men who had seen and done, and had done to them, terrible things. Most were scarred; some limped; at least two men wore eye patches. What blades Hastings had seen, whilst diligently maintained, were scratched, pitted and distorted from use. He found himself wondering if they too had dreamed of the prisoner in his...

"Chains," he said.

"Beg pardon?" said Collins, sliding his sketch book into his hip box and shouldering his musket.

"Did you dream, last night?" asked Hastings.

Collins looked a little unnerved. "Yes. Why'd you ask?"

"What of?" said Hastings. "What did you dream of?"

"Well, I'd rather not say."

"It's important."

"Important, how? It's just a dream."

Hastings didn't know how to explain it, how to make it sound anything other than ridiculous. "Just a superstition in my regiment," he said, trying to sound casual. "We share our dreams before a mission. It's good luck. Whenever we didn't... well, it always ended badly."

Collins shrugged. "I dreamt it was winter and my mother had been sent to the madhouse. She was chained to a bed. I tried to free her but couldn't. Then..." he picked at a few loose threads on the sleeve of his coat, "a man came in. A doctor, I think. I tried to explain that Mother wasn't mad, that she had a fever. I could feel the heat radiating from her body. Surely, he could, too? But he ignored my pleas. He had... an instrument of some kind, a sort of chisel. And before I could say or do anything to stop him, he brought it down on my mother's skull, right in the centre of her forehead. There was a horrible *crack* and a hole bigger than the chisel-thing had any right to make appeared. It was as big as the hole a musket ball makes as it leaves. And..." more tugging and picking at threads. No eye contact. "Worms, but not really worms, something like worms but orange and luminescent, started crawling out of the wound. Thousands of them. And when they were all out, all of the orange worms... there was nothing left of her, nothing left of my mother. Just skin and a nightdress. Horrible." He stopped tugging at threads and wiped a sudden sheen of perspiration back from his brow and into his hair. "Did you? Dream?"

Before Hastings could respond, the tall man with the scorch wound on his scalp told them to gather at the water's edge, away from the rest of the men. Although he had no insignia of rank, the soldiers did as they were instructed.

Fifteen minutes passed, and the men became restless, speculating about what might be expected of them. One man, his voice deep, his accent almost indecipherably Welsh, said, "I don't care what they want us to do. They're fighting over spuds and turnips, back home. At least we've got rations here."

"I've heard Napoleon's already escaped and he's right here, on the island, hiding in a cave," said another man. He had a scar running from the right-hand corner of his mouth, up to his right ear. It was impossible to tell whether or not he was smiling, and so it was impossible to tell if his remark was meant to be in jest.

"All eyes this way!"

It was the tall man, and with him were the chaplain and another man. The other man was small. His complexion and garb suggested he was Persian or some such. The Egyptian, Hastings presumed.

Both the chaplain and the Egyptian -Hastings couldn't now think of him as anything but -held large books close to their chests. The chaplain's was very obviously the Bible. The Egyptian's was larger, thicker and its binding was of ancient cracked leather that was so warped it looked as if the book had been retrieved from the bottom of a lake, then baked in a furnace, and that this process had been carried out any number of times.

The tall man said, "For all intents and purposes, the chaplain is in charge. You do as he says, and you do it immediately. You do not question him or naysay him. When he speaks, it is as if King George himself is addressing you. Are we very clear about this?"

The men nodded, but it was an uncomfortable acquiescence. Hastings found it strange. They had known, perhaps by instinct or perhaps from the way the chaplain had behaved, and others had behaved toward him, that he was in command. But hearing it said out loud and by a veteran who clearly belonged to the higher ranks, it just seemed wrong to Hastings. A chaplain in command of His Majesty's troops? What sort of mission would require that?

With that question circling round his mind, they set off inland.

It was slow going. Although it seemed like there was little but fields between the beach and the mountain, it was strewn with scree and carpeted in lichen and moss, with the scree often hidden beneath that carpet. It was also a lot steeper than it first appeared; they walked alongside a gulch for the most part, the increasing depth of which was testament to just how steep the terrain. After an hour or so of marching, tripping and cursing, they found themselves in a sparse forest. The trees were either thick squat things that seemed to be slumping under their own weight or thin, almost wispy specimens that strained upwards as if attempting to take flight. To Hastings, the squat trees appeared lazy and resigned and the thin trees appeared foolish, as if they were yet to realise they were rooted to the ground.

It was in this wood of lazy and foolish trees that the chaplain gave his orders. Seven men were to continue inland with him, and three men were to stay in the forest with the Egyptian and await the chaplain's return. Hastings found himself in the latter group. Collins fell in with the former.

Hastings watched as the chaplain's group headed further uphill then broke right and, despite the seeming thinness of the forest, disappeared from view. He sat at the base of one of the squat trees and set about cleaning his Brown Bess.

Now that he had stopped walking and didn't have to monitor every footfall to avoid being hobbled by a moss-caped rock, several things struck him about his immediate environment. Firstly, the smell. He'd never come across anything quite like it. It wasn't particularly unpleasant; Hastings was no stranger to unpleasant smells, and much worse than unpleasant. At Quatre Bras, Hastings had gutted a soldier of the French 6th Division, and the man's innards and everything they had contained had spilled out into the long, dying grass. The smell had been so overwhelming Hastings had lost his morning's rations. This smell, here in the forest and maybe even before they'd reached the forest, was not unpleasant. This smell was simply... wrong. For one thing, he couldn't quite pin it down. For a moment he thought it was vanilla; the next, liquorice. Then lemon. Then rose water. Then charcoal or was it candle wax? Or gin? He suspected his sense of the scent's wrongness came because it was none of these things, that it in fact existed at the *precise point* where all of these things -vanilla, liquorice, lemon, rose water, charcoal, candle wax, gin -*didn't* overlap.

The second thing he had become aware of now that he was no longer distracted -though, to be sure, that alien odour was a distraction -was a high, squealing sound. It was so high that it was almost beyond his capacity to hear it at all. It was the kind of sound that would have made dogs lie down, their ears and tails flattened. It seemed to be coming from somewhere up ahead, from wherever it was the chaplain had taken Collins and the rest. He was tempted to compare it to the ringing-in-the-ears that followed artillery bombardment. But it was too clean and sharp a sound and it seemed to underscore all the other sounds around them, rather than muffle them. He could hear birds squawking above him, insects buzzing and whining around him. He could hear the water running deep down in the gully some fifty feet or so to his left. He could hear the barking of seals in the distance. He could hear -but surely that wasn't possible -the breaking of the waves on the grey pebble beach. Somehow, the clean, sharp squeal was making it possible.

Hastings knew that if he gave too much of his attention over to that sound and that smell, he might go mad, might wander off 'confused' and be shot for desertion. So, he decided to strike up a conversation with the soldier sat leaning back against the tree nearest his own. He looked younger than Hastings. Perhaps not yet even out of his second decade and he had a troubled look upon his young face. Hastings wondered if he too could smell that wrong smell or hear that clinical squeal.

"What's your name?" asked Hastings.

"William," he said. "Sorry. I mean, Davies."

"Hastings."

"Pleased to meet you."

A silence moved between them, back and forth, for almost a minute, and then Davies said, "It all feels wrong."

"Yes. It does."

"Not just here," said Davies. "My mum reads palms and tealeaves, has the sight. She says things have felt wrong for more than a year now. She says something has awoken -the Devil, perhaps -and its eyes are upon us and upon the land and the crops. Can you feel them? Its eyes, on your skin? Inside your head?"

"No," said Hastings and turned away from the boy. Better the smell and the squeal to that, to all the thoughts such a conversation might bring crashing down. It wasn't talk of palm reading and tasseomancy, or even of eyes upon the land and the crops, that disquieted Hastings. It was 'for more than a year now' which had disturbed him most. He was suddenly certain he'd been dreaming of the prisoner, catching that elusive scent and hearing that underscoring squeal for months, maybe even for more than a year.

*　　*　　*

The Seal Things

It was almost night when Hastings awoke, heart rattling. For a moment, he wondered what had startled him from sleep; then he heard the scream. At first he thought it was that knife-edge squeal rising to a crescendo, but, as he grasped his musket, he realised it was far too messy and organic a sound for that.

As he rose to his feet, legs unsteady as when he'd first staggered from the ship only a day ago, he also realised that it was not a human sound.

He saw that he was the last to be roused by the scream. Davies, the other soldier and the Egyptian were all standing upslope from him. The soldiers had their musket trained on... Hastings couldn't see what. The Egyptian was reading from the misshapen book. The words made no sense and reminded Hastings of the hawthorn-tangle of consonants that the prisoner had disgorged in his nightmare.

Hastings moved toward the others and, as he did so, saw the thing they were confronting.

At first, he thought it was a large seal or a walrus, perhaps. It certainly had a similar, tapering shape to it. But the colour was all wrong. It was a pale orange -like the fungus in his dream, like the prisoner's eyes -and dripping with a clear, glossy slime. Along its flanks were flaccid tubes the width and length of a man's forearm; from some of these tubes, a black, steaming foam spilled. Its back was studded with bone-coloured thorns, each as big as a paring knife. Its face was... Hastings didn't think the word 'face' was right at all. But it was where a face ought to be. It was more like a ragged wound from which an albino pig's head had only partially emerged. Its eyes were blind, poached things amidst folds of swollen flesh and its mouth, beneath an ulcerous snout, was wide and lipless and filled with row upon row of tiny, jagged teeth. It pulled itself along at an astonishing speed with the arms of a deformed and hairless ape, and hands with far too many fingers with far too many joints.

Davies discharged his musket; the other infantryman did likewise. Hastings wasn't sure whether or not the shots found their intended target, but the seal thing did not slow one jot. It ploughed on, then lashed out with one of those deformed arms, that looked like they'd been broken ten or fifteen times and never properly reset. It struck the Egyptian in the chest, lifting him from the ground and slamming him into one of the indolent trees with a series of cracks that Hastings recognised as breaking bone. And then it just kept moving.

The soldier in Hastings awoke. He reached into his hip box, pulled out a cartridge and bit off its twist of paper. He half-cocked the musket, drizzled a little powder into the priming pan, then closed the frizzen. He lowered the butt of the musket to the ground, poured the remaining powder down the barrel, followed by the musket ball and wadding. He drew out the ramrod, tamped down the wadding and powder with two swift, firm strokes, then replaced the ramrod beneath the barrel. He brought the butt to his shoulder and pulled the cock back fully. All of this took, perhaps, fifteen seconds and the seal thing was almost out of site, dragging itself downhill, trailing slime and black froth.

Hastings heard Davies exclaim, "Oh God! Oh God!"

He returned his attention upslope.

There were more of the things. At least ten.

He trained his musket on the nearest of the beasts and pulled the trigger.

Either he missed or the thing's blubbery hide was too thick to penetrate.

Hasting began to reload, certain the seal thing was going to deal with him as it had the Egyptian. Instead, it dragged itself past him, tearing up clods of earth and shreds of moss and lichen. It didn't so much as turn its wound-borne head in his direction or even regard him with a poached eye. The overpowering smell it left in its wake existed at the precise point where vanilla, liquorice, lemon, rose water, charcoal, candle wax and gin didn't overlap. And it was not only an odour that trailed behind the thing, but heat. Like the heat from the prisoner in his dream.

Two more musket reports upslope, then a scream.

The screaming of men was a sound with which Hastings would never reach an accommodation.

He returned his attention to his comrades.

Davies had dropped his musket and his hands were clasped to his face. The steaming, black foam covered him from the chest up. He dropped to his knees, his arms falling to his sides. His face was gone. And not just the flesh; the bone, too. From brow to chin was a hollow. Within it, the stump of a tongue writhed.

In the time it took Hastings to reload, six or seven seal things passed him, heat roaring from them, and the second soldier, a man whose name he didn't know and would never know, dropped his Brown Bess and ran. At least, he tried to run. The moment his musket was dropped, one of the seal things grasped the back of his head with a hand that was trying to be a spider or a crab. It dragged him along for a few yards then... squeezed. The infantryman's head collapsed like an old fungus filled with glistening red spores.

Hastings continued firing and reloading, firing and reloading, standing his ground, until all of the seal things, as many as twenty, had passed him by and passed from sight. His ears were ringing from the musket fire and from the shrieking of those things. The smell of gunpowder had almost succeeded in masking that other, indecipherable odour he now knew to be the stink of the seal things themselves. But if the seal things were the source of that weird scent, why was he becoming increasingly sure that he'd encountered it before; indeed, that it had been all around him for a year, maybe more?

Then he remembered the chaplain's voice through canvas: *They are in the world already, so many of them.*

But he didn't want to think about that. He shouldered his musket and went to the Egyptian. The soldiers were dead, but it was possible the Egyptian had survived. One glance at the man erased that possibility. A broken length of mossy branch the size of a bayonet had skewered his neck, entering at the windpipe and exiting at the base of the skull. The book, that swollen tome that looked as if it had spent a lifetime at the bottom of the Atlantic before being dried in a kiln, lay next to him. The ornamental handle of a small, slim dagger appeared to have been used as a bookmark. On the handle of the dagger was inscribed a five-pointed star; at the centre of the star was an eye; at the centre of the eye, a flame. Hasting used the dagger to lever the pages apart. On one page was a script he didn't recognise, Arabic, perhaps; on the other was an illustration rendered in a style that combined medieval engraving and Japanese brushstrokes.

"God," was all Hastings could say.

* * *

The Cave

It took Hastings three hours to find the chaplain, Collins and the rest of the men. At first he'd tried following their tracks but the lack of light and the devastation caused by the seal things had made it impossible. Then it had occurred to him that wherever the chaplain had gone was likely the same place from where the seal things had come.

The mouth of the cave was no larger than the door to the ruined farmhouse in his dream. The ground around the cave entrance was slick with slime and still-steaming black froth. From within the cave, a faint, orange glow. Sat to the right of the cave mouth, a figure was slumped. It might have been possible to mistake this figure for a dozing man, if it weren't for the obvious indications of decay, the pistol in his lap and the ragged hole in the top of his head. Hastings had seen the like before. Men so afraid to die in battle they chose to end their own lives. Typically, they'd find a quiet place, somewhere they could, however briefly, find a moment of peace. This particular suicide differed in one respect: from the exit wound, orange mushrooms sprouted.

Hastings loaded his musket and stepped inside.

He found himself in a steeply sloping tunnel. All along its walls sprouted the thin-stemmed mushrooms from his dream, orange and luminous. He had been descending for about five minutes when he almost tripped over the first body. Or what was left of it. It was burnt or rotted, or a combination of the two, until all that remained was an arm and a leg connected by a scorched twist of torso and ribcage. There were a few rags of uniform and, sat in a green-black soupy puddle, a pelvis, as white and clean as an anatomist's model. It could have been anyone, but lying to one side, where the cave floor began to curve up into the wall, was the small notebook upon the pages of which Collins had sketched images that had made Hastings believe, foolishly, that this island in the middle of the South Atlantic was no different from Snowdonia. He would have picked it up, that notebook, slid it into his hip box, but it was sat amongst those orange mushrooms and he couldn't bring himself to go near it.

He kept walking, keeping to the centre of the tunnel, not wanting those spindly orange mushrooms to touch him. After a hundred yards or so, he saw the first of the copper pipes. It was the width of a drainpipe and emerged from the ground close to the tunnel wall. At approximately waist height, it curved and then ran on, parallel to the ground, clamped to the wall at regular intervals.

As Hastings continued, more pipes appeared; then, cylinders, coils, gears, wheels, belts and bellows.

"My dream..." he muttered.

But unlike in his dream, the bellows were still, no cool air emerging. The copper pipes were speckled and, in some places, encrusted with verdigris. The further he walked, the more dilapidated the mechanism became. Belts hung slack, gears lay in the dirt, pipes were cracked. From the cracks, scrawny orange mushrooms sprouted.

Hastings had no idea how long he had been walking for, when the tunnel opened up into a cave, five or six times the height and width of the tunnel. There were chains hanging down from the ceiling; chains coiled on the ground; chains trailing limp from the walls. They all gathered near the same point, at the centre of the cave, where... something lay. The glow from the fungus wasn't strong enough to cast any light on precisely what that thing was. It was, however, intense enough -just -to reach the snarled mess of limbs and muskets and boots and faces and half faces.

One of the faces opened its mouth and screamed.

The chaplain. Still screaming, he disentangled himself from the amber-lit abattoir, stood in a series of twitches and jerks.

Hastings resisted the urge to shoot him, just to stop the screaming that was echoing throughout the cave, as if all the faces, and even the half faces, had started screaming, too. But then, as abruptly as he'd begun shrieking, the chaplain stopped.

"The machine, the vapour compressor, it stopped working," he said, his voice the opposite of a scream, now: low and flat and emotionless. "Bass had warned us it would. He needed parts and materials and people, but the war ate up every resource. He called the war the Great Distraction. Sometimes, he hinted it was a deliberate *distraction*, and that the Corsican was complicit in all of this. The cold keeps it sleeping, he told us. When it is awake the chains hold it, but it can wander in our dreams, where it can proselytise and forge neophytes and compel them to cross the globe to break its chains. And those it could not convert, it would drive to madness and death. Like Bass. Oh God, did you see him? That hole in his head? He *told* us. He *warned* us."

As he spoke he moved forward in the same twitching and jerking fashion with which he'd risen, until Hastings could see that he was missing most of his left arm and his right leg was twisted so that the foot was facing entirely the wrong way. Closer, and Hastings saw the gleaming ropes of intestine hanging from the man's ruptured gut. "But no neophyte came, no proselyte. We came. And we were scared. The men were scared. Of *course* they were. And they shot it. They pierced it and it... and it... opened... and they, those things came out. So many of them. Oh God, Ibrahim, why didn't I listen?"

And then the chaplain started screaming again, a high inhuman sound that seemed to be in imitation of the seal things.

Hasting didn't precisely *decide* to pull the trigger. It just happened.

By the flare of burning gunpowder and in less time than it took the chaplain to crumple to the ground, Hastings saw the thing on the floor. It was, without doubt, the thing from the Egyptian's book, the *huge* seal thing, perhaps four times the size of the elephants Hastings had seen at The Royal Menagerie in London so many years ago. But the thing on the floor was withered and flaccid and empty. The thing in the book had been round and swollen and pregnant.

1816: The Year Without Summer

Turner's Apprentice

By Jonathan Oliver

T*he following correspondence was found amongst the affairs of the renowned art-critic Lucius Fitch on the occasion of the sale of his estate, following his passing across to the hereafter.*

The letters have been reproduced exactly in the order that they had been collected together. They tell a remarkable episode in the life of artist Joseph William Turner. Of his antagonist in this tale, Alexander Pickman, nothing more than that which is presented below is known.

*   *   *

Dear Fellow Traveller,

I don't know what I should call you, but Fellow Traveller seems to fit. You must let me know if you do not like it.

London. One had hoped for so much more from the capital with its subterranean temples, forgotten rivers and countless esoteric societies. To be honest, you'd get just as much insight into the 'mysteries' at an Anglican communion as can be found in the ludicrous pantomimes that here call themselves occult. Even so, my art continues to flourish. The legendary mist-shrouded streets and louring skies of the city have been a revelation. There is a quality to the light that is positively otherworldly, not what I was expecting at all. I can't quite think how to capture it in its full glory; my brush is neither quick enough, nor my eye sufficiently cultured. Of course, I dare not show anyone my latest pieces. I am just about making ends meet sketching for the tourists who flock to the city. One must battle against one's instincts to portray them as they truly are – ignorant apes; simian children who do not truly see that which surrounds them. I trust all is well and that your research continues to be fruitful.

I shall continue to keep you abreast of developments. I live in hope that I shall soon encounter a fellow 'seeker'.

Yours,

A.P.

Dear Sarah,

    Bill has been effing and jeffing, grumbling and moaning, all weekend. It is driving me to distraction having to wait on him hand-and-foot. God knows how I am supposed to run the studio without his help. Yesterday I was double booked three times! I had to turn away two very angry gentlemen who had both apparently been promised the same canvas, which I discovered had sold weeks before! I could barely reconcile myself with the subsequent shame! If I am not careful, the name Turner will become a joke in the art world.

    The doctor has assured me that the best route to recovery for Father is plenty of bed rest. Naturally, I couldn't do without him, and his coughing and wheezing has been keeping me awake at night, wracked by fear that this may be more than a mere cold.

    Bugger this. I'm going to get drunk.

Yours, as ever,

J.W.

Sarah,

It is certainly more than just a mere cold. Two weeks now Bill has been confined to his bed. I've hardly had time to paint, let alone manage the studio. Much more of this and we will soon be in dire financial straits. I wish that you were here with me, and that a sea did not separate us, however temporarily. Bill is forever apologising for the inconvenience he is causing. I fear I have been too hard on him. After all, it's not his fault. A solution must be found, however, and soon.

In desperation,

J.W.

1816: The Year Without Summer

Dear Fellow Traveller,

I had thought to address you as The Egyptian, as one of my associates calls you. One day you may reveal to me your true name, when I am ready.

Good news. An opportunity has arisen for gainful employment. I am to become the assistant, nay the apprentice, to a Great Man. No doubt the name Joseph William Turner will mean little to you, as you are above such concerns, but he is quite the name to conjure with amongst artistic circles. I was perusing the front page of *The Times* when I happened upon his advertisement. It seems that Mr. Turner requires assistance in the running of his studio, seeking a young man of artistic bent.

I begin at the start of next week and will write you with more news as soon as I have it.

Yours,

A.P.

Dear Sarah,

I had almost more applications than I could cope with. I had been advised not to put my name in the advertisement, but word would have got around soon enough. All day long the door has been opening and closing on a seemingly ceaseless parade of earnest young men – *sycophants,* I should say – all of whom are desperate for the chance to work with the 'Great Man.' (I can even now hear Bill chuckling from his sick bed. One hopes that this levity is a sign of improved health).

Finally, I have made my choice.

Alexander is no less intense than his fellow applicants, but he has a certain hunger and openness that appeals to me. He is also available to start immediately and is more than happy to take up residence in the studio. He has been introduced to Bill, and Father did not disapprove.

I feel as though a great weight has been lifted from my shoulders. I can continue to attend to Father's care and, God-willing, we shall soon be out of this.

With affection,

J.W.

Dearest Sarah,

For a young man of modest means, Alexander has amassed a considerable travelling library. Most are works of philosophy, many not in English. He is a little sensitive about his collection, as I discovered when I picked up one of his books and began to leaf through it. There is also a chest that he has warned me off ever touching. "The books within are extremely rare and sensitive to abrupt changes in atmosphere." It is well. He has his eccentricities, as I have mine. He soon understood what is required of the role and has started to make appointments and go through the accounts. Money well spent, I'd say.

Later–

It is to be expected. After all, if one asks for an 'artistic' assistant, one should eventually expect to be shown their work. Perhaps I should have used the words 'applicant should be familiar with the art world' to offset the expectations that I would be looking for creative endeavour from my employee.

We had been drinking. It was late. The wine, Bill's slowly improving health – all attributed to a generally agreeable mood and made me perhaps more open than is usual. When Alexander asked, "May I show you my own work?" I said yes, and now I fear that sleep will be a long time in coming.

Sarah, Bosch's visions are as nothing to what I was shown!

A single canvas about two feet high, perhaps half that across. Against a murky background… actually, *dirty* is the first word that sprung to mind – diseased, even. Against this broken and desolate plane stood something I can barely describe. The Chimera of Greek mythology is maybe the closest comparison, but that beast was composed of animals found in nature, whereas this...

"What do you think?" Alexander said.

I was at a loss. There was no levity in his words, no sign that he was joking, and so I had to provide the laughter, to which he responded in kind, though his eyes held a challenge.

Sarah, I can barely write for shaking. The stains upon this page are wine. If sleep won't come, insensibility is to be preferred.

I have asked him to keep his dreadful painting in his room.

I love you,

J.W.

1816: The Year Without Summer

Fellow Traveller,

I fear that I have gone too far. Last night I showed Turner one of my works. I know that he saw the truth of it, but I have greatly disturbed him. It was the painting of the creature Alhazred mentioned numerous times in his writings, and which came when it was called. I cannot remember its name.

I must rest now and try to make it up to the Great Man in the morning.

Yours,

A.P.

Dear Sarah,

Alexander has set to with such vigour and discipline that the studio is running more efficiently than ever before. Bill is almost returned to full health, but it has been decided to keep Alexander on, so indispensable has he become to the running of our business. He has not endeavoured to show me anymore of his art, much to my relief, and despite his rather peculiar ways, I am beginning to find him pleasant company.

I hope that your jaunt abroad continues to be beneficial.

Yours affectionately,

J.W.

1816: The Year Without Summer

[*Address not supplied. Provenance unknown*]

A.P. Our time is limited. I was under the impression that your man, Turner, was beginning to show promise. I hope that I was right to put my trust in you.

Fellow Traveller

I am taken aback my your most recent correspondence. You needn't be so anxious. How can you think your trust misplaced? Wasn't it by my side that you descended the Seventy Steps? Was it not I that lead you through the streets of Dylath-Leen; saw you at play amongst the million cats and their mistress? Just because I don't scatter my missives with purple prose or endlessly share my dream visions – like a certain young novice I could mention – it does not mean that I don't take my mission seriously. After all, who could deny that I was called here?

In any case, I have made progress. Great progress.

It has been raining for the better part of the week, but on Friday the weather finally broke. An incredible sky revealed itself and Turner immediately took to the garden to paint. The garden has not been attended well, and the trees that border the field at the rear of the house have grown to such a prestigious size that their branches all but eat up the sky. I suggested to the Great Man that he may be better served in planting his canvas somewhere like Hampstead, where the sweep of the sky may be more fully appreciated.

"But I shall lose something of the light," he said.

"Ah, but may the light not be more pleasing in the late afternoon when the sky has more blood in it?"

And so, I took my first journey with the Master, though I don't think he'd been expecting me to accompany him as his manner was, at first, reticent. He was not used to working with an audience, he said. I pointed out that were I to help him manage his business, it was vital that I observe his process.

To Hampstead then, where we sat and looked out over London.

It was getting on for three in the afternoon and the sun had already begun to dip towards the horizon. The sky was fire. Turner began to paint. Such energy! The canvas was attacked again and again. Soon, he was up to his elbows in oils. He was entirely unconscious of my presence, and several times he collided with me as he described a flourish with a little too much vigour. There were periods of great stillness, where minutes passed as he looked at the canvas like a caged beast viewing a tasty morsel of prey just beyond reach, before he lunged in once more – sweating profusely, grunting like a rutting pig.

He is fascinating to watch, but it is in his oils that the true vision is manifest. It has become abundantly clear to me that Turner sees that which is beyond the sky. He must hear the call; how else to explain those prismatic wings, their spread encompassing the horizon, enfolding the dying sun? Or the pyroclastic orgies that pulse through the skeins of shimmering vapour he expresses with such delicacy, yet which hold so much presence, such that I can feel *them* pushing against our world. The city is almost an afterthought; the buildings mere dabs of dreary colour beneath his magnificent sky, signifying nothing of the shabby, squalid lives within.

The whole of the true realm, the only existence worth acknowledging, is in *his* sky.

In short, dear Traveller, it is he whom I was sent to witness and bear home.

Yours, in anticipation,

A.P.

Dearest Sarah

Yes, yet another missive. No doubt you receive these letters in batches on the various stops of your tour. I'm not usually so voluble in my correspondence, but life has been so strange of late, and with Bill still ailing (though continuing to improve, I am pleased to say), I feel that I must reach out to someone *normal* for the sake of my sanity.

I cannot fault Alexander's book-keeping, and he certainly keeps a tidier studio than Bill ever did, but he's just so *present*. He is always asking me questions, always making sure to see to my comfort and needs. He no doubt means well, but I find him disconcerting.

I am away at the Academy tomorrow, so hopefully the society of my fellow artists will dispel this unease.

I love you,

J.W.

1816: The Year Without Summer

Dear Fellow Traveller

I have been up and down the length of this blasted city trying to find a supplier of esoteric wares worth his salt who stocks even one gram of Reichenbach's Reduction. Damned if I can find the bloody powder! Of course, I wouldn't ask you to send a consignment by air – the expenditure of your power, let alone the cost to your sanity, just wouldn't be worth it.

I shall have to perform the ritual without the powder. I just hope that Mr. Turner is a heavy sleeper.

Yours,

A.P.

Dearest Sarah,

There was a curious look on Alexander's face at breakfast this morning. He asked me whether I had passed a troubled night.

"No, I slept very well, thank you," I told him. He seemed dismayed by this.

"No curious dreams?" he asked.

"No, sir. I very rarely dream. Or, if I do, I rarely remember my dreams."

Alexander seemed crestfallen. "Are you well?" I asked.

"I would have thought that a man of your artistic stature would have the most vivid dreams. You only have to look at your many works to realise the depth of your vision."

Bill, who had joined us at the table, and even managed a little toast, laughed. "You don't half talk a lot of rot, Alexander! It may be that you are spending too much time in the studio; the paint fumes must be getting to you."

Later —

I asked Alexander not to accompany me to the Academy today, but instead to remain in London and see to the books. I came here to Sandycombe Lodge directly from the Academy. I couldn't remain in the city, not after what I had seen there.

I had intended it to be a social visit, an opportunity to catch up with a few friends, but I had what I can only describe as an *episode*.

1816: The Year Without Summer

(Do not worry, my love. I have mostly recovered, and the housekeeper has sent for a doctor in the meantime. By the time you receive this letter, I shall be quite well again.)

After an excellent lunch with an old friend, I decided to take in some of the most recent acquisitions at the gallery. I was looking at a naïve pastoral scene which depicted a shepherd standing atop a hill, looking down into a shadowed dell into which one of his flock had wandered. As I took in the composition, the painting *changed*. The errant sheep moved. Of course, how could such be possible when it is a thing of oil and pigment? But I'm telling you, Sarah – it moved!

As I watched in horror, the sheep in the picture made its way out from under the shadows of the trees. At first it walked on four legs, but as it mounted the rise four became eight, and then they weren't legs at all but whip-thin tendrils that propelled the creature towards it prey with a horrid swiftness.

I cried out and staggered back. The firm hand of a colleague arrested my fall. When I returned to the painting, it was as I had first seen it.

I think I have been working too hard

Yours,

J.W.

Frederick,

Good news! The 'old bastard' is not dead. After almost a month of flirting with death, I have decided that it is not for me. Hah! It will take more than the wretched flu to finish off old Bill.

Joseph employed a studio assistant to help run things during my convalescence, but now that I am most of the way better, I do not think that we will need Alexander for much longer. This is a good thing. I do not like the man. While my son is away at the Lodge, I shall take the opportunity to have a quiet word with him.

Soon you and I shall have to catch up on all the carousing we have lately missed.

Yours,

Bill

1816: The Year Without Summer

[Letter to *The Times*]

Sirs,

I had the most extraordinary encounter at the Academy the other day, the details of which may interest your readers.

We all know that Joseph W. Turner is a man – one hesitates to use the word 'gentleman' – of uncouth manner and undesirable social habits, but on Thursday afternoon I actually saw him screaming at a painting. It was a pastoral fantasy of no great artistic merit, so the mind boggles as to what the 'Great Man' found so alarming.

As ever, I find his presence at the Academy simply baffling.

Yours Sincerely,

Professor Greg Aldrich, Esq.

Dear Fellow Traveller,

I must say that I find Joseph's recent absence alarming.

What is more, during this time Bill took it upon himself to be utterly foul to me. Alas, he is now more out of bed than in it and spent most of the day in nit-picking with his relentless questions: as to my place of birth, as to my parentage, my education, where I trained in the arts, what my interest is in his son, why I wanted to work for his son in the first place. Endless niggling designed, no doubt, to aggravate me rather than sate his curiosity.

In the afternoon, the inquisition was given a rest and I hoped that Bill was once more in his bed, perhaps exhausted by his efforts. I therefore spent a productive few hours going over the studio's accounts. As the sun was setting, I felt a presence at my shoulder.

"Joseph tells me that you consider yourself an artist," Bill said, making me jump.

"My art is my own affair," I replied. "Be assured it is as nothing when compared to your son's paintings."

"That, sir, is most true. However, Joseph told me about the unusual nature of your art, that it is disturbed, of a base nature. Not fit for public consumption."

"Does not this say more about your—"

"Having seen your work, I find myself in agreement."

"You have been into my room!"

"It is *my* room, sir, as this is *my* house."

I was struck dumb. I could not formulate a reply, and seeing me so stunned, Bill went on. "You are a deeply disturbed man, Alexander Pickman; a scoundrel. I do not wish for your corruption to take a hold of my son. You have until tomorrow morning to remove yourself and your effects from our home."

On this, he departed. I could do little but stare at where he had stood, trembling with shock and rage.

This *oaf*, this *simpleton* – does he not see the true potential of his son's art? Does he not realise that under my guidance, his son could become a true visionary?

This is a significant setback, and when all was going so well, but do not call for me yet, or attempt to summon those who would do so; it shall be as promised. I shall persevere.

Yours,

A.P.

Dearest Sarah,

I have the most upsetting news. During my absence Bill fell gravely ill once again. I do not understand it. When I departed, he was almost his old self. Alexander said that he had tried to make contact with me when Father had first returned to bed, but he had no clue as to my whereabouts. Now we are unable to wake him, and he burns with a fever twice as intense as before.

Later —

Though near insensible, Bill has been trying to speak. He struggles to sit up, grimacing as though desperate to communicate something of great import. But from his lips comes not English but a stream of nonsense, accompanied by bestial grunts. One sound in particular he repeats – *Eeyar. Eeyar. Eeyar.* I'm trying to make sense of his babbling, for if these are to be his last words, there must be something more to them than lunatic cacophony.

A short while ago, I managed to get him to take some opium. He is quieter now, and the physician has advised me to leave him to his rest.

I can still hear him through the wall.

Eeyar. Eeyar. Eeyar.

Dinner was a maudlin affair. This is supposed to be the season 'of mists and mellow fruitfulness' but the endless bloody rain shakes the windows in their casements. This year has already been meteorologically strange; this month doubly so. Alexander arrived late to supper, flecks of paint speckling his hands. No doubt inspired by the doom-laden mood hanging over the house, he has been driven to create. He spoke very little but smiled frequently and made sure to keep my glass filled.

Now I must sleep.

I am beyond exhaustion.

J.W.

Dear Fellow Traveller

It is only nine o' clock at night, but Joseph is already fast asleep, sped on his way by the elixir I administrated during our meal. Bill's slumbers are not quite so peaceful. Even so, though he does not realise it, he will form an essential part of the ritual.

For these past two weeks, I have been trying to guide Turner to *true vision*, and though he has shown again and again through his art his cognisance of those realms which shadow man's, he has been unable to take that final step into revelation. Is it up to me to be his guide? It is up to me to bring him to kneel at the feet of our master.

Below, I will write down the processes I employ so that they may be of use, or academic interest, to those who come after me. Also, I want to make it clear just how much I have learnt at your feet.

Firstly

I prepare myself.

It is not essential to disrobe, but I find the flesh revealed to be a potent symbol.

Next, the flesh is marked.

Using the sharpest and cleanest knife I can find, I incise my flesh – at forehead, above the lips, at chest, the inside of each wrist and below the stomach. The symbols are as those on the separate sheet I have enclosed within this letter.

[NB: The sheet referred to above was not amongst the correspondence found]

Next

I wait in silence.

I visualise the marks I have cut into my flesh – from the highest to the lowest. This is to establish the alien geometry that will allow Turner and myself to access the realm beyond.

(During this time, Bill's half-conscious ranting has turned into a steady chant as I imposed my will upon the household).

"Ftagn!" The shout is as sudden and final as a slammed door.

I begin the chant.

"Iä. Iä. Iä…"

(I fancy at this point that I hear a choir of alien voices echoing my own).

Defilement/Creation

The picture I have chosen is not one of Turner's better-known works, but it is the perfect focus.

I started, before dinner, to make my changes to Fishermen at Sea. Despite what Bill and Joseph may think, I have had comprehensive training and am a fine artist in my own right.

To the night sky, to Turner's depiction of that merciless void, infinity, I add hints of the terrors of creation; that sublime otherness, the sight of which I am hoping will unlock wondrous possibilities within the Great Man. I peel back the sky to reveal the vista of endless passages, in which one may encounter formless terror made manifest – those that lurk and dance to cacophonous piping; those that slumber within star-strewn seas. Life which is not life.

Turner may encounter, and in turn be encountered.

*   *   *

The processes are finally complete, and I can barely keep my hand from shaking as I write these words. All that remains is the final step, which we shall take together.

Buoyed by this confidence, I foolishly decided to check in on Bill just a moment ago. His place in the ritual finished, he had fallen silent. I had rather hoped him dead. But as I leaned over him, holding my breath as I listened for his, he rose suddenly from the bed, his hands closing around my throat.

"You… *you… blasphemer!*" he spat into my face.

I grabbed the nearest thing to hand (the Bible upon the bedside table) and rendered him unconscious once more. Now he lies snoring, and I hope that he will not awake before Joseph and I are done.

I anticipate that I shall have such revelations to share with you, Fellow Traveller, and soon we shall be reunited.

Yours,

A.P.

1816: The Year Without Summer

Dearest Sarah,

I can hardly believe all that has taken place, but I shall try to make some sense of it.

Two days after my last letter to you, I awoke to find myself lying on the studio floor, Alexander lay beside me, whimpering, while Bill stood over him brandishing a poker. My assistant was covered in blood and strange symbols had been cut into his flesh, presumably by his own hand. Even more astonishing than this sight, however, was what had been done to one of my works. Alexander had taken Fisherman at Night and changed it – *defiled* is perhaps a more apt word. He had scrawled across that placid sky, crudely depicting what could have been a city populated by strange aquatic creatures. Despite the naivety of the execution, looking at the picture brought me to recall the terrible nightmare I had been trapped in for the last forty-eight hours; a dream so extraordinary I must recount it as fully as I am able before I tell you what happened next.

* * *

I remember going to bed after my meal with Alexander and then… it was as though I was falling through the sky; the streaming stars enfolding me, a curiously warm wind buffeting my body. And then an astonishing, source less light that pierced my very being and sang in my bones. *The sun*, I thought. *The sun is God.* Voices surrounded me, speaking too fast for me to comprehend any individual words. I do not think they were English.

My surroundings changed and I found myself to be flying. This sky had no end; there was no ground below or stars above. Skeins of the most beautiful cloud, like delicate, coloured scarves stretched away into infinity on all sides. The colours, Sarah – there are no words in the English language, or perhaps any human tongue, to describe them – and pulsing within the hearts of those clouds, more extraordinary colours still. From them emanated a sense of magnificent power. I knew that were I to draw near them, I would be destroyed.

For how long I flew, I know not. At some point the clouds thinned and then were retreating astern. I was surrounded now by the same featureless blue. With nothing to measure it against, all sensation of movement stopped.

Perhaps, I reasoned, *I have died, and this is all that awaits us in the life-to-come.*

Below me the depthless blue began to darken and assume form, and now I was flying swiftly over a noisome, roiling black sea. I was drawn downwards, and though I fought against it, I could do nothing to arrest my descent. I feared that I would be drowned in those viscous waters, but instead, I alighted upon the surface and it held. I had come to rest in a small area of calm, the surface of the water so still it was as though I were looking into a perfect black mirror.

I looked down at my reflection, to find Alexander standing beside me. Instantly, I turned and wrapped my hands around his throat.

"What have you done to me?" I screamed.

Alexander merely smiled. His teeth were the same black as that terrible sea.

It is not Alexander alone who brought you to this place.

It was as if the universe itself had spoken, and I turned in the direction of the voice to see *it* begin to rise from the black sea. I let go of Alexander and staggered back from the colossal dark column that rose far above us. It began to take form as it ascended: vast arms held crossed before a cliff-like chest, atop which hung that which I suppose I should describe as a head, though where the face would have been was only hollow darkness; blacker than any starless night, blacker even than the onyx sea that seemed to be all that there was of this place. Atop this head, and adorning the figure's shoulders, was a headdress like those worn by Egypt's pharaohs. At the feet of the giant, the sea boiled and frothed, giving birth to the most profoundly ugly things I have ever seen. These squamous horrors capered and danced at the feet of the... *god* is surely a blasphemous term, but it's the only word that does justice to the creature's immensity. These scabrous goblins raised their inhuman voices in worship; some of them piping on instruments protruding sickeningly from their own diseased flesh.

Alexander grabbed my shoulder and hissed "kneel!" and I had no option but to obey.

The giant leaned down – it was like a mountain falling and I tried to raise my arms to shield my head but found I could not move – and I was face-to-face with ceaseless night.

My servant believes you worthy, it said.

"Oh, he is. He is!" Alexander simpered, and I was nauseated by the subservience in his voice.

Alexander would have you be a witness to our coming reign. A prophet, disseminating works of true vision to others of your kind; it is time for them to wake up.

"I knew it from the first time I saw your works, Joseph," Alexander said. "You see such otherworldly beauty."

"You are wrong!" I spat back. "The beauty I portray is of this world... of *my* world."

I would show you more, Joseph Mallord William Turner. I would reveal to you visions that would put you far above any other earthly artist. Together we could journey from the seas of Ubo-Sathla into the exquisite realms. I would return you to your world a changed man, one bearing a gift of immeasurable value.

Alexander had thought he had seen in me the same unnatural impulses that burn within his breast; he thought he had found a kindred spirit that he could present to his blasphemous god.

"Your disciple was mistaken," I said.

The giant reared back, as though I had spat into its face. The creatures capering at its feet turned and bared their fangs. The ground began to undulate; the sea rising up until we were surrounded on all sides by towering cliffs of night.

"Don't be foolish, Joseph," Alexander said. "Do you not realise what it has cost me to bring you here? Do you not appreciate the sacrifices I have made for you?"

I was filled with a dreadful terror, Sarah. A fear that I would be locked inside this insanity forever, and the next time you saw me would be through the bars of a cell, as I rocked and drooled against a padded wall. Though you know that I am a far from pious man, I am not ashamed to say that I closed my eyes and began to pray.

Partway through my benediction, I was stopped by a dreadful sound. Alexander was screaming, his mouth open so wide I thought his jaw would surely dislocate. The sound pierced all, stilling the waves that were threatening to topple and drown us; the black sea became as stone, cracks zig-zagging through its surface with deafening retorts. The creatures that had been about to turn on me whined and pleaded as a sharp wind rose and blew them to dust.

And the god himself was falling. Just before he struck, I opened my eyes.

*   *   *

1816: The Year Without Summer

Bill was standing over Alexander's prone form. The young man was writhing in pain on the studio floor. Father had clearly taken a blow himself as his hair was plastered to his scalp with blood. Despite his condition, I was delighted to see him back on his feet.

"Get out!" Bill snarled. "Get of our house and remove yourself from the city. If you return, I shall find you and I shall murder you."

Alexander was sobbing as he got unsteadily to his feet. He reached out to me, beseeching. "I'm sorry, Joseph. I tired. We could have achieved so much together."

"Do as Father says," I replied. "Leave."

Once Alexander had gone, Bill and I stood in the midst of the chaos, looking at each other. Then I did something I have not done since I was a child; I rushed into my father's arms and wept as he held me.

Lovingly Yours,

J.W.

[From a scrap of paper found on the desk of a Whitechapel hotel room, the occupant having apparently fled]

[...] you must forgive me, and do not give up your faith. I had thought Turner such a promising initiate. I will not fail you, or our master, again.

[There follows an illegible passage, some of which may be written in Latin]

I have been hearing the hounds for several days now; their baying comes across an unfathomable distance, but I know that they are drawing ever closer. Don't let it end like this. *Please.*

Though I have not turned to look, I am sure the walls of the room behind me are beginning to unfold. I hear the skittering of crystal talons upon a driftglass floor.

I can see —

1816: The Year Without Summer

Dearest Sarah

It was so good to be reunited with you after everything that has taken place of late. My letters must have worried you sick, especially as you were not in the country when you received them, and therefore not in a position to come to our aid. However, you have now seen that Bill and I are well recovered and in the best of health and spirits.

It is over a month now since the conclusion of our troubles with Alexander. I wonder what has happened to him. One hopes that he is safely ensconced in Bedlam with others of his kind.

These last few weeks have been a time of immense productivity. I am painting most days and only finishing when the call of my bed becomes irresistible. Though it was no doubt brought about by whatever strange drug Alexander administered, I often find my thoughts returning to that curious dream, and those skies.

I have always been adamant that is the beauty that surrounds all of us that I would depict in my art, but what if, I wonder, were I to introduce a little of that dreaming realm?

Yours, in loving faithfulness,

J.W.

Dreams of Tierra Caliente

By Dickon Springate

P resident Vicente Ramón Guerrero Saldaña, a proud and honourable man who was beloved by his countrymen and the miraculous victor of nine shy of five hundred battles, awoke on a cold and rough stone floor. His recent kidnapping was to be his final harsh lesson in the treacherous world of Mexican politics, where party members had deposed their own incumbent president for challenging their ignorant prejudices against his fellow mulattos and for threatening to bring an end to the inhuman treatment of their downtrodden slaves who tilled their fields and estates.

His head pounded and his eyes throbbed as he came to once more; the bruises on his manacled ankles and wrists barely registering as pain by comparison. With little give in his chains, all he could do was continue to slump against the wall in the foul-smelling jail and wait for his guards to come. As he did so, he thought he heard a faint hiss coming from beyond the barred window. He could not be sure if the sound was real or imaginary, but the mere suggestion was enough to quicken his pulse and bring back terrible thoughts of October 1816; a period in his life he had done his best to obliterate from his memory, yet here, and with only a single cue, they came flooding back, vivid in description, and the bitter regret that came with it hurt like it was happening anew.

*   *   *

It all began on that fateful morning, as he sat around a campfire, tucking into a bland plate of frijoles and huevos, nervously awaiting the arrival of the Jarochos, while in his mind he was missing the tender embrace of his beloved and heavily pregnant wife, Guadalupe.

The journey from his fortified redoubt near Chilpancingo had been a gruelling two-week trek on horseback through federal-controlled territory. Normally, he would never have entertained such a dangerous idea, however the leader of the rebels wrote with such steely resolution that he felt he could ill afford to ignore someone whose words echoed his own convictions so closely. So it was that he had relented, after leaving plans and provisions with his most capable and trusted lieutenant-commander, Isidoro Montes de Oca, to continue the good fight in his absence.

Having finished his meal, he gathered his cloak around him and headed out into the street. He always preferred to talk a walk in the early morning, before the midday roasting sun made leisurely strolls uncomfortable, and he also liked to guess the profession of passing townsfolk, by their chosen attire. This particular morning, while he mused over a pair of fancily dressed young ladies, he turned a corner and noticed that a rather peculiar congregation had formed a little way up the muddy street ahead of him.

Slowing his pace, he saw an old, blind beggar at the centre of the throng, garbed in tattered rags and lecturing to a crowd of street urchins. The scarred old man clearly had the tearaways' attention, as instead of jostling and playfully wrestling each other, they sat quietly around him, leaning in, listening to his every rasping word. Guerrero wondered what possible sermon could have these gutter snipes so enrapt, and his curiosity made him pause to see if he could make out any of the old beggar's words.

Maintaining his distance, he smiled when he realised that this was a retelling of how the city of Tenochtitlan had been founded.

Nodding along to himself, he marvelled at the way in which the wanderer wove his animated story, using his old, gnarled limbs to great effect and bringing much wonder and amazement to the proceedings.

His curiosity satisfied, he was about to turn away when the beggar declared that it was all thanks to the Mayan deity, Kukulkan.

In not praising the Aztec god, Huitzilopochtli, for their divine intervention, the old man had made Guerrero a little uncomfortable, as his version jarred with what he knew to be true, yet the tone and cadence of the old man was not erratic or spontaneously inventive, but measured and rehearsed, as if he had told this particular story a thousand times or more.

Guerrero was about to interrupt when the old man's recital reached the part where the eagle lands atop a pear cactus, and he was further confounded when the old man declared that the eagle had already been bitten by the snake, and that no sooner did it land it then keeled over, stricken, and was subsequently swarmed over and devoured by dozens of hungry baby snakes.

The tale was so close to the original that, up to that point, Guerrero would have struggled to separate one legend from the other, however, when the beggar finished his story with the claim that the city was ruled by the Snake Kings before being handed over to the Aztecs, he was sure that it was nothing more than a carefully reworked imagining, as part of some cautionary tale or other.

Once the beggar had concluded his retelling of the legend, the children got up silently as one, and hurriedly scampered off in all directions. Mindful of his purse, Guerrero drew his hands about him as they jostled past, swivelling his head back and forth as he attempted to track each one. As the last of the children dispersed, Guerrero realised that the blind beggar had also vanished. Unsure what had just happened, he continued to glance this way and that, hoping to catch sight of the old man and question him, but of the old man there was no trace, and nobody else had been paying the group any attention.

Sticking his hands in his pockets, he felt something scratchy and, pulling it out, noticed that a tiny scrap of brown parchment had been slipped in while he was busy surveying the children. Opening it he saw that it was not a note as such but scrawled in ink was a glyph of an upright snake, in what appeared to be Mayan script. Turning it over in his fingers he could see that there was nothing on the back; no clue or hint as to the meaning of the glyph. Slightly unsure as to exactly what had just transpired, he repocketed the scrap and resumed his walk; eventually returning to his men and waiting for the rebels to arrive.

At the appointed hour, the representative of the Jarochos, named Jorge Pérez, arrived, flanked by four of his own men, including one strikingly mulatto companion. Guerrero greeted them warmly, and after introductions had been made, the men sat down together to discuss their military aims and objectives. It took only a short while for Guerrero to see that, although they did not hail from the wild hot lands of his birth, they were clearly not peace-mongering Poblanos who thought more of politics than lives.

Towards the end of their meeting Jorge recounted a particularly gruesome beheading and piking of one of his men, a not altogether uncommon atrocity, but one that reminded Guerrero of discovering his dear friend Galeana, and made him shiver at the thought. Despite the distance between their two camps, Guerrero could tell that they shared a visceral hatred for their common enemy, and so a loose alliance was agreed upon.

With formal duties complete, Guerrero felt free to ask a question, for during the meeting, he felt sure that the tall mulatto he had noticed earlier was adorned with a tattoo that was similar to the crudely scribbled glyph he had in his pocket. Attempting to surreptitiously get a better look at the tattoo did not go unnoticed, but thankfully Jorge was of good humour, and eager to show good faith he smiled warmly and called over his companion. Introducing the man as Ehēcatl, and clarifying that he was not a mulatto, but of Nahuatl descent. Shaking hands with Ehēcatl, Guerrero could now see that, although the tattoo was now old and stretched, when it was first cut it would have been a near identical match for his glyph. Curious to know its origin, he asked Ehēcatl where he had got it. Ehēcatl casually shook his head and sighed, saying that it was probably something his father had done to him as a young child, however as his father had died many years before he could not be certain. Almost at a loss, Guerrero asked the only other thing he could think of; for the name of Ehēcatl's home town. Cholōllān was the reply, and with that, the group bade each other farewell and departed.

With the meeting complete and the Jarochos returning to their hideout, Guerrero retired to his hut and considered his next move. From his younger years spent smuggling and transporting alcohol, Guerrero knew all the towns and cities for two hundred miles, as well as the majority of unobserved trails in or out, but the name of Ehēcatl's town was not instantly familiar. Wondering if perhaps Cholōllān was another name for the small town of Cholula, Guerrero allowed his men the rest of the day to relax and celebrate, but planned on taking a detour on their way back.

* * *

In the morning, he and his company woke early, before even the rooster had begun its crowing, and begun the ride to Cholula. Once they had cleared the foothills that surrounded Ixhuacán, the land became flatter and more even underfoot, allowing the horses to stretch their legs and gain more speed across the open country. They rested for the night beside the volcanic lake at Totolcingo, and set off again early the following day in order to reach Cholula before dusk.

As night began to fall, the distant howl of the coyote could be heard over the faint crackle of fallen leaves and shifting scrub that were the tell-tale signs of cacomistles foraging for food.

Approaching Cholula from the north, Guerrero sent two of his men ahead to see if there was a safe taverna for them to share a meal near one of the many disused churches that they would use as a dry place to bed down for the night. The men found the little sleepy town's main road all but deserted, with most of the townsfolk either at home or congregating in a few central bars to drink mezcal and listen to the local tamborileros into the early hours.

Shunning the vibrant town centre, the pair of riders found an old taverna still open which, fortuitously, backed right onto an abandoned church. While one rider returned to act as guide for Guerrero and company, the other tied up his horse out of sight and entered the taverna.

When Guerrero and his men reached the town, they easily made their way through the still back streets to the taverna, where their companion was waiting. Having tied up their own horses, they quietly entered and found a table near the bar where they could order some hot food. The taverna's interior looked even older and more decrepit than its frontage suggested, which was something Guerrero found hard to believe, but its condition went a long way to explain why the only two souls in the place appeared to be the bored young waitress and the fastidious barkeep, who repetitively wiped the already clean worktop.

After a few minutes of mundane chatter, Guerrero suddenly heard a soft cough and realised that the place was not empty of patrons after all, for, mostly obscured by a tall pillar and shrouded in shadow, was an elderly man sitting quietly with his back to his group. Whether by chance or design, the layout of the taverna was such that he was sitting beyond the glare of the wall-mounted candle lights, and almost invisible to anyone who stood illuminated by them, yet Guerrero was sure that from his location he would also be able to hear every word being said by anyone up at the bar.

Deciding to overtly ignore the cough, Guerrero waited until the barkeep was at the other end of the taverna before surreptitiously throwing a few subtle nods and winks to the others; sharing the fact that they were not alone. By the time the waitress had turned up with their plates of beef mole and rice, the unseen cougher had drained his drink and, having slowly lifted himself from his chair, departed without so much as a nod towards the owner.

Weighing up the options regarding when and how to withdraw from a given situation had always been one of Guerrero's greatest military strengths, and he felt there was something odd about the old man's manner, which worried him. Indecision hung in the air for a moment as he sought to divine the answers by staring into his mole, until he at last concluded that, regardless of the man's true purpose, the prudent thing would be to ride on.

His decision made, Guerrero flashed his captain a telling gaze, and then, with closed lids, shook his head just visibly enough to pass across the message that there was something amiss. Having fought beside him many times, his captain knew well enough to trust his commander's instincts, and so under the guise of going to relieve himself outside, he exited and went to ready the horses.

Having finished their meals, the men settled up and left, intending to return to their horses and ride out as quickly as possible. However, as they rounded the corner, they could plainly see their captain deep in hushed conversation with a young boy, while all their horses remained fastened by their reins.. From this distance, Guerrero could tell that the captain was on his guard, but sensed no immediate danger, so, trusting his captain's instincts. they continued walking until they were together once more.

Beaming a wide, honest smile which only an innocent child could attempt, the youth said that he had been given a whole

Spanish dollar to deliver a message to the finely dressed gentleman from the taverna, and that he would be given another dollar if he would guide the gentleman to where the old man would be waiting for him. Unfolding the piece of paper that the boy offered him, Guerrero saw again the familiar standing snake glyph, only this time, it appeared to be wearing some sort of clothing.

Guerrero's men did not comprehend the message, but they knew him well enough that if Guerrero felt it was not a trap, then it was probably not a trap, and so noting that he was debating whether to go or not in a relaxed manner, the others dismissed any thoughts of danger and instead turned their minds to unpacking the horses and bedding down for the night.

Had the note said anything else, Guerrero would most likely have chosen to ignore it, but the glyphs were no coincidence, and although its true intent remained unclear, he felt certain it was benign.

Instructing his captain to set the watch for the night, Guerrero agreed to go with the boy and meet the man who had sent him the note. Still smiling, the boy placed his small hand within Guerrero's loose grip and began to skip playfully as he led him through the narrow, cobbled streets, splashing and jumping in little puddles as he went.

As the pair reached the centre of the town, a small, squat man garbed in Mayan dress stepped out from a concealed alleyway and silently beckoned them over.

One look at the man's upper right shoulder told Guerrero all he needed to know, for there, again, was the upright snake glyph tattoo.

"The boy stays here, for you must come with me alone," instructed the Mayan.

1816: The Year Without Summer

Already committed to solving the riddle, Guerrero nodded his acceptance and the pair progressed through the narrow streets until they at last came to a steep incline, where his guide requested that he wait while he prepared the opening.

By now, the sun was deep below the horizon and the thin moon, high in the night's sky, was hidden behind thick cloud banks, casting only an occasional mottled reflection on the ground, so Guerrero heard more than saw what happened next. First, he heard clods of earth being tossed aside by hand. Then, he heard wood being scraped over earth, hollow and echoing like there was a chasm or opening behind it. Finally, he heard the swooshing of thick material behind pulled back and to the side, allowing a thin beam of light to stretch out from within the hillside.

The guide beckoned Guerrero to follow him once more, and the pair descended into the ground through a tunnel of cold and hard earth, before suddenly reaching an opening of perfectly chiselled rock; solid and clearly part of something much older that the surrounding buildings.

The air down here felt cool and stale, but not dank or clammy, suggesting to Guerrero that, although definitely underground, they were still clearly above the water table. The way forward, though dimly lit, was not at all treacherous, and some part of him knew that that the flooring was probably swept clean on a fairly regular basis. Eventually the walkway ended with a thick curtain drape, through which Guerrero's guide instructed him to get on his knees and carefully shuffle forward a couple more feet. These last few feet took him through a small opening in a wall, into what felt like a furnace, as trails of steam seeped from around the edges of the curtain. After the darkness of the walk and the corridor, the gloom of the dimly-lit anti-chamber was, mercifully, not too harsh on his eyes, itself only lit by a few candles placed in small recesses along its length.

It took his eyes only a few moments to adjust to the gloom before they could make out the room's interior, covered with murals of both Aztec and Mayan, but most noticeable was that he was not alone. Barely a few feet away was a figure sitting cross-legged. Even for one who was used to the hellish heat of the flatlands around Chilpancingo, the temperature was such that Guerrero began sweating profusely almost immediately, and so he took off his outer layer to ease his discomfort.

From somewhere behind the old man emerged a young boy, no more than five or six years of age, who respectfully, eyes averted, handed both men a glass of wine before retreating from view while the two men sat facing each other.

Seemingly indifferent to the unbearable humidity, the cross-legged figure sitting serenely in front of him was a man of incredibly advanced years; his carefully-folded white guayabera tucked away beside him. Taking a moment to study his face, Guerrero saw that it was adorned with Mayan tribal paint in artfully decorative patterns of black and blue lines, waves and dots. The man's eyes fascinated Guerrero the most, however, as, in the dim light, they appeared a dazzling light blue, unlike anything he had ever seen, and as the man spoke, they seemed to swirl, drawing him in, and soon Guerrero was hanging upon his every syllable.

The old man did not fully introduce himself, save for stating that he was of Mayan ancestry and that he was known to some as the keeper of histories Then, after taking a sip of wine, he began to tell Guerrero about his lineage, a history full of royalty and power that existed beyond the modest upbringing that Guerrero had assumed was all there was to know about himself.

For the next few hours, the two sat, wrapped within the unravelling of Guerrero's past, one speaking slow and steady, pausing only to let his latest revelation sink in, and the other listening with a growing sense of wonder and amazement as he discovered more about his direct bloodline in one night than he had in the previous three decades. At times, it was reminiscent of the tale the blind beggar told, except this time, it was not kept light for a younger audience, but filled with names and dates.

The keeper of histories detailed a long line of names on Guerrero's mother's side that led not only to Aztec nobility, something that Guerrero had long believed to be true, but also to the legendary Mayan Snake Kings, except of course that according to the keeper of histories, they were very real and incredibly devious. The Snake Kings, Guerrero was told, were ruthlessly ambitious, controlling the entire region with an iron grip, thanks to being not only masterful tacticians, but capable of mythical sorcery such as the ability to cloud a man or summon an army of snakes. These divine powers, were said to be derived through sacrificial rituals and prayers made to their mighty serpentine deity Kukulkan.

As the night wore on, the young jug carrier seemed to instinctively reappear just as they were about to run dry a second and third time to refill their glasses, and then just like before, having topped up their glasses he would retire into the recess and out of Guerrero's line of vision.

On the fourth occasion, Guerrero took a sip and realised that his glass contained something different. He had quickly grown accustomed to paying no heed to the attendee, and so diverting was the story the elderly man was weaving that he had not noticed the change in colour of the contents until he had already gulped and swallowed a huge mouthful. The room began to dim to a dark shade of grey as all the light and colour were seemingly sucked into the steaming coals, yet the storyteller seemed unaffected and continued without a pause, even as Guerrero struggled with consciousness.

Guerrero's eyes grew heavy and, to keep himself from nodding off, he tried exaggerated squeezing of his eyes and sideways head shaking. He blinked once, then twice, and then a third time, only this time his eyes closed slower than intended, and it seemed a strained effort to open them again.

When he blinked a fourth time, Guerrero was no longer feeling thick-headed and sluggish, however nor was he seated on the floor of a steam-filled room, for, together with the keeper, he was now walking as part of a procession through the forest. As the old Mayan led the procession away from the dwindling torches of the town and out towards the dense forest, not a soul spoke as they walked along a hidden path in single file.

All around them, the jungle was alive with nocturnal feeders, with few paying much attention to the solemn procession as they passed. Guerrero almost tripped a few times, as they progressed without torches to light the way, but eventually his eyes adjusted to the reflection cast by the weak moonlight and he stumbled no more.

Eventually, the cortege reached a large clearing and immediately walking around the edge of the clearing, encircling a large stack of logs. When the column head met up with its tail, they stopped and turned to face its epicentre, having formed a large ring. Then a few minutes later, from all directions, Guerrero could hear more movements as other silhouetted figures stepped out of the forest darkness and formed a second, outer ring, just apart from those inside who had journeyed with Guerrero.

Despite being beside the keeper of histories, Guerrero could not hear clearly what he said, but after a few incantations, the logs and kindling burst alight, spitting out purple sparks that darted in all directions as the flames leapt ten feet in the air. The suddenness of the ignition caught him totally by surprise, and he could only imagine that the logs had been somehow doused with a flammable agent and expertly laced with just enough exotic gunpowder to burst into flames without exploding the pile and showering them all with flying wooden debris.

With greater illumination, Guerrero could see that the newcomers were all nubile young beauties, long-haired and bare breasted, each carrying either a small round, wooden drum or two large jugs of a deep red liquid. Despite there no longer being any need for stealth, the group remained in silence, with each person apparently knowing their role, and the women passing their drums to the men before squatting on the ground with the jugs between their knees.

Thanks to the now blazing fire, Guerrero could also get a good look at the young men whom he had followed, noticing that, unlike their leader, their bodies were adorned with thick red and green body paint which seemed to glow eerily in the pale moonlight.

The keeper of histories began to chant once more as the drummers began beating out a slow and continuous rhythm that accompanied a mysterious piping melody that seemed to come out of nowhere and echoed all around the clearing. Scanning the gathered assembly, Guerrero vainly tried to spot the pipe players, but the concert of the combined harmonies suggested something akin to a war party on the move.

One of the men had brought along a magnificent hooded eagle, and at the appointed moment he carefully passed it to the old Mayan, who leaned in close and began to whisper as he gently hefted the bird's perch in the direction of the three winds. With a dawning realisation, Guerrero surmised what was about to happen and so did not flinch when the keeper of histories unsheathed a small knife and slit open the eagle's neck wide open. After spraying the fire with its blood, the keeper of histories threw the carcass onto the ground, drawing the attention of a couple of small snakes that another of the men had just released from a tall straw basket.

With the minority of the men still keeping the continuous beating of their drums going, the remaining men split into two groups. The first formed an even tighter ring around the fire and began to dance and stamp their feet in time to the drumming, while the other half went to sit beside the alluring young girls. Pairing up, the couples began to carefully disrobe each other, placing their discarded pants and headdresses in tight piles upon the ground.

With a final few brief commands, the gathering took on a lustful tempo of fever pitch as the drummers began to strike with such fervour and fury that they threatened to tear their instruments apart, and the dancers began to jump and cavort in time around the roaring fire; each landing creating a mini tremor that shook the ground and would have been noticed by anything sensitive for miles around.

The now naked group enthusiastically quaffed scarlet wine from the brown earthenware jugs and then, without further direction, began to embrace and caress each other with wild abandon, showing a carnal desire towards any man or woman within reach of themselves; their screams of passion and ecstasy merging with the beating of the drums.

For his part, Guerrero stood both within and apart from the party, as he possessed neither a drum to beat, nor was he covered with the body paint of the dancers. Yet as he thought this, he noticed for the first time that he was actually covered in black and blue paint, similar to those covering the old Mayan, and, furthermore, he was wearing a white cloak held fast about his neck by a pair of large red and gold discs.

As he stood there in rapt attention, the old man turned to face him, a filled wooden cup now held between his hands. He took a small sip and swallowed. A second mouthful he spat through the air in three deliberate squirts, moving from east to west, before carefully passing the half-filled cup across.

Having come this far already, Guerrero was not about to balk at this point, so with a slight nod, he accepted the cup and raised it to his lips, glancing down to notice that the liquid had a pale green colour and an aroma that he could only detect as vaguely floral. Taking a larger mouthful than he had intended, he swallowed it all down and instantly regretted it, as the noxious green liquid coursed down his throat and burned like liquid hellfire as it made its way towards his stomach. It tasted bitter and cactus-like, though different from agave which, of course, he had tried many times. His extremities began to tingle as a thick enshrouding fog engulfed his mind and deafened his ears. As the thunderous rhythm of the manic drummers began to gently ebb away into oblivion, the flickering flames that sparked and rose from the great firepit seemed to merge into glowing glyphs that pranced a comical jig before consuming one another.

As his conscious mind began to retreat to the safety of a darkened slumber, he was vaguely aware of several pairs of soft hands caressing him from behind, while yet more pulled free the restricting fastenings of his pants and cape. He fell backwards and landed in a pile of what felt like giant verdant leaves that bellowed around him, shifting to support his weight. Reality faded away and, for a time, was replaced by an alternate existence; a kaleidoscope of lucid colours and a sense of floating in a cool lake while a trickling waterfall splashed onto his head from somewhere high above. Blissful and dumb, he lay there, incapacitated, helplessly inarticulate and completely nescient of the gyrating movements of the several fawning attendees that enveloped him and traced teasing lines across his bare skin with their fingernails or flowing hair.

*   *   *

In the intervening years between that ritual and the present his waking memory never fully returned to explain exactly what had occurred after he accepted the old Mayans sharing cup, but fragments of the vision he imagined under its intoxicating influence would attempt to invade his normal slumber.

On these rare occasions, he saw himself as a young bull, proud and energetic, standing in an open field of giant flowers as far as his bestial eyes could see. Beneath a violaceous sky, his bullish form was in a playful mood as he would gaily trot about until a particular dense growth of blooming flowers would arouse his interest, at which point he would charge headfirst at the blossoming grove, impaling it upon his horns, and, in return, it would explode into a bellowing shower of bright petals and golden stamen.

Seemingly, there was never any end to his ardour or desire to frolic and plough through the flowers, though thankfully, in this other reality, the flourishing fields and amethyst skies were equally endless, thus he would continue to attempt to satisfy his desires again and again, until, in the end, the vision would gently fade into darkness, much as it has begun; never leaving more than a fleeting sense of a hazy, half-recollected memory.

*   *   *

Guerrero awoke the next morning with his men, in good spirits and with a clear head, but with no memory of what had happened, beyond facing the old Mayan and sharing a peace cup. What the ritual's intent had been or if it had been successful, he had no idea, nor did he know how he had returned to his encampment after the fireside dancing had ceased. Many things still seemed a blur to him, but strangely, one thing in his mind was clear and fully formed; the details for an audacious twilight raid upon a federal encampment.

Filled with an incredible sense of purpose, Guerrero summoned his captain and, over the course of half an hour, he outlined his plan, acknowledged its deliberately-chaotic nature and explained that, in addition to the usual preparations, it would require as many snakes as could be found for fifty miles.

Having received his instructions, the captain sent riders on their fastest horses to fulfil the necessary order while Guerrero and the remaining men continued on their way to their redoubt near Chilpancingo.

Arriving a week later, Guerrero was pleased to see that all his preparation had been attended to, as, in addition to the usual weapons were several small barrels of gunpower and fifty thick, hessian sacks full of angry and frustrated serpents. Affording himself only a single day to recover from the journey, Guerrero met briefly with Montes de Oca to discuss the final details of the plan, before returning to his tent and writing a letter of love to Guadalupe.

The next day, Guerrero and his men packed up their provisions and headed out into the sierra, bound for the federal barracks near Iguala, ensuring they stuck to only the smallest mountain trails to ensure they passed the line of Spanish cannons undetected.

As the group came within sight of the barracks, they ceased their progress and made their own temporary camp safely beyond the treeline that skirted the camp and patiently waited until nightfall before attempting to launch the assault. The minutes seemed to drag on for an eternity before the hour had become late and the guards had become lazy, but both elements were vital to the success of the plan.

If his men were to have sufficient time to plant the double payload of snakes and gunpowder and then escape without being seen, a mix of daring and subterfuge was required; the former being achieved by luring out one of the roving patrols, and the latter by stealthily killing the guards. Once Guerrero's men had donned the captured guard's uniforms, they continued on the same patrol that the guards had been on, maintaining a distant but clear visibility with the other patrols, while all about them under cover of darkness darted their comrades, ferrying their deadly cargo to their objectives.

Once the dispatched teams of snake trappers had all returned, Guerrero wasted no time in setting into motion the second part of his plan. Calling back his false patrols, they lit the long trail of poured gunpower and ran, whooping and hollering as they did do.

As the barrels ripped themselves apart, the camp came alive with frantic activity as the screams and shouts of disorientated men came from every quarter. This cacophony, mixed with the stench of human fear, was more than most of the snakes could handle, and so, acting out of self-preservation, they struck out at the dazed waking troops, sinking fangs filled with venom into exposed legs, feet and buttocks. The unexpected nature of their assailants caused a fresh outbreak of panicked cries, with the few victims who did not instantly succumb to their venomous wounds screaming out in bewilderment and attempting to fight back with anything that came to hand; often setting fire to their tents in the process.

Safely far away and retreating ever further into the depths of the forest, Guerrero knew not how many casualties they had inflicted, only that they had struck another blow for independence and, this time, had blessedly returned without losing so much as a single soldier. Indeed, it was several weeks before the first stories of the full horror at Iguala reached Chilpancingo, but by this time, Guerrero had already departed his redoubt; concerned with more pressing personal events.

Not a single soul among the garrison had ever heard the old Mayan legends or the warnings to never harm serpents during this time of year and, following Javier's execution at the hands of the disbelieving inquisition, not a single soul was spared from annihilation. However, before his ignoble trial and inquisition, this was the sworn account of Javier Sánchez; the only surviving soldier left alive at camp Rafael. It was the only version of events he ever told, and it never varied, except for the tiniest of insignificant details.

The following testimony and all references to the barracks were immediately discredited and struck from all military records, but local traders who had often visited the camp still remember its location and delighted in telling ghost stories to their children of the camp that never was.

*   *   *

'On this date, being Tuesday 29th October, in the year of our lord 1816, I, Javier Sánchez, born of the town of Urarte, Basque Country in España, do hereby swear that the following is a true and honest account of the events that transpired at Camp Rafael, located just north of Arcelia in Nuevo España.

A few hours before dawn I woke to a series of small explosions that sounded like they were coming from just outside my tent. I hastily threw on my uniform and staggered outside as I continued to adjust my buckles and braces.

Once outside my tent, I could see the after-effects all around me, as a number of men appeared to have been wounded while others seemed to be screaming and shouting about snake bites. It was then that I saw the first of a multitude of serpents that had inexplicably infested the barracks. Going for my musket, I loaded and fired twice at the nearest serpents, narrowly missing one with my first shot and then, disappointingly, scaring the second off with a noisy misfire.

Despite the absurdity of our slithering opponents, and the recent explosions, the actual engagement ended up being little more than a skirmish and the base itself remained largely undamaged, barring a few disrupted tents and a handful of snakebite victims.

While the officers tried to pick out the cause of the serpent uprising from the confused and conflicting accounts of the bleary-eyed soldiers, a smattering of enlisted men returned to grab a little more sleep while the majority, now painfully awake, simply shrugged off the chill of the early morning and began to think about an early breakfast before the inevitable reveille sounded. I was of the latter.

Then, a few minutes later, while we were all sitting around waiting for the day to start proper, private Luis Ortega, who was still flexing the fresh bandages covering his rump, paused in his chewing, having spotted what I can only assume he thought was a wounded snake that wasn't quite dead. Carefully, so as not to attract its ire, he rose from his stool and, fetching up his empty musket, turned it end over end and, holding it by its barrel like a club, began to creep upon his unsuspecting prey.

The sight of a near-nude Luis tottering around on his tiptoes, stalking an imaginary snake, was enough to make the few soldiers who witnessed the spectacle, myself included, point and snigger.

Having cornered his quarry, Luis began to swing and swipe his weapon against the ground, sending us into fits of laughter, and when he approached his tent, where Ricardo was asleep, we all looked on, but did nothing except slap each other in jest and wait to see what Luis would do next.

I swear that none of us appreciated the danger nor saw the deranged look in Luis's eyes until it was too late, and so when he shouted out 'Adiós señor serpiente' and brought his musket forcefully down upon the Ricardo skull, we were all too far away to react in time to save poor Ricardo. Hearing the gut-wrenching crunch of wood shattering bone, we charged across and tackled Luis to the ground.

It is here that I admit to having no clear recollection of what happened next, as diving on top of the pile of bodies, I must have caught a stray flying elbow to my temple, as I was knocked unconscious and remained ignorant of the next hour or so.

When I eventually recovered, I was woken by a blinding pain lancing my head and found I was half buried beneath a pile of immobile bodies. Ignoring the stench of exhumed entrails and stale urine, I dragged myself out and almost fainted when I was confronted with the shocking tableau in front of me, for, during my unconsciousness, the entire base had become a desolate ruin.

Everywhere I looked lay the evidence of a most desperate struggle for survival, though who the architects of this destruction were, I could not imagine, as all the uniformed bodies were from our own regiment. The many neat rows of sleeping tents now lay flattened and smouldering, and there was still a waft of spent gunpower that emanated from somewhere downwind. Getting to my feet, I went in search of a survivor, anyone who might explain what had happened, but the further I ventured, the more I was greeted with nothing but scenes of inexplicably gruesome death and destruction.

The oppressive silence was maddening, as it seemed that even nature itself had abandoned this place to the dead, with the bloody remains of butchered chickens and hogs scattered around the canteen, and the heavy gate that led to the cavalry and riders' enclosure hung crookedly ajar.

With nobody left alive, and with too many bodies to move alone, I returned to what was left of my tent and began to pack my bags, intent on leaving the base and making a full report. It was while I was in my tent, preparing my possessions for travel, that the dispatch riders arrived at the base and spotted me. After briefly relaying to them all that I had seen, we agreed to depart with all haste and, with me riding one of their spare horses, we made our way back to Mexico City.'

* * *

Before the troops returned from the encampment with news of another victorious raid, Guerrero received an urgent rider bearing a message that had been sent from his father-in-law. It simply said to come home quickly.

Leaving his lieutenant in command until his return, Guerrero took just a couple of trusted men as protection and immediately headed home. Not sparing the horses, the trio rode hard all day and night and arrived mid-afternoon the following day.

When he reached his house and saw his wife's parents waiting for his arrival, he jumped out of the saddle and, leaving the reins to his men, ran over to greet them; noticing immediately that both were in a solemn mood, heads bowed, wearing all black.

His mother-in-law threw her arms wide and hugged him firmly, tears welling up in her bloodshot eyes and streaming down cheeks that were still red and puffy from a long and restless night.

"What is it, Mama? What's wrong?" asked Guerrero, his voice wavering and his composure already cracking. "Is Guadalupe OK?"

In response, his mother-in-law could only murmur through soaked lips that failed to reassure him as she kept kissing his cheeks and refused to release her embrace.

His father-in-law laid a comforting hand on Guerrero's shoulder and spoke in a low, compassionate tone, though it sounded hollow to him as his tough military façade began to shatter and crumble; "Both Guadalupe and Dolores are alive and resting, but the night has not been kind. I am so sorry, my son."

His wife and young daughter were alive… but their unborn baby… his imagination filled the gaps between the words his father-in-law had spoken.

Guerrero's face turned white as he stumbled, almost trampling his mother-in-law as the pain and grief overtook him. Together the three of them staggered and tumbled awkwardly through the doorway, as he could not loosen his grasp, yet he needed to find his beloved Guadalupe.

"Lupita!" Guerrero called as he charged through the mansion his control already broken and betraying a trace of panic, despite his best intentions.

"She needs her rest!" her father called meekly after him, though he knew nothing could stop Guerrero from going to see his wife.

"Mari!" shouted Guerrero once more as he reached their bedroom and turned the handle.

"Mi Esposo," came the shallow, feeble response as he opened the door. "Our poor baby… a snake… oh Guerrero, our poor baby…" Her words were a meaningless jumble that trailed off as she no longer had the breath to repeat them.

Guerrero bounded across the room and, kneeling down beside her, grasped her left hand in his and kissed it deeply.

A snake. Even as he bent low to kiss her again, the word stuck in his mind and a dreadful, horrible possibility occurred to him.

"What about the snake?" Guerrero found himself asking, as a rising fear awoke in his heart and threatened to swallow his tongue.

"It… it bit me… it murdered our baby, and then it slithered away and just… disappeared," whispered Guadalupe, her long hair fanned out in a jumbled mess upon her pillow.

Guerrero turned deathly white as he realised what neither she nor her parents could possibly know that the blood of their innocent baby was on his hands. It was his idea to use snakes against the federals, knowing that it would surely warrant a swift and merciless retaliation from the deity Kukulkan. And so, in the end, it was he who should suffer the most at the vengeful hands of the wrathful deity.

He thought about telling Guadalupe, about coming clean about everything and begging for forgiveness, but her words echoed in his brain, 'It murdered our baby', and surely she was correct, for whatever had done this to her was a murderer. This was not the act of a brave soldier in the heat of battle, but a sly, cold-blooded butcher, who had crept in silently in the dead of night and stolen that which was most precious to them.

He didn't want to talk about his part in all this. He couldn't, for the pain was too raw and the shame too great. Yet he knew he had to say something.

"How did this happen?" Guerrero asked as softly as he could, his voice barely a whisper.

"I don't know," was Guadalupe's answer, though needing to hear more, he gently persuaded her to continue.

Relenting, Guadalupe told how it was not the snake biting her belly that had woken her, but the erratic heartbeat of their baby, as, for the briefest juncture, it had raced like a dozen stampeding horses, then just as abruptly, it pulsed no more.

Startled awake, she had looked up in time to see the pearly white tail of a snake slipping off the bed and flopping onto the floor. Despite being doubled up with pain and suffering, she had the wherewithal to call out, and as her mother burst open the door, they both saw it slink away through a tiny crack in the wall.

Shouting for her husband to come quickly with a broom, Guadalupe's mother had grabbed her daughter's hand and tended to her fevered brow while they waited a few moments longer for Pedro to arrive. Armed with a stiff broom, Pedro had looked over to where they were pointing and then quietly made for the second bedroom, cautiously using the long handle to force the door ajar. Ready to strike, he inched slowly into the room, but there was no sign of the snake; the pearly intruder had seemingly vanished into thin air.

As Guadalupe finished her tale, Guerrero's worst fears were confirmed.

Together they held each other and began to cry once more.

*   *   *

Submerged deep within his own thoughts, Guerrero failed to notice that the inmate chained up on the floor next to him had whispered his name three times, and he would probably have ignored a fourth, had it not been for the infernal, imagined hiss coming from outside the barred window once more.

"Psst. Señor Guerrero," whispered the stranger. "Are you awake?"

"Yes," Guerrero replied, though his voice sounded far away.

"Great. I have good news for you, Señor," the stranger continued. "You have friends on the outside and there are plans afoot to free you."

Guerrero cast his eyes over the man. He could not fail to notice that, although there was no remarkable facial likeness, the stranger was also a mulatto, and of similar size and build to Guerrero.

"Our jailers are stupid Spaniards who cannot tell us apart. Your friends have paid me well to—"

"Stop and do not say another word, my good man," interrupted Guerrero, using an authority and personality he had seldom had occasion to use in recent weeks.

"But you do not understand, Señor," protested the man. "A payment has been promised and I must—"

"Whatever has been agreed, I will ensure you receive," broke in Guerrero yet again, politely yet forcefully. "For me, this day was long in its coming, and though I do not relish the taste of Spanish lead, I already have too much blood on my hands to ever be clean again. I will absolutely not be party to any more shedding of Mexican lives."

"Guerrero please. I beg of you…", the man clasped his hands together, clattering his chains as he begged to be heeded.

"No Señor. It is I that must beg you. Please, I am sorry, but my mind is made up, and all my friends and their politics will have to accept my decision. I have always chosen my actions with courage of my convictions to stand by and accept any consequence. Today will be no exception."

With that, Guerrero turned away and refused to speak, content to face his doom and ensure that no more lives would be taken in his name.

1816: The Year Without Summer

Journal of Able Seaman Garrick

By K.C. Danniel

From the journal of Able Seaman Garrick, left in the good care of his wife.

7th November, 1816

The HMS Zebra has just disembarked into the gentle waves from the Isle of Ascension. I'm relieved at every mile we voyage from the Cape of Good Hope. It should be named Lucifer's Cape because the air smells of thick campfire musk, you'll forever swelter under the sun, and hellish beasts, neither tigers nor lions, lurk amongst the settlements and its bush people. If tonight's cool winds keep, we may reach Portsmouth before December. My home, far away from the devil's monsters living in Africa.

*   *   *

9th November, 1816

Each day I thank God I've awoken to live another day after each battle the Zebra wins against the Atlantic Ocean. I thought being out on water meant I could escape the harsh winters and summer-less weather back home for a moment, but the sea's temperament is worse. This year, torrent storms push vicious tides at the Zebra while the sour sea tosses her around as if she's a worthless toy boat. As a result, the sea has taken eight crew members with her. A gigantic surge threw three men overboard, their bodies forever lost, and another strangled by loose sail lines. Hurricane winds impaled an able seaman with an unsecured cannon rammer and, last month, two of my messmates fell from the gaff of the foremast trying to repair a sail during a sudden storm. And if it's not Mother Nature we are to heed, it's crossing paths with war-hungry Algerians. Still, against the odds, everyone here prays for safe travel.

Every morning I'm grateful for a simple pleasure provided on board–breakfast's sweet oatmeal. It provides me peace of mind during our unpredictable cruise. The pleasant aroma of warmed honey trapped inside the berth deck stirs my memory. Specifically of plump bumblebees dawdling around the white rose garden my Alice tends to in cool spring breezes. Only 21 more days until I embrace my loving wife. I wish her near at this moment. More so than ever. Just the touch of her breath could cure the reoccurring dreams haunting my sleep as of late. Admittedly so, a letter from African natives and a Moravian Priest are at the root of my nightmares.

Before I boarded the Zebra at the Cape of Good Hope, a slave named Stephen grabbed a hold of my sweat soaked uniform. At first I wanted to confront him, but I stopped myself as his cracked lips quivered, and his red eyes filled with tears. Upon the orders of his master, Stephen had delivered a bundle of letters addressed to

Reverend Latrobe and was awaiting his return from Gnadenthal. Last minute, the slave needed to send off two additional, grave notes. He begged me to deliver them, not to avoid punishment, but to save a settlement burdened by demons. As if out of thin air, my friend Wilson snatched the letters from Stephen's trembling hands. Wilson promised to send them off. Remarkably, with not a trace of grog on his breath, Wilson said it's in God's plan that he helps. However, as of a fortnight ago, Wilson had gone against his word. I should've known better.

Since we were lads, Wilson always stuck his nose where it never belonged. Still unapologetically curious, he craved to know the horrors inside the letters. As we continued up the ramp towards the ship Wilson talked over my suggestion to hand them over. He said they'd make for great tales. He could return them later because it's a Reverend's duty to forgive and besides, them letters aren't properly sealed. They're asking to be read.

*　*　*

10th November, 1816

During lunch my fellow messmates and I chatted about women, foreign encounters and reckless adventures back home until Master-at-arms Smith and Lieutenant Davies entered our converted mess. The sight of any officer is unusual in our space. It's to be free from command. Their black boots thumped against the floor boards as they strolled towards our claimed spot, centre of the deck. With their arms resting behind their backs and chins held high, both reached the edge of our blanket. Our group silenced and without delay stood at attention. Soon after, the room fell silent except for the clank of the bells, muffled commands and creaks of the wooden ship.

MAA Smith's presence only meant trouble. His duty is to punish crew members for any misconduct because the rule of order is the law on Royal Navy Ships. Never to be tested. Never to be broken. It keeps the crew alive on these untamed seas. LT Davies called over for the Mainmast Captain, Wilson. At Davies' right, Wilson maintained his attention, with long arms at his side, feet together, wide shoulders back, and his cleft chin pointed upwards. His slit green eyes locked onto mine. Hot sweat tickled down my temples and my lungs struggled to fill with air. Everything and every person in the room blurred. I imprisoned myself inside my mind. The fear of having my pay stopped, being confined, or worse, flogged in front of the entire crew, caused me to lose my balance! I couldn't hold any more guilt let alone suffer another horrific nightmare any longer. As I opened my mouth, ready to admit wrongdoing, a clank of the Zebra's broken bell interrupted my admission. Shouts travelling from above proclaimed a strange sail had been spotted.

At once LT Davies instructed everyone to stand by until further orders. Before departing upstairs, he faced the crew and said he wasn't ever here. Aye Aye, Sir, we responded. Soon after, excited chatter erupted. Smith then rested his hand on my shoulders while hunching over to examine my eyes. His lips were pursed, and his soft jaw jutted out. Again, I tried to confess, but only a dry heave of lobscouse belted out. Wilson's face wrinkled into a fierce frown, Smith's upturned to a smile. I remember him saying, glad to see you're sober, lad, you had but a drunken stare. Another hand, missing a ring finger, gripped my shoulder. Ice-cold blood flushed through my heart. It was Wilson. Instead of a threat, he mentioned in high spirits that LT Davies just wanted to announce in person that I'm to train as a Top Mainmast Captain. Ship Captain Forbes called for an increase of skilled sailors in the event we lose valuable seaman from a battle with the Algerians or another coming of a great gale. Wilson added that Smith and Davies had wanted an excuse to peek at the forbidden berth deck. There was nothing to worry about. Then Wilson's fingertips dug into my shoulder, waking my paralysed mind and body from stupor. Through his clenched teeth, he warned me to keep my mouth shut. Four purple and red bruises now spot my shoulder.

Dear God, Wife and Rev. Latrobe. Please. Forgive me.

*   *   *

From atop the aftermast I could see porpoises racing alongside the Zebra looking like a school of tiny fish and seamen moved like busy ants as they carried out their duties on the deck. From the south, across the relaxed sea, the jagged mountain peaks of Ascension existed no more. To the north, large grey clouds reached the heavens. The storm brewed and grumbled, glowing a vibrant violet as lightning struck the sea behind the strange boat.

When the temperature dropped, squalls hungry for destruction created choppy waves that crashed against the ship. Many onboard liken them to the fins of a sea monster that stalks the Atlantic. Thrice the size of a porpoise, it has a painted white tip fin and endless rows of teeth its mouth. Everyone on deck anchors themselves on the account of a drunken seaman that fell overboard. We saved him from the sea beast, but his leg was ragged from the knee. Exposed, splintered bones and torn muscles flailed in the wind. Poor man bled out on the deck. One of his close friends was in such a shock from the accident that he grabbed a Marine's musket to shoot the shark dead. Seconds later, a hoard of those rabid water dogs guzzled every bit of the dead beast as the Zebra kept its course. Still, streaks of red stain the stern edge from where we shimmied the injured man onto the deck. No amount of scrubbing has cleared it yet.

As the storm drew near, the hairs on my arm stood on end. A purple bolt flashed, temporarily blinding us all. In the distance, a wall of rain fell from the sky consuming the unknown ship until it disappeared. The storm reminded me of the crazed slave women from the letters. Her thrashing body engulfed in hail stones and illuminated by the same violet light amid horrified witnesses.

Again, the warm air dropped to a chill. The squalls took a toll on my balance above deck until I adapted. I gripped the railing, eyeing which Jacob ladder or line to grab a hold of in case of a sudden fall as freezing rain drops smacked my face. The sting my body endured couldn't have compared to the balls of ice pelting the slave's possessed body. As I thought of her, I failed to notice the extreme tilt of the ship. My soles slid across the slick deck, but my grip on the rail kept me from plummeting through the sail lines. After the ship balanced itself again, I shouted orders through the speaking trumpet to the crew. Later that night, I observed the conditions of the flapping sails until something odd caught my attention. Hideous tentacles crept above the dark sea's surface. Could it be the monster the slave woman had seen?

I swear on my wife that what I saw was no squid. The whites of its eyes glowed red and hundreds of them covered the entire creature. One tentacle alone was thicker than three carronade cannons lined side by side! It dripped from slimy skin folds and wrapped itself around the base of the boat! My stomach clenched at the site of its ill-shaped body, like that of a mound of runny sludge. A longer look caused me to swallow my dinner a second time as it tried to rush up my throat.

As the storm flickered the beast dashed below. Its deep blue silhouette beneath the surface disappeared into the violent waves leaving behind a mass of bubbles. How didn't anyone see it? It wasn't the alcohol because the past few days I'd chosen to earn an extra per diem for the day rather than have one sip of grog.

*   *   *

16th November, 1816

Recently, Wilson's behaviour has been erratic. At moments his temper is short, he snaps cruel insults in the mask of jeers, and he barks commands at crew members on deck as if they're incompetent. Under secrecy, my messmates and I had allowed Wilson to sip our rationed grog to keep his spirits high and to lessen his vindictive verbal lashes, but lately he has refused our offers and his rage festers anew. His mental state concerns me, therefore, I've decided I will copy the Reverend's letters because my gut knows Wilson would rather toss them overboard before doing what is right in the eyes of God. My heart hopes that Wilson will heal and come around soon. Between the supply crates I've found a spot to hide. I shall copy these letters in a hurry before I'm discovered by a crew member or bit by a dirty rat.

The first letter was folded neatly within a cream-coloured envelope. Drips of white wax once sealed the flap. Written in tiny messy script with many inkblots and smears is:

*   *   *

1816: The Year Without Summer

{Letter undated}

DEAR REVEREND LATROBE,

On first of May you at slaves woman's cottage. The one with the rotten tooth not pulled right. You there with Brother Stein, Kya, and family. Do you remember?

We knew bad come that day for your God we worship together showed signs. He not weep joy this year because our gardens grow dust, everyday tigers hunt our people, black clouds come our way with a mist on ground. It hides our settlement.

The mist scared Kya to tell truth.

Last she remembered is small ache in tooth one day before pull. First, she sipped tea with Dacha root. It makes pain disappear. Then Kya says she not home. She went far away to another settlement. She become different soul. An evil soul.

Kya said her arms not hers but long wet tree roots. Her hands are crab claws size child two year old. Feet not there. Maybe under dress of a body of fish scales. Her mouth drip live worms. She see her face but no English word for it.

She in a tall room. Freezing like hail from sky. Roof higher than sky and same white mist on floor. Walls are of stone like our garden statues but smooth and with carvings larger than our church. Many white circle lamps light up room. Inside room she see many like her. Others different. Missing eyes, one arm, or all hands. They bleed green. They look in pain but not cry. More swim in big cure bottles. Two laid still in a corner in a green puddle laying on broken bottle pieces.

Inside woman's mind, beasts say one of their own escaped. They next. They will live forever too. Beast say no more hiding from Elders, but now from Shoggoth monsters. Beast also say they older than Moravian God. Even older than people. In past they meet Khoikhoi leaders and our people They say, reason our tribe speak same language but less. Kya said they talked more but she returned in her body while tooth pulled. She not know what happened or why she gone then back. Inside mouth torn, pain big, but not the same as beast pain. Beast burn inside body. Beast sick and body cursed by god like cripple man with elephant leg, or child with large head and no eyes.

Husband of Kya wanted everyone to leave. No more tooth pull. Husband knew wife was not there. Now happy she returned.

At midnight women not here again. Body here, her soul somewhere else. Her body moved like sick cattle. She spoke forgotten language she not learn. Little we understand. She said, We live. We Come. She not walk or work. She not eat or drink. Is this truth? Brother Latrobe is she ill with possession? Please help us rid evils.

We wait your return.

GNADENTHAL PEOPLE

*   *   *

Like Wilson, I too have experienced ill-possessed episodes. Many times, I've been awoken from slumber by nightmares of my own teeth being yanked by a faceless preacher. It is Brother Stein, tall as a giant, reciting a passage from an over-sized bible. In his other hand is a rusty tool clamped onto my wisdom tooth. As he extracted, I saw what looked to be red soaked plant roots covered in thorns attached to the end of my crushed tooth. My gums shivered at every inch the core slipped out the hole it once occupied. All the while Stein pulled he preached proud and loud, shaking the cottage walls and furniture. He drew thick stretched roots over his shoulder and elbow like a sailor gathering rope.

Inside the dark cottage I'm surrounded by my messmates standing in a white mist. They pointed with elongated fingers at me. The eight men that died on this year's cruise were amongst the crowd with their injuries still fresh. They laughed and mocked my pain. In the distance bush people wearing white robes soaked in green sludge stand at attention repeating Brother Stein's sermon in the same exuberant manner. Further still were the demons, towering over everyone, crouched in the house with their three eyes and their mouths of wriggling worms. Their wart covered claws clicked maniacally as the walls and ceiling raised to the clouds. Pulsing from the walls were strange carvings glowing green, lighting the room. Dear Alice, I need you.

The ship's bell clanked again, eight rings thereafter. My supper has ended. I must find time to copy Brother Stein's letter.

*   *   *

Again, I have left supper unnoticed, hopefully for the last time. I'm back in the hold to copy Brother Stein's letter. It's written in elegant calligraphy. There's a broken white wax seal stamped with a Moravian Church emblem. It's a lamb holding a crossed flag with a bent leg and a halo crowns its head. The letter reads:

*   *   *

16th October, 1816

DEAR REVEREND LATROBE,

I want to apologise, in advance, for this letter isn't what you might expect. I've thought for many days about the frightening incident we both saw at the Slave woman's house. I must share the events that took place after our early departure.

Woken from a deep sleep, I was startled by the Chief Eldress of our church, Nancy Paulding. Her frail hands clenched around mine as she hurried me to the entrance of the church. Before me stood a trembling Hottentot. Kya's mother travelled alone to share grim news about her daughter's well-being.

That night, thunder rumbled behind me as I made my way through a thick white mist. I couldn't see past the length of my arm, but my memory of the settlement and Kya's muffled screams guided me towards her home. While running, I prayed that a starving tiger wasn't nearby because I travelled alone, carrying only a bible, a cross, and a trinket of holy water.

1816: The Year Without Summer

As I approached the cottage, I heard the woman's deep throated scream and the crack of furniture being broken apart. I knocked on the door and was allowed in with haste. Inside, the slave woman thrashed her body against everything. She even rammed into people trying to protect her from self-injury.

The Hottentots have a special language, but it was as if she wanted to speak only with their unique click sounds. She even used broken pieces of furniture to create the same pattern of noise. Then she yelled and spoke as if she had no control of her tongue. It was at that moment I believed she was possessed by a demon. I decided it was my duty, bounded by my religious vows to save her from the evils of Satan by performing an act I'd never practised. Exorcism.

After we had restrained her to a bed, I asked for aid from the most physically and emotionally strong persons in the room: her husband, brother, and older sister. Others were instructed to seek shelter for I feared the demonic being might enter another person of weak mind and spirit. As soon as the door slammed shut, Kya spoke a language that has not been used for generations. Her husband tried to translate.

She said, we won't be sacrificed, we will live and be forever free.

She spoke in a devilish tongue. I demanded the evil spirit to reveal its name to cast it away. I prayed the Lord's scripture. I showered her with holy water. It didn't surrender! The louder I shouted, the stronger she threw her body against the bed, jerking it yards from where it once rested. Soon after, the ill woman was provided a traditional Hottentot tea infused with the roots of Vlachdorn or, as the English know it, Flat-Thorn. Kya gurgled as her family force fed the drink. I begged them to stop before they drowned the possessed woman.

She regained her strength and shouted about memories of horrid beings. Without warning, hail pounded the side of the cottage. Ice the size of apples penetrated the straw roof striking the body of the slave and others inside as cool white mist and freezing air seeped through the gaps. The air was so cold that I saw Kya's breath create little clouds as she hyperventilated.

As we took cover, Kya's thrashing became more intense. The torn sheet restraints ripped from her arms and legs as she escaped. Similar to a new-born horse, she stumbled off the bed, past the door. Straightaway her brother tried to chase her but the pain he suffered from the hail brought him back inside.

You see, Brother Latrobe, we have been in an unusually persistent drought for many months. The storm was not only unexpected, but I believe to be a sign from God, trying to help with the exorcism. Until the worst occurred. Satan grew stronger for the cows, sheep, horse, and goats that were outdoors hollered and the people indoors screamed all at once as flashes of purple lit the sky illuminating the possessed woman as she ran towards the Hottentot's sacred grave.

After the storm cleared, mounds of ice soaked in bright red blood surfaced and exposed the unblinking eyes of motionless livestock reflected underneath the moonlight. When I approached Kya, balls of scarlet hail rolled from her chest as she breathed. I shovelled the ice aside then flipped her on her back. Her eyes were swollen and black, purple welts covered her body and poured blood like open blisters. The moment I pressed my hand onto her burning forehead, I experienced something I must share with you.

The slave woman's accounts of the devil and his cursed children were true because I too travelled to the same Hell.

Somehow, I had been transported inside a smooth marbled tower with an unreachable roof. So tall I'm unable to compare it to any human-made structure or one of God's earthly creations. Illuminated orbs lined the walls which exposed carvings of the most eerie characters etched with inelegant curves and odd geometric shapes covering every inch of slab. I could only suspect a satanic text, for it was too ghastly to be anything divine.

From the corner of my eye, the east wall glowed green. There, a row of ten glass bottles as large as our wagons lined the wall. Inside at least half, wart covered seeds the size of calves floated at the bottom. The seeds pulsed like a beating heart suspended in a pale green liquid. Attached to each container were two spiral glass tubes as thick as my thigh, supplying bubbles of air and spurts of black grit. The living seeds secreted an unusual bright green ink which diluted the grit in an instant. Then, with ease, the seed absorbed everything until the water was clear.

The other half of the gigantic bottles held smaller versions of the demons Kya described. Two must have been destroyed somehow because a couple of the demons laid on top of shattered pieces. Green liquid seeped from their wounds as they, I presumed, had passed. As I backed away in fright, the clicks and taps grew louder behind me. Over my shoulder I saw Satan's evil creatures tower over me.

The horde of demons' bulbous heads balanced on withering elephant trunk-like necks. Their python thick arms stretched out as they clicked their clawed hands. Their bell-shaped bodies were wrapped in rows of slime covered scabs as they approached me, gliding on the tile below. Then I saw my reflection. I could not shut my eyes if I'd been able! I had three large eyes staring back at me, piercing through my soul!

Just as quick as I arrived, I returned to where I had once stood. I awoke in the arms of the slave woman's father and brother. On their account, the moment I touched her I lost my balance and babbled the same as her. They were worried that I too had become possessed. At once, they snatched me from her body. The father read a random scripture from the bible and yelled the demon's name. Yith. What sprinkles of holy water I had left was thrown upon me. Afterwards,

I realised my surroundings, back on God's Earth, cradled in the Hottentot's arms. In front of me I witnessed the stars sparkle above and lying next to me I heard Kya's final breath.

Her family mourned until sunrise. That night I had hoped to perform a Moravian ceremony in one last attempt to save her soul, but a traditional Hottentot ritual was held instead. Kya's experience and the hell I was trapped in were both real. Please, upon your return home, send more missionaries. We need more help!

God deliver us from evil.

STEIN

19th November, 1816

Manning the foremast today, I tried to hold onto the memories of my wife to help erase the images of Kya and Brother Stein's encounter with Yith. I guzzled my ration of wine to help me sleep. I regretted my actions as I swore that again I saw the gigantic sea monster, but the fool of me confused it for a great whale covered in layers of barnacles. With a deep breath of relief, I laughed at my troubles before a whiff of rank grog interrupted my inner peace. I followed the stench, but, before I turned around, something from behind grabbed my ankle and caused me to slam my back and head against the foremast deck.

The Zebra swayed with the waves and my mind jostled along with it as Wilson stood above me with his worn boot on my throat. His foot pushed on my windpipe. The crew below were unaware of our confrontation, lost in song to stay awake. Wilson knew I had rummaged through his belongings because the letters were shoved to the left of his ditty bag, not the right side that had been patched. My attempts to convince Wilson that his lack of sleep had him confused only made him yank me upwards by the collar to shove me against the railing's edge. The threat on my life appeared imminent; I wanted to make peace with Wilson, my best friend. I forgave him in hopes he reconsidered his actions. Instead, he threatened to tell Captain Forbes that I stole and kept the Reverend's property.

My bones shook at the possibility of being a disgrace to the Royal Navy and my family. Without hesitation, I confessed. I wanted to read the letters for myself to see if what he said was true because the nightmares haunt me to this day. He delivered a punch to my left shoulder that sent me over the railing's edge. My top hat floated past the busy seamen into the ocean. All I could think of was Alice and how sorrowful I was, and I hoped that God shall forgive me. I descended until my body was jerked upwards. Together we fell backwards onto the deck. He chuckled, sneaking a sorry between his laughter. As we stood, Wilson said he would make sure I'd never touch the letters again. He produced them from his jacket. Tied to them was a chunk of obsidian we had gathered from the Isle of Ascension. True to his word for the first time in months, Wilson chucked them into the sea.

* * *

21st November, 1816

Even if Wilson won't admit to his sufferings while awake, his ramblings and thrashing through the night have. For a moment I even believed he was possessed by Yith! He screamed its name over and over, alerting the surrounding crewmen. I was there to tame his nerves with my last bottle of wine I had stashed away, but he refused saying, it only makes their bloody arms grow longer.

* * *

22nd November, 1816

The first night in many weeks I slept well. God answered my prayers. This morning I awoke with vigour and strength; ready to take on the duties of the day, but I wasn't prepared for the loss I would experience later that afternoon. The strange ship finally approached us. To our fortune it was a merchant ship. Everyone on board worked together carrying boxes of grape shots the captain purchased. Wilson stood right next to me, reminiscing about our past and teasing the crew as we passed the ammo down the line of arms. By lunch, he wanted to be alone, he needed space. Before he left, He mentioned that his nightmares were getting worse, that they appeared even when sober. He could feel their slimy arms grip his skin, and the smell of copper and iron filled his nose when the dead ship mates got too close. I reassured him that we would speak to the Reverend and that there's nothing to worry about anymore and he should report to the commander that he's ill. I reminded him that I've been properly trained by him and can take over in the meantime.

After lunch I saw Wilson man the topmast, but it seemed as if he was swatting back a swarm of bees, shouting, then stabbing the air with his knife. He leaned back over the rail as if something had him by the neck, chocking the poor lad to death. Through my speaking trumpet I called for him. His eyes squinted above red cheeks as he smiled. His lips mouthing forgive me before leaning over for good. His body fell and tangled through the ropes and snapped against three thin masts like a rag doll. Wilson's body collapsed on the top of his head onto the freshly holystoned deck. Frantic seamen hollered for help as he lay still except for an occasional twitch of his legs and arms. A puddle of bright blood spread across the deck.

Stars dotted the sky and the moon was nowhere in sight. Wilson has yet to recover. His right arm was amputated, his head shaved and covered in stitches. He doesn't speak, but drools. I sat at his side, holding his uninjured hand. A knock on the door from Reverend Latrobe broke the silence. Not a word was shared between us, together we watched Wilson barely breathe.

The Zebra bell clanked. After the eighth strike Wilson opened the one bloodshot eye he had left, the other having collapsed inside his skull. He stared at the ceiling mumbling, drool spilling from his swollen purple lips. I interrupt the dreadful moment to tell the Reverend about his stolen letters and the demon called Yith.

1816: The Year Without Summer

Esoteric Tides

By C.P. Dunphey

T he men dragged Ambrose from the orlop, his limp feet thumping against the stairs leading below the deck of the Bombay Anna.

The crew had decided his imprisonment would be for the best, considering the ramblings and paranoid scuttlebutt he had been attempting to spread amongst the crew like an infectious disease. He spoke of a creature below the ship, holding the entire vessel rigidly in its grasp. The crazed man had suggested the crew make sacrifices, employing their already brimming paranoia as a backdrop for his own insanity. Many had taken note of his deteriorating mental state for some time, his affiliation with an ancient Polynesian cult in Java leading to his treatment as an eccentric. Their recent return assignment to Java was undocumented by the Crown or John Company, official records describing another transport to China. The assignment ended disastrously, and the farther the distance between them and the island grew, the more Ambrose succumbed to madness.

His words were spoken between rotted teeth and through lungs that pressed stale air out of his pointed ribs with each breath. Captain Jonathon Read commanded that he be taken away, though he knew deep within that something very strange was happening aboard the ship. Regardless of his own intuitions, it was impossible to deny that there was indeed something beneath them, preventing the ship from moving. If this thing was alive or not, Read was uncertain.

At first, the logical explanation was that of coral reefs. It was not uncommon for ships, even as large and sturdy as the Anna – a transport vessel - to hit a reef while navigating across the deep ocean. But the precise circumstances made this unlikely.

The Anna had not moved in two weeks.

No matter the turning of the helm or the directing of the sails or the strength of the winds filling the sails, the ship would not budge. As much as the captain wanted to consider Ambrose's explanation- as any explanation would suffice if it meant freedom from this secluded location and the bleak horizons of the sea-the last thing he needed was hysteria amongst his crewmen. He felt their creeping mutinous thoughts with each sunrise, knew that their intentions were growing ever more malicious with each passing day.

What puzzled Read more than anything, was the state in which they found Ambrose. The sailor had slowly become more and more unpredictable with each visit the captain made to his cell in the brig. His mutterings grew unintelligible and frantic. Through some means, the lunatic managed to steal a fork from one of the other crewmen-likely one of his last sympathizers come to visit in hopes to check on the welfare of their mate-who was tricked into providing the rusted utensil.

Ambrose dug into his flesh with the fork, pulling tendons and ligaments out of his wrist. With the blood, he scribed a blasphemous and ill-envisioned portrait on the wall of his cell: some horrendous beast with long tendrils outreaching from its body like the arms of a star, and undulating waves surrounding its figure. When finished with his illustration, Ambrose reached out of the porthole with his bloody gatherings, clenching his fist so the blood would leak further from his lacerations. When one of the crew ventured down to see him, they swore that they saw a large shadow wrapped around Ambrose's wrist, pulsating as if it were vacuuming all the fluids from his frail body.

After the third day, Ambrose's hair had turned a silvery grey, the wrinkles upon his face portraying a man thirty years his senior. By the fourth day, he was completely unrecognizable. He hadn't eaten or drank any water since he was banished to the orlop, insisting that food and water were meaningless when considering the fate that awaited them all.

It never slipped the captain's thoughts that these strange events only began once they chartered their course back to England after the Dutch drove them out of Java. The screams of his fellow countrymen combining with the enemies' as some malevolence overtook them, ringing through the cold night as they escaped the island, did little to sway even him from conjuring intruding and superstitious theorem. Even more suspect was Ambrose's direct involvement in inciting these events, and his intimate correspondences with the natives. Yet, regardless of the gruesome circumstances that occurred on that beach, the captain needed to maintain discipline and control over his rattled crew, lest he invite mutiny.

Captain Read instructed the men to hoist Ambrose to the bower. Their brows furrowed, mouths gaped, for which Read had a snide response.

"Some of you believe the words of the mad Ambrose. Some of you think that there is indeed a creature below the Anna, holding her in its grasp. While I am ready to wait until the rest of our fleet finds us with their search parties, many of you have more treacherous plans. Some amongst you think a solution could be found, granted you were given command. You want to know if something is beneath us? Then we shall look for ourselves. Don't be surprised when the anchor comes back, with Ambrose's corpse clothed in coral."

The men shrugged, a few of them immediately dismissing Read's idea as rubbish, others turning away and refusing to face the captain. Their tendencies towards supernatural hysteria enraged Read. None of them saw this action as a merciful act in the way that he did. Ambrose may have gone mad, but his dying wish was to enact sacrifices to his new deity. Regardless of the insanity that plagued his fragile mind, this is what the late sailor would have wanted.

"Piers and Geoffrey! Operate the windlass."

Two scraggly sailors-some of the last men aboard the Anna that Read still trusted-sprinted to the winch and held onto the mechanism, their faces pale, reluctant.

Read joined two other crewmen in strapping Ambrose's body to the anchor. Wet chains lapped around the dead man's figure, his limp hands loosely hanging from the metal structure. His corpse bore the malnutrition and decomposition of weeks old carrion, though it had only been a night at most since he passed. They gripped the chains, pulling the ties taut. Read approached a sailor on the quarterdeck and asked for his belt. The disgruntled man hesitated, finally unbuckling his belt and handing it to the captain. Read tied the belt around Ambrose, the last notch still leaving slack around the corpse's emaciated, skeletal waist. The captain cut a new hole into the belt, fastening it to the anchor. The sailor had already cut several new holes himself.

Geoffrey and Piers started to operate the windlass, the clunking and clattering of chains against wooden frames descending the anchor into the depths below them. The men raced from the quarterdeck to the bulwarks, gazing into the deep blue below. There was no motion on the waves, silence pervading all else. The anchor splashed heavily into the ocean, drawing for a few long minutes until its descent abruptly stopped.

"Cap'n. These seas are at least forty fathoms deep. Why'd it stop? The bower only reached about fifteen. There's a whole lotta slack left," said Geoffrey.

Read squinted against the bright, indigo horizon, pondering the possibilities.

"Damned reefs," muttered Read.

The other men heard the captain's words, regardless of their whispered volume. They shifted, eyeing Read.

For several minutes, the crew waited, until finally Captain Read ordered for the bower to be raised. Geoffrey and Piers spun the windlass, cranking the heavy chains as they skidded across the hull of the ship. The men all peered into the depths, the anchor finally arising from the dark, sloshing waves of the sea.

"Look!" shouted one of the sailors.

Read hung over the bulwark, his eyes widening as he gasped.

Ambrose's body was nowhere to be seen. Only fragments of flesh and lofting broken bones hung upon the bower, torn remnants of tattered garments strung drenched across the anchor. The metal frame itself was gnawed, as though some serrated-toothed behemoth had chewed partially through the thick rusted iron. The torn remnants of decaying fish carcasses dangled from the tarnished iron, reminding Read of their unsuccessful attempts to net supper each night.

"There is something beneath the ship! Ambrose was right!" cried one of the sailors.

The men scattered away from the gangway and some spoke of maddened theories and conspiracies. A few claimed it was the "kraken" come to claim their ship, and others spoke of the ancient deity Ambrose had muttered of repeatedly before his death, of the ancient monolith he uncovered with the natives in Java. Read stood frozen, paralyzed not only by the gnawed anchor, but also by the realization that he may have been responsible for Ambrose's death. The crazed sailor may have been right . . .

"Halt your ramblings, immediately!" Read bellowed over the crew.

They all paused dead in their tracks.

"We need to start a fire."

* * *

The crew gathered emptied barrels and extra equipment from the lazarettes and chopped the wood into large chunks, carrying them to the stern. Read fashioned a large circular cradle with a steel plate beneath it and lit a massive torch before spilling oil into the pit. Geoffrey approached the captain's side, brushed his shoulder with his own. Read turned to his crewmate while he fastened the masts tightly to be void of the flames.

"What is this for exactly, Cap'n?"

"The smoke will billow upwards, miles into the sky. The British fleet will take notice. St. Mary can't be too far away. They will be very inclined to save their fastest cargo ship, if they believe her to be damaged . . . or worse."

"Do you think a search party is really on the way? Only a few people know we're here. The rest of the Navy thinks we're in China."

"Aye, they'll come to us. These seas are treacherous, lad. Many others have found themselves lost in its currents. Even as far off course as this."

1816: The Year Without Summer

Read lifted the torch and dipped it into the pit. The logs sparked and then cracked with inferno. Smoke billowed up into the air, gently whipping against the sails. For a brief moment, the billowing smog seemed to take the shape of a winged serpent, then no more.

"We shan't be here much longer. They'll be able to see this signal for miles."

"Won't the smoke cloud the ensigns?" asked Geoffrey.

"The British will respond regardless. Either their ship is sinking, or it is a Dutch shipwreck for the taking. Either way, they will come."

"Aye, but there is a storm on the horizon."

The clouds ahead darkened, bending and whipping speedily towards the Anna.

*　　*　　*

That night, Captain Read slept in his chambers. As his mind drifted into the dark recesses of his imagination's canopy, a void grew in intensity around his consciousness, gripping his arms and legs and nearly pulling him apart. In the epicenter of the emptiness, a tendril whipped through broken air, piercing his heart and releasing his floating blood into the darkness. Read attempted to scream, but only raspy air spilled from his throat.

The tendril pulsated, much like the one that had allegedly eaten from Ambrose's wound, and expanded within his ribcage, snapping and breaking each bone until it inverted his flesh, pried it open like a dissection. Another tentacle split from the foggy shadows, this one smaller and with a pointed tip that opened to an even smaller feeler. It reached Read's face, retracting in apparent disgust before inching forward once more.

Read could not speak, move, or breathe. His body was completely isolated, immobilized, some dark hands of the void grasping at his limbs. The smaller tendril crawled across his face before stabbing into his forehead, carving a horrid shape into his scalp. The wounds burned, and fire erupted across his skin, the entirety of him swallowed into a towering blaze before whimpering back into nothingness.

From the ashy mist, the sound of titanic flapping wings, a rush of incinerating air. A black obelisk in the shape of . . .

The captain awakened, sweat covering his body and his hands trembling. The burning sensation still writhed across his limbs and chest, haunting his nerve endings. He stepped out of his bed and walked to his mirror, wiping the sweat from his brow with a white handkerchief.

A thumping sounded from the deck above, hard footsteps running across the bow.

Read stood from his chair and gathered his wardrobe before quickly ascending the stairs to the upper deck. When the crack of moonlight casted upon his features, Read's nightmare of immobilization took physical form. What awaited him above deck enflamed his mind, pinching at his consciousness for explanation. His hands trembled erratically, the railings beside him the only object he could grip with the intensity he felt.

Several of the crew hoisted the bodies of dead men to the kedge and grapnel, before dropping their corpses into the depths below. Their naked figures flexed under the moonlight, blood cascaded across their legs and arms and faces, crude symbols carved into their foreheads. They pulled and pushed the windlasses, screaming in crazed speech and cackling like mad witches over a cauldron.

"What bullocks is this? What have you bastards done?" said Read.

In unison, the men turned. They halted their actions simultaneously and glared into the captain. What haunted Read most were their eyes: hollowed shells with the reflection of the gibbous moon constant in their depths. They appeared as animals in the dark, their eyes reflective lenses.

The naked crewmen stood statuesque beneath the night sky, the array of stars and constellations shining weakly upon their bloody visages. One man sprinted from cover, likely hiding beneath a loose mooring line. A swarm of the crazed sailors tackled the man, thrusting short shivs into his stomach until his resisting ceased.

Read stumbled backward, falling onto the staircase and tumbling back into the lower decks of the ship. His fall ended at the orlop, the cells of the brig reeking of putrid death. The captain looked up from the floor beneath him and saw bloody scriptures written across the walls of each cell, a deity dastardly drawn, its tendrils reaching out from its centre, grasping caricatures of the crew. Out one of the portholes, an anchor descended.

The captain sprinted to the opening, fitting only his head through the aperture. Gazing into the moonlit depths, a shadowy mass lurched upward as the anchor splashed into the water. Small shadowy arms grasped onto the chain, pulling the cadavers underneath. Read shook and pulled himself back into the brig, clasping his mouth shut with his hands as he turned to see the crazed naked men standing in the cell with him. Their eyes, even in this dark chamber, glistened, hollow and fluorescent bulbs locked inside empty rooms.

Two of the crew emerged from behind the crowd, throwing Geoffrey and Piers to the floor in front of Read. They crawled like wetted rats to the edge of the cell. As far as the captain could see, these men were not affected by whatever madness the rest of the crew had succumbed to. Either they were immune as Read was, or the three of them had been reserved for a more gruesome fate.

The lunatized men started to hum a deep, vibrating rhythm, their chests bouncing with quickening heartbeats. Streaks of blood glowed and shimmered across their pasty flesh.

"What do you want?" asked Read.

"To feed," they said as one.

"What the hell are you? Where are my crew?"

"We are the crew."

"And the others?"

"Ascended."

"What will you do with us?"

The cluster of insanity hyperventilated further, rapidly, humming between muffled whispers that were directed at no specific listener.

Read walked towards the beings that were once his crew, testing their intentions. They did not move, remaining frozen in place like vibrating ice sculptures. The captain prayed they would melt.

"I'm locking the door behind me. Stay in the cell until the search party arrives," said Read.

"But they'll kill us!" cried Piers.

"For some strange reason, I don't think they want to hurt us. At least not yet. If you feel threatened, burn the ship to the ground." Read grabbed a lantern and torch, handed it to Piers.

His two most trusted crewmen looked up, fresh tears cracking through their muddied cheeks.

"Trust me," reassured the captain.

Geoffrey and Piers mumbled acknowledgement as they locked themselves inside the cage.

He ascended the steps, leaving the huffing, asthmatic madmen in the brig and hoping they wouldn't find a way into Geoffrey and Piers' cell. When he reached the upper deck, Read locked the shaft behind him, trapping the crazed savages in the orlop. Amidst the flickering of the signal's fire, blood painted the deck. All the anchors were dropped, likely to never be seen again. The Anna still hadn't moved from its spot, itself anchored to whatever lay beneath the fathoms.

Daylight crept through the sky, twilight beckoning for its reach over the tides. Down below, the sounds of the crewmen humming and breathing echoed through the hull. Between their strange incantations, the captain swore he could hear the ghastly wailing of the soldiers on Java's beach. Their cries were blood-curdling echoes, reverberating through the dark. Rest was impossible to attain. By morning, the humming had transformed to primordial shrieking and howling below his feet, like a trapped pack of wolves clambering to be freed into the night.

Something evil and wicked had taken over the vessel, corrupting his entire crew and driving them to insanity. Yet, he could not explain their eyes. Those hollow, glass-like, bright orbs that tormented him every time he slipped into unconsciousness.

Once the horizon spilled blue streaks across the sky, Read took out his spyglass. Warm rain lightly sprayed across the deck. He threw more timber onto the fire, prodding the smoldering ash to rivet the flames anew, fastening the masts again to hang tightly away from the inferno. When dim daylight finally broke across the sky-the rain growing in fervor-the captain found relief in the sight of an entire armada of ships speeding towards them, still several leagues ahead.

The captain leapt up and down, fastening the sails the best he could to display their ensigns through the vomiting smog. Several warships sped ahead of the rest of the fleet, inching closer to the

Anna with each passing second. Below, the humming increased, the howling halted. Their words started to blur into an intelligible chorus. However, Read would not waste time trying to decipher the ramblings of madmen.

He hoisted the masts and spun the sails before raising a burgee up high with the British flag upon it. Lightning danced across clusters of black clouds that stormed ever nearer.

The armada closed in, racing directly towards the Anna. Read shouted for them again and again, hoping they would hear his words.

"Ahoy! It is I, Captain Read! Help us off this bloody ship. Something is below us, holding us still!"

The warships shifted their direction, coming alongside the Anna. Sponsons and portholes opened, the barrels of cannons extending from their parts. British flags sputtered in the wind aboard the first and second rank ships, men behind them shielding their ears after lighting their fuses.

"What the hell are you doing? Have you also gone mad?" said Read.

The droning below reached a crescendo, and now, Read recognized the lyrics. They were from a song that Ambrose sang before his death, an old shanty of sorts.

> *"Our sleep is disturbed,*
>
> *With visions strange to know,*
>
> *And with dreams on the streams,*
>
> *When the stormy winds do blow."*

1816: The Year Without Summer

They repeated the lines again and again, the words echoing in Read's mind as remembrances of his dream from the night before replayed repetitiously. Tendrils reaching from the darkness, tearing his limbs apart; his chest opening, dissected while his body hangs, pulled from invisible pincers; his forehead carved with some archaic symbol; these images plundered through his consciousness as he fell to shaking knees and garbled speech.

The black monolith appearing through the mist.

Read crawled across the deck as cannonballs ripped through the hull of the ship. He shielded his head from the debris, looking up to find all his crewmen standing around him, both living . . . and dead. They circled, naked with white eyes gleaming luminescent, humming that damned tune. Splinters of wood and pieces of the Anna's frame flew about the deck as armaments rapidly ripped through the hull. Chaos ensued as the ship leaned, ready to capsize.

Other crafts closed in, circling the vessel as the warships had. They did not come close-as it was now apparent that they had no intentions to board-but remained just within range of their cannons. Mortars fired, and explosions tore across the Anna. No matter the destruction, the decomposed bodies of his dead crew remained as still as the living, their voices chambering louder than the deafening crackling and creaking of the vessel as it split and collapsed, in and upon itself.

Read leaned towards the deck, his hands over his ears. "Why?"

"To feed," a voice came from behind the circling dead.

A deteriorated and dismembered Ambrose limped towards Read, splinters of the ship shooting into his sides with each detonation. He broke through the crowded gathering and knelt to face the captain, the exposed bones of his knee settling rigidly onto the deck.

The corpse of Ambrose snapped his broken and skinless fingers. Two more of the dead crewmen emerged from the rest, dragging Piers and Geoffrey before the captain, both men muttering and shaking uncontrollably.

"Don't feel bad, Cap'n. The Father needed a few untouched for it to work. The purest, 'twas his command." Ambrose looked around him at the monstrous crewmen, emphasizing them with his mangled hands. "We were touched on that shore. You three wasn't, eh? Manning the Anna until we returned from the jungle. That's why you lot were saved last. The Crown . . . well, they know that this had to be done. They don't want our country to ascend just yet, they would rather everyone else did first. 'Tis why they're sinking us. Why they sent me with ye in the first place. Esoterics, that lot. We were never meant to make it back," said Ambrose through a loosely hanging mandible.

"So, this is our atonement, aye?" asked Read.

"Ye, of sorts. Though it shan't be mistaken for what this really is. The Father promised the King riches-wealth beyond his imagining. 'Tis a small price to pay, this crew, myself. You."

Ambrose looked up, strings of flesh hanging across his mangled throat, bobbing with the wind.

"It's almost complete," he said.

"What's almost complete?" said Read.

The dead man grabbed Read by his jaw with spindly bones, turned his head to a burning plank as it fell from the sail. The captain followed the debris with his eyes, watched as its flames licked at the deck, which he now noticed held the lines of a symbol drawn in oil. A serpentine trail of fire ignited, walls of flame surrounding the captain and his undead crew.

Read looked around him, drew the symbol in his head, looked to the carvings upon Ambrose's flesh.

"Aye, it is indeed time. A lot of bloodshed contained in these foundations," said Ambrose as he knuckled a protruding bone on his wrist, "A lot of pain. Suffering. Things we did back on the beach. What we made the Dutch promise when we offered them Java. After we slaughtered their men. With all that, comes satiation, Cap'n."

Ambrose stood, limped away to the bulwark, stepped onto the ledge. The others mimicked him. Geoffrey and Piers wallowed in stuttering curses.

"What of the monolith? Please! I can't get it out of my head. What did you find on the island? What did you bloody do? Answer me that," said Read.

Then, they jumped.

Read wept as the ship broke into pieces, the weight of the water filling its skeleton, funnelling the vessel into the darkness below. He knew what awaited him in the depths. His nightmare was coming to fruition.

The Anna finally folded and cracked, capsizing each end into the ocean below. The cannon fire stopped, and the circling ships held steadfast.

Shadowy forms reached from the depths, grasping the shipwreck and pulling it deep into the chasms below.

The reality that awaited Captain Read was worse than even his dreams could conjure. Chaos and madness gripped him and the visceral horrors that would grasp his body for all eternity only ensured the torturous fate he'd so fervently fought.

With the crew of the Anna in its mouth, each man serving a purpose for its disgusting, morbid desires, satiation was found. The entity from the fathoms would find satisfaction, even if only until the next offerings.

As the tendrils wrapped around each of Read's limbs, the escutcheon of the Anna descended before him. Where the title of the ship was once engraved, a new name was primitively inscribed across the metal, carved with erratic and ominous craftsmanship.

"DAGON"

1816: The Year Without Summer

Meet the Authors

Geoff Groff lives near Kalamazoo, Michigan, USA.

He has been an avid reader since he was able to read and first delved into the weird fiction genre about a decade ago.

Some authors that left their mark within him are; Douglas Adams, Isaac Asimov, James P. Hogan, and H.P. Lovecraft. He has also been a homebrewer for 20 years.

**

C.K. Meeder was raised in Miami, FL (USA) near the squid-laced water.

CK is an LGBTQ+ writer with a BA in Illustration, having produced works for indie zines / publications and gallery displays. He currently resides in London, UK.

**

Robert Poyton is a martial artist, writer and musician and founder of Innsmouth Gold, an outlet for HPL related music and fiction.

Originally from East London, Rob now lives in rural North Beds with his wife and a menagerie of furred and feathered creatures, none of which has developed tentacles...yet!

Meet the Authors

K.T. Katzmann lives in Florida, surrounded by Cthulhu idols and crazy people. His first published novel featured a vampire and Bigfoot who fall in love while working for the NYPD. Despite all this, he is somehow still allowed to teach children.

He counts among his greatest influences the works of H.P. Lovecraft, Douglas Adams and Roger Zelazny.

**

Brett J. Talley is the author of several acclaimed horror novels, short stories, and collections. Twice nominated for a Bram Stoker Award, Talley's works include That Which Should Not Be, He Who Walks in Shadow, The Fiddle is the Devil's Instrument, and the Limbus, Inc. trilogy.

**

G.K. Lomax is a dyed in the wool Englishman who hails from Essex and finds nothing better than buffing up his general knowledge or watching grown men wearing jumpers try to hit a tiny ball with a very big stick.

Describing himself as a writer, versifier, pontificator, holder of untenable and contradictory opinions, he also has nostalgic twinges for simpler times.

Author of Quicksand Tales plus numerous other short stories.

Meet the Authors

Stacy Dooks hails from Calgary, Alberta in the fabled Canadas.

Raised on a steady diet of Saturday morning cartoons, comics, VHS rentals, and what his mother called 'those weird books', he nevertheless grew into a surprisingly stable individual with a passion for science fiction, horror, and fantasy in all their myriad forms.

**

Chuck Miller is a native of Ohio, a long-time resident of Alabama, and now lives in Norman, Oklahoma.

His previous works include the Black Centipede, The Incredible Adventures of Vionna Valis and Mary Jane Kelly, The Bay Phantom Chronicles, The Journal of Bloody Mary Jane, and The Mystic Files of Doctor Unknown Junior. He is also the author of two Kolchak: The Night Stalker novels.

**

M.J. Sellars hails from Liverpool, UK.

He was forced to begin writing stories as a child when Liverpool's libraries struggled to satisfy his appetite for horror, fantasy and science fiction.

He has contributed stories to publications such as All Hallows, Murky Depths, Nocturne, Fusing Horizons and Best Tales of the Apocalypse. His first novel is Hyenas.

Meet the Authors

Jonathan Oliver is the award-winning editor of horror anthologies Magic, End of the Road, House of fear, The End of the Line, 5 Stories High and Dangerous Games.

His fiction has been published in A Town Called Pandemonium, Sharkpunk, Game Over, Respectable Horror, and Terror Tales of London amongst others.

He lives in Oxfordshire with his wife, their two children and a cat.

** **

Dickon Springate hails from the town of Gillingham in Kent, UK, where he lives with his Mexican wife and enjoys watching movies and trying as many new board games as he can find.

He has had numerous forays into the world of the written word, most recently founding the indie publishing house Beyond Death Publishing.

** **

K.C. Danniel is based in Orlando Florida, and when she isn't drawing or obsessing over zombies and cats, she writes horror fiction.

Her poem, "Monster Hunter Meated" was published in Carrying On, a poetry anthology inspired by the TV show Supernatural.

She's working to complete her self-published anthology, Ello Midnight.

Meet the Authors

C.P. Dunphey is a Staten Island-born expat dwelling in the dirty south, and is perhaps best known for his novel Plane Walker and as the founder of Gehenna & Hinnom Books.

His work has appeared and is forthcoming in publications such as Vastarien, Weirdbook, and the anthology 32 White Horses on a Vermillion Hill.

**

Meet the Artists

Mihail Bila is a gifted young Romanian digital artist who is also a London-based architect with a passion for CGI, architectural visualisations and concept art.

Dystopias and horror fictions always fascinated him, so combining these two fields of interest, with a focus of H.P. Lovecraft's writings, seemed a natural fit for his talents.

** **

Shayna Rose Diamond grew up with a particular appreciation for myths, monsters, and martial arts. This pull towards the unusual (and often horrific) balanced bizarrely with her hippie, Buddhist upbringing, and developed into a rather loving conglomeration of obsessions which still gladly haunts her steps to this day.

Diamond Ink is a graphics business Shayna founded in 2015 after selling a range of digital and physical pieces of countless subject to individuals, publications, and businesses alike.

** **

Additional images and artwork provided with kind thanks to Sardonicus, Russel Smeaton, Sian Brighal and Steve Lillie

Acknowledgments

The Inspiration for the book, and the concept of taking real historical people and events and weaving various Mythos backstories around them, was the result of a late-night tea and whisky fuelled discussion about H.P. Lovecraft's literary habit of lacing his stories with links and threads of the past. As such, this anthology owes a heap of debt to David Southwell.

My dear wife Adda, who was forced to endure the countless postponing or cancelling of fun activities following my too frequent and lame response of "I can't right now, I need to write" and yet somehow managed to prevent herself from strangling me, must surely deserve an award for her continues patience and support, but as I have none to hand perhaps a mention herein will suffice until I rectify the lack of a suitable trophy.

With those very obvious needs attended to, I now turn to thank the many authors, artists, photographers, proof readers and beta readers who helped turn a murky concept into a very solid and real thing. Your work, often at short notice, was and is very much appreciated and honestly this would not have been completed without you.

Finally, although there are many others who justly deserve a mention if the section be long enough, I cannot wrap this section up without a quick word of thanks to the following people :-

Ben Wasserman, Wendy Hyland, Nancy Paulding, MaVi Peralta,

Itzcoatl Ima Cervantes Ibarra, Molly Alcroft and

Sheryl & Rick Gilbert

With Special Thanks to the Kick Starter Backers

Jim 'The Suited Gent' Drew, Aimee Williams,

Alexander von Schlinke, Matthew Carpenter,

Gevera Bert Piedmont, Sarainy, Adam Thornsburg,

Raven Shadowz, Eva Bradshaw, Andreas Zuber,

Morgan Scorpion, Chris Basler, Adam Selby-Martin,

Ben Wasserman, Christopher 'Vulpine' Kalley, Casey Kirkpatrick,

Arran Dickson, Joe Kontor, Keisuke Inoue, Tim Hull,

Leigh Oakley, Dirk Bester, Lee Carnell, Karen Peralta,

Cory Aughenbaugh, Griffin Endicott, Jack Dennings,

David Charlesworth, R.B. Randolph, Gil Cruz, Claus Appel,

Dale Hirt, Iona, Chase Hopper, Mark Lukens, Deckan Sprengoot,

Stephanie McNamara, Andrew Ferguson, Neil Hemfrey,

Abby Wright, Ewa S-R,Liz Peters, Sam Springate, Azhmodai,

Josh King, Jeffrey Vaca, Wayne Callar, Callum Stoner,

Angiel Melie, Megan King, Lorenz Thor, J. Patrick Wentz,

Philip Lebow, Brian Bander, Eric Priehs, Keely Milburn Taylor,

Mark R. Froom, Charleen Briggs, Thomas Bailey, Tom Stead,

Kristen & Lawrence Dennis, Rhel, Henri Dennis,

With Special Thanks to the Kick Starter Backers

Steve Summersett, Jinnx, Edward Drummond, Joshua Hill,

Paul Lilley, Christopher Henderson, Shawn Hakl,

Christopher Dean, Ben Gasparini, Henry Espy-Roberts,

Serenity Kaysdatter, Abby Wright, Nancy Paulding, Jeff Narucki,

Patrick Wheaton, Mihail Bila, Robert Derie, Tim Lonegan,

Morgan Griffith-David, Colin Mackay, TheKeegan8r,

Elizabeth Young, C.P. Dunphey, Chris "ChrisAkira" Atkins,

Nathan Rosen, Lisa M. Gargano, Bob Burke, Randy Stafford,

Patrick Wheaton, Johnny Apple, Spencer Fry, Mog MacLaughlin,

Chris Jarocha-Ernst, Trevor A. Ramirez, Joseph Gustafson,

Joerg Sterner, Lewis Evans, James McKelvey, Christopher Meyer,

DeAnna Visalle, Owen Springer, Ewan Thomson, Will Hart,

Rebecca Moore, Travis Stluka, Robb Wijnhausen, Ivan Donati,

Lee Cox, Mikko Salomaa, Alexander W., Melinda K.,

Natalia Morse, Lord Hancock, Ed Kowalczewski, Jedidiah Nixon,

Dagmar Baumann, Cullen 'Towelman' Gilchrist, Per Stalby,

David Southwell, Bentley Burnham, R.R. Hunsinger,

Elizabeth Hasara, Starbucks Marc, Kyler Cole

THAT WHICH SHOULD NOT BE

BRETT J. TALLEY

"Four and a half suspenseful, frightening tales in one. Talley is wonderful at crafting suspense." - Kirkus Reviews

"Rivals that of any successful commercial author in contemporary horror fiction."
Dave Gammon - HorrorNews.net

"It's a great read. Pick it up you won't be disappointed."
- Mike Davis, Lovecraft eZine

"Brett J. Talley has written a wonderful homage to occult horror." - Colleen Wanglund, Monster Librarian

JOURNALSTONE
YOUR LINK TO ARTISTIC TALENT